About the author

Scott Hunter was born in Romford, Essex in 1956. He was educated at Douai School in Woolhampton, Berkshire. His writing career began after he won first prize in the Sunday Express short story competition in 1996. He currently combines writing with a parallel career as a semi-professional drummer. He lives in Berkshire with his wife and two youngest children.

DEATH WALKS BEHIND YOU

Scott Hunter

Death Walks Behind You

A Myrtle Villa Book

Originally published in Great Britain by Myrtle Villa
Publishing

Acknowledgements

A *big* thank you as usual to Louise, my wonderful editor, without whom I would be in serious trouble …

Cover Design:

Books Covered

To my children ...

Hu seo þrag gewat,
genap under nihthelm,
swa heo no wære...

How that time has passed away,
Grown dark under cover of night,
As if it had never been...

The Wanderer (Old English Poem)

Prologue

Linda Harrison wouldn't have described herself as an outdoor type but she did enjoy her early morning perambulations, a word her new husband had coined to describe her forays into Cernham Woods. Linda and Matthew were owners of a hyperactive Cocker Spaniel and a pair of young Boxers. Linda was only too aware that forgoing their morning constitutional would mean that the three dogs would spend the rest of the day tearing the house apart, a reality she'd had to deal with on more than one occasion when illness or practical necessity had conspired to keep her indoors. Matt knew this, of course, but he persisted with his teasing, as though her morning routine was little more than some selfish indulgence.

"Pippa! Stop that!" Her thoughts were interrupted as the young spaniel plunged into one of Cernham's many puddles. "Out!" Linda scolded the bitch who was clearly having a wonderful time. "Not *another* bath, I can't believe it! You are one high maintenance dog, girl." Alf and Bennie, the Boxers, sniffed around the puddle's perimeter. Thank goodness they weren't water dogs like Pippa.

Linda strode on, wrapping her scarf more securely around her neck. Although the year was turning and spring was imminent the dank air held little promise of warmth. As she turned onto the long path by the fallow field she shivered, a long, body-shaking shiver that left her wishing for her wood-burning stove. Matt was a great wood cutter and she took comfort in the knowledge that their log pile would last well into the new season. Linda smiled to herself as she thought of her husband's ritualistic preparations: chopping and splitting, hewing and stacking, his lean, wiry frame stalking the garden, axe in hand and a glint in his eye.

"Come on, guys!" She called the dogs after her. There were few folk around this morning, but it was dull and misty so Linda wasn't particularly surprised. Sensible people would wait for the sun to burn off the mist before braving the elements, and besides, many of the dog walkers with whom she came into regular contact only appeared in the woods after the morning school run, or later in the day before the teatime chores were squared up to. *No school runs for us, though*, Linda said quietly to herself. At forty-two the sands of time had pretty much run out for her. However, Matt didn't seem to mind. They had each other, the dogs, a nice cottage. All in all, much to be thankful for.

Footsteps behind her interrupted her reverie. She turned and acknowledged the half-grunted "Morning" as a cagouled shape walked by, green Wellingtons slapping on the muddy farm path. Not one of the regulars. And no dog. Linda deliberately slowed her pace to put a comfortable distance between herself and the stranger. She rarely worried about walking on her own, but it was wise to be vigilant. She paused at the next gap in the hedgerow to watch the mist rolling across the fields. It was a beautiful, almost other-worldly sight. A kite called mournfully for its mate somewhere high above and she felt a warm sweep of contentment. This was England, *her* England, and no one would shift her from it. You could keep your holiday cottages in Tuscany and the south of France. This was her country and she loved it, whatever the weather.

Linda smiled contentedly. She still pinched herself every morning to confirm that the unexpected transformation of her life was grounded in reality and not just the product of her own menopausal imagination. Whirlwind romance? She'd heard of such things, of course, but hadn't considered the possibility that it might actually happen to *her*. A weekend visiting a friend in Exeter had turned her life upside down. There they were, herself and Susan, enjoying a quiet drink. And there was Matt – tall, strong, rugged, watching her from the bar. Ten minutes later he'd asked her out (much to Susan's amusement). Ten weeks later they were married. A small ceremony, no fuss – one or two friends, no family to speak of. Linda's parents had died a long time ago and she had been raised by her aunt, now a frail old lady in a nursing home.

Pippa appeared at her feet, sniffing and whimpering. "What's up, girl?" She bent to stroke the spaniel's head. "Where are the two Bs?"

She peered ahead, looking for the Boxers. No sign. That was unusual; they usually stuck together, never roaming too far as Pippa was prone to do.

"Alf? Bennie?" She picked up her stride and followed the path away from the field into the woods. "Come on, guys, where are you?" She rounded a corner where the path twisted away towards the chalk pits. *Aha*. Behind a tree, a flash of movement. "Alf?"

As she drew nearer a shape detached itself from the shadows and blocked her way. The walker she had seen a few minutes ago. Or was it? The face was covered, didn't look right... She drew back in alarm, looked around for her dogs. Where were they when she needed them? The mist was thicker here; for a moment she thought her imagination was playing tricks, but then she saw the figure again just ahead, standing perfectly still. It was shaped like a man, but *– somehow it wasn't right...*

Linda's heart was pounding. Should she turn and run? A weapon, something ... she felt the Boxers' chain around her neck and her fingers went to unclasp it. The next moment something reached out of the fog and caught her by the arm.

Linda pulled away with a strength born of sheer terror. She felt fingers grasping at her coat, a brief scrabbling resistance and then she was free, stumbling and flailing through the trees, branches whipping and stinging her face. *Don't look back*, she told herself. *Don't...*

She ran until she felt as though her lungs would explode. Disoriented, she came to a halt, pressed her back against the trunk of an old oak and scanned the woodland for signs of pursuit. The woods were eerily still. Where were the dogs? She daren't call them. *Calm, Lin, calm...* Linda's breath gradually slowed to something approaching normal. Where was she? In her headlong flight she had lost all sense of direction. She began to walk cautiously to where a gap in the trees suggested one of the many well-trodden paths might pass close to her present location. And then she heard it: the soft crunch of leaves underfoot, the slow searching tread...

Oh no, please... Linda bent low, darted away into the undergrowth. After a few seconds she recognised where she was – close to one of the smaller chalk pits. She remembered an ancient tree perched on the edge of the pit, its roots forming a knotted cage beneath the lip. If she could find it, slip inside, curl up, cover herself with leaves... She almost stumbled over the edge of the pit in her terror. Where was the tree? Was it as she had remembered? *Yes... there...*

Half-slipping, sliding down the chalk face she grabbed at the roots and checked herself. There was just enough space. Heart thumping, she squeezed in and lay down in the nest of foliage, sweeping handfuls of leaves over her legs and torso. For a while there was no sound except birdsong, the occasional scamper of a rabbit or squirrel. Then she heard it. *Slap, slap, slap*, marking the perimeter of the chalk pit. She lay still, hardly daring to breath. The footsteps circled once, twice. And then receded.

Linda shivered. How long should she wait? A few minutes, maybe... What was that? Something skittering into the chalk pit, snorting, rooting around. *A dog.. Oh no, no...*

A wet nose appeared through the mesh of roots. A spaniel's nose. *No, Pippa. No...* She reached for the dog but the bitch backed away, alarmed to find such a large moving object half-buried in the mulchy floor of the chalk pit. Pippa barked, and barked again.

No...

Linda grabbed at the roots to extricate herself but a cold hand slid between them and caught her deftly by the leg. She screamed and tried to pull back but the grip was inexorable and her voice was muted by the mist. As she was dragged into the open she made a grab for the scarf hiding her attacker's face, but he was strong and strangely elusive, moving with an assured, swaying grace. Her heart skipped in fright as she saw that his head was oddly misshapen, with stubby, antler-like protrusions jutting from the skull… and then he was behind her, twisting her arm, making her gasp at the sudden, shocking pain. She felt something snap and the pain intensified. Probing, abrasive fingers slid around her neck, squeezing and palpating her flesh. She kicked back once, twice, tried to catch hold of his clothing, but he was quick, far too quick, and her hands were left clutching at nothing.

The pressure on her neck increased. Her legs thrashed wildly but then became limp as she gave in to the inevitable.

I'm going to die…

Linda felt resistance go out of her like the final sigh from a pricked balloon; she was floating now, embracing the darkness. Somewhere far away she heard the shrill, whistling call of the kite as it plunged and dipped in the gusting thermals high above, searching intently for its prey.

Chapter One

DCI Brendan Moran nudged the door open cautiously, unsure what to expect. He fumbled for the light switch and blinked as light flooded the small room. His eyes took in the scene with approval. It was just what he had hoped it would be: small, snug, quiet, clean and simply decorated. There was a wood-burning stove beneath the mantel, a criss-crossing of oak beams above and an atmosphere of profound peace.

"Brendan, old son, I think you've picked a good one for a change." He dropped his bag on the stone floor, shrugged off his coat and draped it across the back of the small settee. The clock on the wall told him it was 8.45pm. The whole journey had taken around five and a half hours, door to door. *Not bad going*, he congratulated himself, especially considering the state of the roadworks on the M5 and the predictable holiday traffic on the A30. *And what's more*, he reflected happily, *the pub is still open…*

"Staying long?" the landlord asked as he pulled Moran a

pint.

"Ten days," Moran replied, handing over a five pound note. "Just a short break."

Moran allowed his eyes to range around the room. The pub was half-empty; a few couples were eating at tables, one or two locals supped ale at the end of the bar, chatting quietly. Not a drug dealer in sight, Moran thought contentedly. This was why he had come to the West Country, and it looked as though the West Country was going to deliver.

"Where're you from?" The barman handed Moran his change.

"I live and work in Reading, in Berkshire," Moran said. "Not much life, actually; mainly work."

"I know it," the landlord said. "Big town. Ten days'll be long enough for you here, I expect. Not a lot goes on in Cernham."

"No?"

The landlord shook his head. He was of a similar age, Moran estimated, broad-faced and profusely sideburned. "No," the man laughed. "Been here all my life and I'm still waiting for something to happen."

"That's just how I like it." Moran smiled and raised his glass. "Long may it continue."

"I'll drink to that," the landlord nodded and picked up a half-pint pewter tankard conveniently to hand by the till. "All the best for the season."

"And to you, sir." Moran inclined his head mock-formally.

"If you're around tomorrow night we've got the Morris side in."

"Oh really?" Moran raised his eyebrows. "Bit early, isn't it?

I thought Morris dancing was a Whitsun event."

"We celebrate seasonal change here when the time is right, not when some church calendar tells us to."

"Well, I suppose that's your prerogative," Moran replied cautiously, worried in case the landlord had taken offence.

However, his new acquaintance had adopted a pensive posture, one hand stroking a sideburn, the other clasping his tankard proprietarily as if someone might suddenly challenge his right to drink from it. "Nature's what it's all about, y'see, not all that God business. End of winter, start of the growing season. That's what's worth celebrating in our part of the country. That's what's real. Load of hypocrites, these church people, the lot of them."

"Perhaps," Moran said non-committally, reluctant to be drawn into a religious discussion. He was saved by the arrival of a new customer, a woman in her early forties who greeted the barman with the ease of long familiarity.

"Usual, Celine?"

"Terl, what else would I be having?"

Moran's ears pricked up. He could tell a Cork accent a mile off, even when it was diluted by a splash of Cornish lilt.

"Evening." The woman smiled pleasantly at Moran as she waited for Terl to fetch her drink. "Warmer today, isn't it?"

"Very pleasant," Moran agreed. She was rather attractive, her long dark hair, loose and unpinned, framing a slim, well-balanced face in which was set the most extraordinary pair of green eyes Moran had ever seen. "Forgive me for asking, but do I detect a Cork accent?"

"Oho. Very astute," she replied with a grin of acknowledgment. "I was born and raised in Cork – in another life. I'm Celine, by the way." She extended a slender hand which Moran squeezed briefly.

"Brendan Moran."

"You can't get more Irish than that, eh?" Celine laughed. "Thanks, Terl." She unclasped her handbag and perched on the adjacent bar stool, rooting around for her purse.

Moran fought quietly with himself. His track record with women was poor. He wanted a peaceful holiday, not more complications. Besides, there was the unresolved issue of Shona...

"I'll get that," Moran heard himself say. He passed Terl another five pound note.

"Oh. Thanks." Celine had found her purse. "If you're sure? That's very kind."

"My pleasure," Moran smiled, cursing himself inwardly.

"So, you're on holiday?" Celine settled herself on the stool.

At least she's not wearing a ring, Moran reassured himself. "Yes, that's right. First for quite a while."

"Now, let me see," Celine stroked her chin and looked him up and down. "I always enjoy this bit."

Moran made a face to hide his discomfort at her top-to-toe examination.

"Got it." She clapped her hands and grinned. "Policeman."

Moran groaned. "That obvious, eh?"

She sipped her drink. "Always is. You can tell by the eyes."

"The crows' feet?"

She laughed, a tinkling, resonant sound Moran found appealing and not a little beguiling. "I've seen worse," she told him. "But it's not that, it's the *depth*."

At that moment the door of the pub crashed open. A

small blonde woman in jeans and a red blouse stormed up to the bar and banged her fist on the counter. Heads turned and mouths froze in mid-conversation.

"Listen up," she shouted, "will *somebody* in this joint please tell me where I can find Linda Harrison? Or are you all as clueless as her six-pack-centrefold husband seems to be?"

"We found each other again. On Facebook," the woman explained. It turned out her name was Blanche, and her capacity for whisky, Moran had noticed, even in the short time since she had arrived, was impressive. "We hadn't been in touch for years, but you know how it is; you're noodling around the internet and you think, 'I wonder what happened to … dot dot dot.'"

Moran nodded. But he didn't know. The last thing he'd consider as a leisure activity would be 'noodling around the internet'.

It had taken a while to calm Blanche, but Celine had risen to the challenge with an impressive display of empathy, a well-attuned listening ear and a few practical, if obvious, suggestions.

"I just don't understand it," Blanche continued. "She told me she never went anywhere these days."

"Tell me again what her husband said," Celine prompted.

Moran listened with half an ear. He hadn't come to Cernham for mystery. Fatigue had crept up on him and he began to concoct excuses with which he could comfortably extricate himself and leave the women to it.

"…and he just looked at me with this blank expression and said, 'I'm not my wife's keeper. How should I know where she is?' Rude, rude, rude." Blanche knocked back her drink and gestured to the barman. "I'll have another scotch."

Moran chuckled to himself at the way Terl scuttled to obey; Blanche's Uncle Sam assertiveness seemed very much at odds with the pub's cosy Englishness.

"I know Matt," Celine told her. "Body builder, outdoor type. He never says much, so I wouldn't read anything into it. Typical man, really; avoids conversation if he can."

Moran coughed.

"There are exceptions to the rule of course," Celine laughed. "Sorry, Brendan."

"No need to apologise." Moran took his opportunity. "I'm going to head off, so if you ladies will excuse me." He drained his glass. "I hope you track your friend down," he said to Blanche. "I'm sure she'll turn up soon." And to Celine, "Nice to meet you."

"You too, Brendan. See you around, no doubt." Her eyes sparkled.

Moran nodded. "No doubt."

The cottage was snug and comfortable. Moran busied himself unpacking his few belongings and rustling up an egg on toast from the meagre supply of groceries he had collected at a Tesco Express somewhere en route. He whistled tunelessly along with the local radio station as he worked, feeling pleasantly tired and relishing the prospect of a long, untroubled sleep. He began to toy with tomorrow's agenda; a late breakfast perhaps, followed by a walk along the coastal path, lunch in some local café, and if further afternoon exertions warranted, tea and scones to round off his first day. Total R and R, just as Dr Purewal had recommended. Recharge the batteries, disconnect the brain, feel the stress slough away. Moran stopped what he was doing and let his hands fall to his sides, only too aware of how fickle his mind could be: past experience had proved its inner workings to be well versed in the art of dissembling. *R and R, Brendan? Is that why you're here, or is there a subconscious agenda you're not owning up to?*

He switched the radio off and let the silence close around him. *You know why you're here, Brendan Moran. You're here to make a decision. To continue, or not to continue?*

There. It was in the open now. He'd confronted it.

Moran sighed. *That is the question...* Retirement, or onward? Onward to the next case, and the next, and...

A series of staccato knocks on the front door made him jump. *Who...?*

In two strides he was fumbling clumsily with the latch. "Brendan?" A female voice penetrated the woodwork. The door was stuck. He heaved and it sprang open.

Celine pushed into the cottage, her face paler that he had last seen it, mascara smudged and hair awry. "Brendan. You have to come. I'm sorry to ask, but – it's the American woman, Blanche. Please–" She grabbed his arm, pulling.

Moran drew back in alarm. "Hey, hey, hey. Hold on a second. Come in, sit down and–"

"No! You have to come *now*." Celine's eyes blazed into his. "She's dead, Brendan. *Dead*."

Chapter Two

Celine's assessment of Blanche's condition was, Moran reluctantly admitted, entirely accurate. The American was slumped forward in her car, a silver Lexus, and there was no pulse to be found during Moran's customary checks. The saloon was parked next to the low cemetery wall two hundred metres from the pub, a dimly-lit corner of the village. Had it not been for Celine's curiosity the body could well have remained undiscovered until the morning. He straightened up from his examination.

"I'm afraid you're right. We'll need to call the police."

Celine was shaking. "I thought I'd done that already." She looked at Moran.

"No. This is a matter for the local police. I have no jurisdiction here."

"Can you tell what happened? I mean, look, there's not a mark on her."

"No, I can't. The police doctor will come and perform a more thorough examination. The best thing we can do is make the call and leave them to it."

"But don't you want to know what happened? I mean, she might have been *murdered* or something."

Moran rested his hand gently on her shoulder. "Look, we don't know that. She may have died from perfectly natural causes. There's no point in speculating, trust me." Moran found his mobile and tutted in frustration. "No signal."

"There never is here. We could try the pub. They'll still be clearing up."

"OK, after you." Moran fell into step beside Celine. "When did she leave the pub?"

Celine shook her head in consternation. "A few minutes after you. I chatted to Terl for a bit and then left myself. And there she was. I knew straight away she was … you know."

"I know."

Moran rapped on the pub door. The lights were still on and presently they heard the sliding of a heavy bolt followed by the jangle of a security chain. Terl's head appeared, silhouetted against the jaundiced interior light.

"What is it?"

Moran explained.

"You'd better come in." Terl stepped aside and motioned them through. He closed the heavy door behind them and headed for the bar. "You could use a drink, I expect. I'll knock up PC Frobisher – our local bobby."

"No," Moran said. "This needs more than local expertise. I'm calling Exeter."

"Are you sure?"

"Of course I'm sure." Moran tried to keep the exasperation from his voice.

"All right. Phone's just there," he told Moran. "Come round the side."

As Moran picked up the receiver he noticed Terl helping himself to a generous measure of vodka from the optic range. Celine was fiddling with a packet of B&H, tapping an unlit cigarette on the gold packet. Terl offered her a light and she inhaled the smoke greedily.

Moran made his report and replaced the receiver.

"Now what?" Celine asked.

"Now nothing," Moran told her. "Now I go back to the car and wait for the police. Then I go to bed."

"How can you be so calm?" She blew smoke and took a swig of whisky.

"Seen it all before, I expect," Terl offered with a half-smile.

Moran shrugged. He just wanted to go to bed. "Yes, I suppose I have. Thanks for the drink."

"I appreciate your help, Brendan." Celine stubbed out her half-smoked cigarette in a heavy glass ashtray Terl had conjured from somewhere. "Sorry I had to disturb you."

"You did the right thing. I expect the police will want a quick word. I'll send them along. No point in both of us hanging around in the dark."

She smiled briefly. "Thanks."

"Well, good night. Thanks again, Terl."

"Cheerio, Mr Moran."

Moran stepped out into the night. He'd forgotten how dark it could get without any light pollution. It wasn't just dark, it was opaque.

His footsteps echoed flatly on the road. The Lexus was just round the next corner, by the church. With any luck the police would be there soon. It wasn't as if they had far to come. *This is bizarre*, he mused. First day off for months and what happens?

He turned the corner and stopped in his tracks. For a moment he thought he'd made a mistake, taken a wrong turning. But there was the low cemetery wall, the bulky shape of the church. No mistake. *He* was in the right place, but the Lexus certainly wasn't.

The car had vanished.

"Renting the place are you?" The young detective sergeant cast his eyes around the cottage interior. "And you arrived this afternoon, you say?"

Moran gave the policeman a withering look. "Yes, I did say."

"All right, sir. We're nearly finished. Just trying to get everything straight, you know how it is."

"Yes, I know, DS Wilmot. Forgive me. It's been a long day."

"That's all right, sir."

Moran watched Wilmot jot a brief note. He was young, sandy-haired; not long in the job, Moran concluded. Keen. Moran's eyes were grainy with fatigue; he knew that his patience was nearing its end.

"You're absolutely sure that the woman was dead, sir."

"Absolutely."

"And you have no idea where the car might be?"

"Of course I have no idea."

"And no idea who might have taken it?"

"None. How *should* I know? I've only just arrived."

DS Wilmot rested his pad on his lap and gave Moran a sympathetic smile. "Sir, if I might suggest a possible solution, don't you think it's entirely feasible that you may have been mistaken? Perhaps this lady was resting; maybe she had simply dozed off? And while you went back to the pub she simply woke up and continued her journey?"

"No. She was dead. Dead people don't wake up, in my experience. Except for Lazarus, and that was two thousand years ago."

"Laz...? Oh, yes, I see." Wilmot's businesslike expression barely flickered. "But you do see my point, sir."

"Yes, of course I do. But I am a senior police officer, DS Wilmot. I know a dead person when I see one."

For the first time, Wilmot looked uncomfortable. "Point taken, sir, but it does seem odd, doesn't it, that someone would drive away in a car containing a dead body."

"Yes, I am compelled to agree."

"Especially as they would first have to move the body in order to drive the car."

"Yes." Moran stood up. "Look, DS Wilmot, I've told you all I can for the moment. May I suggest that I pop in tomorrow morning to have a chat with your senior officer?"

"I'm afraid that will be a bit of a problem, sir. DI Steele went off sick last week. We have the flu going round at the moment."

"So, you'll be dealing with this yourself?"

Wilmot's expression told Moran all he needed to know; the young sergeant was struggling to keep his head above water. Moran felt a pang of guilt. How were his own team faring in his absence?

"Myself, sir? Yes, that's correct."

Moran rubbed his eyes with the heels of his hands. "Look, son, why don't you have a word with the lady who alerted me in the first place? Her name is Celine. She may have learned something during the course of her conversation with this woman that'll shed a little light. And I'll come and see you first thing."

Wilmot tapped his biro on the chair arm as he considered Moran's suggestion. A moment later he nodded. "All right, sir. I'll expect you around half past nine, if that would suit? You know where to find the local station?"

"No."

Moran waited while Wilmot scribbled directions in his pad and tore out the leaf.

"A little different to Thames Valley HQ, I shouldn't wonder," the DS said. "Suits the place, though. Quaint, I call it. I don't come out this way much but it always makes me smile."

"Is that so? I'm not that big on comedy, I'm afraid," Moran said. "Especially after a death." He ushered the sergeant to the cottage door. "Good night, DS Wilmot."

"Good night, sir. I'm sure we'll sort it all out tomorrow."

Moran closed the door, puffed out his cheeks and exhaled. *Happy holidays, Brendan...*

Moran knew he was asleep but the dream had him in its grip and he couldn't wake up. He knew the story; he had heard it from his maternal grandmother's lips. He also knew that he didn't want to hear it again, because it had always unsettled him, made him uncomfortable. It was a story about his great-grandfather, but in this dream Moran found himself cast in the central role.

He was returning from some errand, following the old track through dense woodland. It was eerily quiet. Presently he found himself in a clearing; in its centre was a neatly constructed circle of sticks and broken wood. He approached it cautiously, but also with a flutter of excitement. He knew what it was: he had found a meeting place of the hidden ones, the spirits of the forest – the little folk. He bent, selected a curved shard of wood from the ring and backed away. Was he being watched? He felt daring, slightly giddy, and then suddenly fearful. He shouldn't be here. He wasn't supposed to see this. He turned towards the gap in the trees that would reunite him with the path, but as he reached the edge of the clearing a sudden weakness in his legs pulled him up short. *He couldn't stand…* He sank to his haunches and keeled over, his useless legs splayed out behind him. Panicking, he dug his hands into the mulchy forest floor and hauled himself away. How far to home and safety? A mile? Two? He began to crawl, using the stolen stick for leverage.

A lifetime later, bruised and terrified, he emerged from the trees by the rutted forest road. Doggedly he crawled on, still with over a half a mile to go.

It was fully dark by the time he reached the village. No one was about, nobody came to help him. Summoning his last ounce of strength he dragged himself to his mother's doorstep.

She was waiting for him on the threshold, silent, angry.

"You know what you have to do, Brendan."

It was a statement, not a question.

"I can't." His knees were raw, his hands bleeding.

"You must."

And she turned her back on him; shut the heavy door against his futile attempts to enter.

He cried for a long time but his mother was pitiless. He felt the rough wood in his hands and knew that if he didn't go back, didn't make good the damage he had done, he would never walk again.

It took him twice as long to crawl back along the lane, to re-enter the foreboding woodland, to negotiate the labyrinthine paths of his childhood. He cut himself on shards of flint, briars and brambles, splinters and stones. He was scared witless, hungry, near to collapse, but he drove himself on, knowing that his mother was right.

He crawled and rested, crawled and rested. Once he dozed on a pillow of dead leaves but then some nocturnal noise scared him awake and the nightmare journey continued. Just when he thought he couldn't go on, the moon sidestepped nimbly from behind a cloud and he found himself within sight of the clearing. As he hesitated with lungs wheezing and heart thudding he became acutely aware of some heavy, invisible weight of expectation, as if the old gods themselves had gathered to witness his penance completed.

He placed the wood carefully where he had found it and half-rolled, half-crawled away from the ring. He reached the edge of the clearing and felt the blood rush back into his legs. He got up, unsteadily at first, and began to limp through the moonlit trees towards the village and safety. As the strength in his legs returned he broke into a run. Branches flicked his face as he flew by and the wind soughed in the high boughs like voices telegraphing his progress.

Now he was nearly home, nearly at the forest perimeter. Legs pumping, he followed the track around a narrow bend and came crashing to a halt. Was it his imagination? He took cover behind a broad oak and peered into the gloom.

No, he wasn't seeing things.

Just ahead, blocking his way, a tall figure waited silently, shrouded in darkness. He saw the horns, the misshapen head and froze in terror…

Moran awoke with a start. The moon painted the tiny bedroom with a wash of delicate silver. For a moment he had no idea where he was until the events of the previous night came back to him in a rush. The missing body, the Lexus, Celine…

He tossed and turned for the remainder of the night as the church bell tolled in the near distance, marking the passing hours until dawn.

Chapter Three

The local police station was unassuming in the extreme; a small terraced building three doors from the local grocery store. Moran entered and found himself in a reception area furnished with three slatted chairs, a low table covered with a spread of old magazines and a tatty counter behind which a shirt-sleeved police constable was sipping tea and tapping his pen thoughtfully on the Formica top. A name plate announced his name as PC William Frobisher. He looked up with a surprised expression as Moran closed the door behind him.

"Can I help?"

"I'm looking for DS Wilmot," Moran said. "I have an appointment."

The PC looked at his watch. "DS Wilmot? I wasn't expecting him. But he's got to get here from town if he's coming, so I imagine he'll be a while yet."

"He said half past nine."

"Why don't you have a seat, sir? I'll give Exeter a ring. And the name is?"

"DCI Brendan Moran."

"Oh. I see. I do apologise, sir. Just a moment."

Moran sat down, disgruntled. He was tired and irritable. After the briefest of conversations the PC put the phone down.

"Sorry, sir, DS Wilmot sends his apologies but he can't get here today. He's been seconded to something urgent, apparently."

"What?" Moran went to the counter. "Look, someone died here last night. It's got to be dealt with."

"Died, sir?"

"Yes. Died. Can I make a call?" Moran reached for the receiver.

The PC deftly removed the phone from the counter. "I'm sorry, sir, that's not possible."

"What the hell do you mean, not possible? Look, a woman died in the village last night. In *your* village. The car and the body are missing. Now let me make a call."

The PC sniffed. "I have no record of this, sir."

Moran felt his blood rising. "I was interviewed by DS Wilmot in the early hours of this morning. He'll have made a report. Now, please can I phone Exeter?"

The door opened and closed, and a cheery voice said, "Morning, William. Everything all right?"

Moran glanced behind him. A man in his late forties wearing a worn hacking jacket and a genial expression stepped forward with hand outstretched. "Richard de Courcy."

"DCI Brendan Moran." De Courcy's grip was firm and dry.

"I was explaining that police procedures work a little

differently in our neck of the woods, Mr D," Frobisher said.

"Good man, William. Quite right." De Courcy turned to Moran. "Local lad, our William. Followed his father's footsteps and took over as our local bobby after poor George was diagnosed." De Courcy turned a sympathetic eye to Frobisher. "How is dad, William?"

"He's not too bad, Mr D. I'll pass on your good wishes."

"Be sure to tell him I'll look in later in the week." And then to Moran: "we look after our own here, DCI Moran." De Courcy reached over the counter and patted Frobisher on the epaulette.

Moran noted the familiarity with which the young PC addressed the newcomer. Familiarity *and* respect. But there was something else in his tone – unless Moran was imagining it – and that was the unmistakeable timbre of fear.

"I simply wish to make a phone call, PC Frobisher." Moran kept his voice even and reasonable.

"No harm in that, William," de Courcy said. "He is one of yours, after all, eh?" His face creased into a smile, the crow's feet becoming more prominent at the corners of his eyes, which were blue and clear. "Anyway, I just wanted to let you know that I found another body this morning."

Moran's heart skipped.

"Torn apart like the last one," de Courcy was saying. "If I didn't know better I'd say it was a wolf, or one of those wild cats they keep reporting on the news." De Courcy registered Moran's shocked expression. "A deer, old boy. We've had a few killed over the last couple of months. Woods are well stocked with the delightful beasts, but some bloody animal is knocking them off."

"Thanks for letting me know, Mr D," Frobisher said. "I'll

see if we can't get one of those experts down from Exeter to set some traps."

"Good man, William. Got to put a stop to it, eh? Nice to meet you, Mr Moran. You're here on police business, I take it?"

Moran shook his head. "A holiday, actually."

"Oh, splendid. Staying long?"

"Until next Wednesday."

"Very good, very good. Well, enjoy your break. It's a lovely spot. We're proud of it, aren't we, Will?"

"We are indeed, Mr D."

Moran wondered if PC Frobisher was going to salute de Courcy on his way out. When Moran returned his attention to the counter he saw that the telephone was back in its original position. He was left with the distinct impression that his call had been authorised not by Frobisher, but by de Courcy.

Frobisher appeared to have lost interest, shuffling papers at the far end of the counter. Moran picked up the receiver and made his call. He was told that DS Wilmot was unavailable and likely to remain so for the rest of the day. Moran gave up, nodded curtly to Frobisher and left. As he walked back to the cottage it started to rain.

Preparing a late breakfast – porridge to start, followed by toast, orange juice and a pot of coffee – Moran asked himself some questions. They were not comfortable ones.

Is your brain up to its old tricks again, Brendan? Is this whole thing some kind of Charnford Abbey flashback?

He knew his brain to be an unreliable witness. After all, during the investigation at Charnford Abbey it had constructed a fully-formed, highly attractive persona of its own devising in the shape of English teacher Holly Whitbread, as real to him as the solid abbey walls had been – and yet Holly had been a phantom, a product of his own imagination. He still couldn't believe it, still caught himself thinking about her during those quiet, unguarded moments before sleep. And along with these uncomfortable recollections came the fear that he might be heading for a permanent loss of faculties, poised on the crest of some cerebral breaker which would shipwreck him on the rocks of full-blown mental illness forever.

But he actually felt fine. Sure, the leg pained him a bit and the limp would always be there, but apart from that, physically he had never felt better. This morning's weariness was merely the product of a restless night, nothing more. Moran buttered a slice of toast and crunched it thoughtfully. The woman, Blanche, had been real. And dead. He would stake his professional reputation on it.

The question was what to do about it. Moran swirled the last third of his coffee around the bottom of the farmhouse mug. *See, swirl, sniff, sip, savour …* the five Ss of wine tasting. Well, he'd seen and swirled. Now it was time for a little sniffing.

He locked the cottage door behind him. His watch told him it was eleven fifteen, almost opening time.

Moran paused at the spot where the Lexus had been parked and bent to examine the ground. The rain had cleared and the sun warmed his back as he looked for tell-tale tyre tracks, or any personal indications that Blanche had indeed parked her hired car here by the cemetery wall.

However, the ground was firm and clear of mud. There were no signs of a struggle, nothing left behind to give any clue as to what had happened. In short, no evidence at all. Moran harrumphed and continued along the lane to the Green Man.

The interior of the pub was gloomy and Moran squinted as the door creaked shut behind him with a soft thump. An overweight barmaid in a low-cut top was leaning across the bar with a copy of *Hello* magazine open in front of her. The only other occupant was a white-bearded regular reclining in the far corner with a folded paper on his knee and a pewter tankard at his elbow. He grunted a greeting and immediately returned his attention to the paper.

"What can I get you?" The barmaid straightened up, adjusting herself.

Moran tried to fix his eyes somewhere between neck and forehead. "I'm looking for someone by the name of Celine. Do you know where I might find her?"

"Celine? Nope. Sorry."

"She was here last night," Moran said. "Chatting to Terl."

"Don't know her." The girl shook her head.

"Is Terl about? Perhaps he—?"

"Terl's off today," the girl cut in abruptly.

"I see. When might he be back?"

"I have *no* idea." She sighed. "I just work here on Sundays and Mondays. I don't see Terl very often — just so long as he leaves my wages, that's fine. Where he goes and what he does is up to him."

"Right. Well, thanks anyway."

Moran left the pub, narrowly resisting the temptation to slam the door behind him.

Best just forget it, Brendan. There's probably some rational explanation. Maybe she wasn't dead; maybe she was asleep after all...
Maybe.

He guided his car out of the village and drove the three or so miles to the nearest main carriageway. A petrol station beckoned from the far side. Moran crossed the junction and pulled in. His mobile phone showed two bars on the signal meter. That should do. He dialled a number.

"DI Pepper."

The voice brought a smile to Moran's face. His new DI, Charlie Pepper, was a fiery Midlands girl whom he had grown to admire and like in equal measure over the preceding months. She had shown her mettle during the Ranandan case, fighting off a murderous attack in her own home and playing a leading role in pulling the teeth of an internationally active drug ring. He could imagine her at her desk, twirling a strand of short blonde hair between her expressive fingers as she held the receiver to her ear. "Hello, Charlie."

"Guv? I thought you were on holiday."

"So did I. Look, Charlie, I have a small favour to ask, that's all."

"Oh yes? You're supposed to be taking it easy. You know, R and R and all that."

"I am. I have a very pleasant cottage, a local within a stone's throw, copious woodland stocked with all manner of wildlife, a dozen or more public footpaths to explore—"

She interrupted him. "But something's bugging you, right?"

Moran chuckled. "Right."

Charlie sighed. "Go on, then. What do you want?"

"I just need a few airline passenger lists checked, that's all."

"Airport?"

"Not sure, probably Heathrow, or maybe Bristol."

"More, please."

"OK. I'm after the name of a passenger whose first name is Blanche, married, surname unknown. Airport of origin unknown, but definitely the US."

"You're pulling my leg, right?"

"I wish. I'm sorry, Charlie, I know it's not much to go on."

"Arrival date?"

"Sorry."

"*Guv!*"

Moran grimaced and held the phone away from his ear before going on. "Sometime over the last couple of days. Another thing; she hired a silver Lexus. That might help."

"Yeah, right."

Moran could almost see Charlie's keen eyes sparkling as she scribbled down the scant details. He tapped the iPhone over to loudspeaker.

"I don't think you can fly direct to Bristol from the US, anyhow." Charlie's voice filled the car. "I think the flights are via everywhere: Paris, Amsterdam, Dublin."

"See, you know more than I do already."

Charlie gave a sigh of mock-disapproval. "OK, I'm on it. Only if you tell me what's up, though."

Moran briefly explained the events of the previous evening.

"Sounds weird, for sure. Leave it with me; I'll see what I can do. DS Banner is at a loose end right now. He can make a start."

Moran grinned. DS Banner, the team's resident male chauvinist, was still acclimatising to taking orders from a senior officer in lip gloss. He was going to love this one.

"Thanks, Charlie. How's things?"

"Not too bad. The Chief is keen to find the last of the Ranandans' buddies. We reckon one or two are still lurking around the town centre."

"You be careful, DI Pepper." Moran clocked the intonation of concern in his voice and realised with a jolt that to describe Charlie Pepper as someone he 'liked' didn't tell the whole story. Not at all.

"Banner'll look after me, never fear." Charlie gave a throaty laugh.

"I'm sure he will. Listen, Charlie, my mobile network doesn't seemed to have extended its reach to this neck of the woods. You can reach me at the Green Man, Cernham. Leave a message, OK?"

"No probs, guv. Try to forget it for now. You're on hols, yes?"

"I'll try. Take care. Bye." He rang off.

Moran sat for a while, deep in thought. The Ranandan drug ring had not been your run of the mill local operation; it had been a significant strand of a massive international cartel. He knew they had only succeeded in cutting off one of many tentacles, and the continuing presence of eastern bloc heavies in the Thames Valley worried him. These people didn't play games. He had lost three officers on the Ranandan case, and the possibility of further casualties was unthinkable. He sat quietly and listened to the buzz of passing traffic. What was the name of that creature from

Greek mythology? The Hydra, that was it. If you cut off one of the heads, two more sprang up to take their place.

Watch out, Charlie, he whispered under his breath. *Just watch out...*

Chapter Four

Moran's eyes shot open. He stiffened and then relaxed as he remembered where he was. He'd decided to have an afternoon nap, but judging from the fading light filtering into the cottage he had slept for much longer than he had intended. However, he had to admit that he felt a great deal better for it. *You're getting old, Moran, that's your trouble…*

He went into the snug little kitchen and made a pot of tea. He felt rested and at ease – *chilled*, Charlie would have called it. So, what to do this evening? It was a no-brainer, really. The pub was nearby and the landlord amenable. Besides, there was always the chance that Celine would drop by, and it wouldn't do any harm to chew the fat over Blanche's disappearance. By now there might even be an explanation, or at least some indication of what had happened. *You're on holiday, Brendan,* he told himself. *You have a mild interest in this, not a professional one.* DS Wilmot could pick up the thread when his 'urgent' secondment had been completed.

Not my problem, Moran repeated to himself, mantra-like, as he gave the teapot a final stir and turned on the prehistoric-looking TV set, which crackled into life in a buzz of horizontal static. He'd read somewhere that a small percentage of TV interference was caused by tiny electrical remnants of the Big Bang. It seemed a fantastic proposition that the beginnings of the universe could be observed from a remote holiday cottage while enjoying a cup of tea, but the astronomers seemed certain of their facts.

"Yes, but you can't tell me what actually *caused* the Big Bang, can you?" Moran said aloud. He wouldn't have described himself as a religious man, but he was careful to maintain what he considered to be a healthy interest in the science versus religion debate. As far as Moran was concerned, science only went so far in explaining the way things were. For instance, the boffins knew that gravity existed because they had laws which could predict its behaviour, but ask a scientist what gravity actually *was* and they would struggle to answer. As for religion, Moran had left his Catholic upbringing behind after his fiancée, Janice, had been killed in an IRA revenge attack, while recent events at Charnford Abbey had cemented his view that those involved in organised religion of any sort were just as flawed, if not more so, than their non-believing counterparts.

He took a thoughtful sip of tea and watched the television flicker and buzz. No mobile signal, no TV channels. They were well and truly cut off from the rest of the world here in Cernham – which was why, he supposed, the pub was so important in the community; it was the centre of social activity where you found out who was doing what to whom.

Moran strolled to the door and opened it, sipping his tea and basking in the mild spring air. He cocked his head. Was that music? He listened again and remembered Terl's Morris dancers. That was religion, of a kind. Nothing wrong with celebrating nature's rebirth. *You'll end up a bloody druid, Moran,* he grinned to himself as he finished his tea. He zapped the TV off, donned his jacket and followed his ears.

The music and applause grew louder as Moran passed the churchyard. He smiled in anticipation. Morris dancing was one of the dafter but more endearing traditions of his adopted country. He turned the corner and there they were: a motley crew of colourfully dressed crazies, dancing and twirling as if their lives depended upon it. With their red braces, hats adorned with bright flowers and waving handkerchiefs they were a wonderfully eccentric sight. A crowd of villagers had gathered, beer tankards in hand, to cheer them on. Moran pressed through and entered the bar where he ordered a pint of local ale. The pub was transformed from his lunchtime visit and doing a roaring trade. Moran was gratified to find Terl back on duty, noting with relief that the surly lunchtime barmaid was conspicuous by her absence. Sleeves rolled up and forehead perspiring, the landlord was hard at work and clearly enjoying the boost in trade. He acknowledged Moran with a brief nod. Moran returned the greeting and went outside to enjoy the Morris men. He could talk to Terl later when the rush was over.

Moran found a gap in the semicircle surrounding the dancers, sipped his ale and tapped his feet to the rhythm. The musicians were doing a great job, accordion, tabor and violin belting out the tunes with gusto. With a jolt he recognised the accordionist as Celine. Her hair was arranged in long plaits and she was wearing a multi-coloured skirt and white blouse. Around her neck were garlands of spring flowers and her cheeks were rouged with exaggerated ovals of outdoor heartiness. She caught Moran's eye and winked. However troubled she had been the previous evening, she seemed to have made a good recovery.

The Morris men clattered their sticks in time to the rhythm of the tabor. The music bore some similarity to the pipes and drums of Moran's youth. He remembered watching the marches and the pipe bands, as well as the eventual and inevitable escalation into dark days of violence and confrontation. He didn't want to go there, and quickly switched his mind back to the present.

The dancing ended to enthusiastic applause from the crowd. The dancers clapped one another on the back and made their way inside in twos and threes to replenish their tankards.

"Hello again, Inspector Moran," Celine greeted him with a coy smile.

"Hello. You play very well."

"Thanks. Listen, I'm sorry about last night. I panicked, you know. I shouldn't have disturbed you."

"Not at all. You did the right thing. Did DS Wilmot keep you long?"

Celine looked puzzled. "DS who? No one showed up last night. I presumed you'd spoken to the police. I waited a while with Terl and then I went home."

Moran's brow furrowed. "Right. I see."

"Are you OK? You look a bit nonplussed."

"Do I? Sorry." He ran his finger around the rim of his glass. Should he say anything? There could be no harm in sharing his concern, surely? He took a breath and told her straight. "After I left you last night I went back to wait for the

36

police. The car had gone."

"Gone?"

"Yep. It wasn't there."

"But—"

"I know. She was dead. I'd swear to it in court."

"How bizarre."

"Quite."

The dancers began to make their way outside carrying their replenished jugs of ale. Celine gave him a tight smile. "Look, I've got to play again. Can we talk later?"

"Sure," Moran said. "Have fun. I'll be here."

He watched Celine take her place as the dancers reassembled. The music struck up and the dance began anew, but this time there was something different. The accordion struck up a mournful, minor key melody, almost a lament. The dancers moved slowly, respectfully, heads bowed. Celine's face was downcast, troubled. To Moran it seemed as though spring and all thoughts of new life had been banished. A cooler wind ruffled his hair and he shivered, turning up the collar of his jacket.

This was no dance of celebration. It was a dance of bereavement.

"Message for you, Mr Moran."

Terl handed Moran a slip of paper. The dancers had long since departed and the pub had emptied. Rather than eat in the isolation of his cottage Moran had elected to stay for a bar meal, a simple variation on the theme of burger and fries, which he had enjoyed well enough. Celine had declined his offer of dinner, excusing herself by citing a busy day and the necessity of a decent night's sleep. She seemed troubled, but Moran didn't want to pry. However, he did intend to do a little digging with Terl over coffee.

He fished out his glasses and read the note:

Flight UNA2194, Boston-Dublin-Bristol
03/05/2013, 06.37 arrival
Passenger: Ms Blanche R. Cassidy
DOB: 22/06/1968

The only 'Blanche' I could find.
Hope it helps, C.

Moran folded the note and tucked it into his inside jacket pocket. Not a phantom, then. A real person – and now, possibly, a missing person. A missing *dead* person, he corrected himself.

"Same again, Mr Moran?" Terl made as if to pull another pint.

Moran raised his hand. "I wouldn't mind a coffee, Terl, if you'd do me one?"

"Americano? Espresso?"

"Espresso, please."

"Coming up."

Moran finished his beer and reviewed the situation. An American woman arrives in an excitable state, proclaiming the disappearance of a friend who had confirmed the time and place of her visit. She berates the husband for his lack of interest or concern, stays for two drinks and leaves. An hour later she is found in her car by a woman from the pub who fetches an off-duty policeman. He confirms no pulse. The American woman is dead. Twenty minutes later the car and the body are gone.

"So, no sign of her, then?" Terl placed a cup containing the smallest volume of coffee Moran had ever seen on the bar and slid it towards him.

"No. Not so far."

"Can't switch off, eh?" Terl grinned widely. "I've never met a copper who can."

Moran conceded the point with a wry nod.

"Probably nothing," Terl went on while vigorously polishing a wine glass. "I'll bet she just passed out for a bit, woke up, drove away. Probably holed up in some Exeter hotel. I wouldn't worry."

She was dead...

Terl continued. "Anyway, I'd leave it to the Exeter constabulary if I were you. Enjoy your break. Disappearances are the last thing you need, eh?" Terl selected another glass and held it up to the light.

"I suppose. It's odd, though." Moran pushed the espresso cup across the bar. "Can I trouble you for another? A double, maybe?"

"Coming up."

As Terl prepared the coffee, Moran's brain raced. Should he contact Exeter again? No one seemed to be taking his report seriously – if, in fact, DS Wilmot had thought it necessary to file a report at all. The more Moran thought about it, the more convinced he became that Wilmot was sitting on it, treating Moran's interview as either low priority, or worse still, a false alarm.

"Thanks." Moran accepted Terl's second attempt at an espresso. It wasn't a bad effort, stronger than the first, and this time there was more of it. He took a sip and gave a murmur of appreciation. Settling the cup into its saucer he looked squarely at Terl. It was time to probe.

"What do you know about Celine, Terl? Seems like a nice lady."

"Yeah. She's all right. Good company. She's lived here for years – part of the furniture. Like me." He laughed.

"No partner?"

Terl leaned over the bar. "I said you couldn't switch off, didn't I?" he grinned, but then he became serious. "She's been unlucky, right enough. I wouldn't get any ideas, Mr Moran. Best leave alone, I reckon."

"Just curious."

"Right." Terl nodded. "Pull the other one." He selected another glass, misted it with a swift exhalation and resumed his polishing.

"Know a chap by the name of de Courcy?" Moran watched Terl's face closely.

"Everyone knows him," Terl replied.

Moran nodded, noting Terl's slight flinch at the mention of de Courcy's name. He pressed on. "Local squire? Lord of the manor?"

"Something like that." Terl let the bar cloth fall to his side and shook his head slowly. "He wishes."

"Oh?"

Terl ran a meaty hand through his hair. "His mother is still alive. Lord Cernham's widow."

"I see. The son and heir kept waiting. Prince Charles syndrome."

"Exactly that." Terl selected a small glass and banged it roughly against the Johnny Walker optic. "Join me?"

Moran declined. "Seemed like a nice fellow. Worried

about a deer carcass or something."

"Was he?" Terl affected disinterest. "Where'd you run up against Mr D, then?"

"The police station."

"Ah." The scotch went down in one.

"Funny, I got the impression that the officer might have been a little … in fear of him?"

"Is that so? I doubt it very much. Mr D is a nice fella. Likes to keep an eye on things, see that we're all doing our jobs properly, you know."

"Of course. Quite right. Good to have someone keeping an eye on things." Moran finished his coffee. "Well, time to stagger home. Thanks for a pleasant evening. I enjoyed it."

"Pleasure, Mr Moran. Take care, now."

Moran paused outside the Green Man and inhaled the fresh, clean air. Somewhere nearby a vixen's bark split the silence, a strangely alien sound that stayed with him as he wound his way back to the cottage. It was only as he turned the key in the lock that he realised why the noise had unsettled him: it had sounded like a cry for help.

Chapter Five

"Thought you might want to see this." DS Stephen Banner dropped a pile of papers onto the desk and made as if to leave.

"Wait. Summary, please. I haven't got time to wade through all that." DI Charlie Pepper brushed her hair back from her eyes with an irritated flick. She'd been meaning to get a trim for days but since the guv had been off she hadn't had time to think, let alone book a haircut.

"Sheldrake's legacy," Banner said as he about-faced reluctantly and waited, arms folded in front of Moran's desk. "I pulled all the info together, did some cross-referencing. Found something interesting."

"Namely?"

Banner sighed. "The Chinese guy from Chalvey, the one who was killed on the motorway? We traced him."

"Did you now?" Charlie's attention was now fully focused on Banner. The Detective Sergeant was smartly dressed as usual, hair fashionably gelled and designer stubble well-tended. Charlie supposed that some women would find him good-looking, but she wasn't one of them. "Tell me more."

Banner shot a glance at the papers, the unspoken implication being that she should read them herself rather than waste his time.

Charlie kept eye contact until Banner spoke.

"Huang Tian Hao."

"Go on."

Banner sighed again. "Born 1967, Wuhan. One brother. More of him in a minute. First caught trafficking 1989, a local affair. Sentenced but got off on some technicality. Reappeared on Interpol's radar six years ago as a much bigger fish. Suspected of international trafficking with links to Bosnia but nothing proven."

Charlie gave a low whistle. "And he was the guy in the Chalvey house. DC Hill's killer?"

"Seems so," Banner said.

"And the brother?"

"Huang Xian Kuai. Well unpleasant," Banner said. "Interpol believe he was at the centre of an incident in Poland where ten people were murdered. Individually." Banner chewed his bottom lip before continuing. "By having various body parts removed while they were still alive."

"Who were they?"

"Some Polski drug baron got too big for his boots. Tried to double-cross Kuai, cut him out. Kuai rounded up the whole gang, sat them in a warehouse and made them watch each other's executions."

Charlie shivered and folded her arms. "OK. So this is relevant because?"

"That's the worrying part." Banner scratched his cheek. "Someone spotted Kuai recently."

Charlie frowned. "Where?"

"Here. In Reading."

If Charlie had ever wondered what a man who had lost everything looked like, this particular prison visit answered the question succinctly. Ex-Chief Superintendent Alan Sheldrake gave the appearance of a man who had been to Hell and back, not just once, but a few times for good measure. His skin was stretched over his face like parchment and his regulation jacket and trousers hung on his body like a set of cast-offs stolen from some Oxford Road vagrant. He allowed himself to be led into the centre of the room and crumpled into the chair, head bowed. When he eventually looked up she saw that his eyes were sunken, empty mirrors with the flat impartial focus of a man who had lost all hope of redemption. She reminded herself that the man sitting before her had been responsible, albeit indirectly, for the deaths of three police officers.

"You've been told why I wanted to speak to you?"

A nod.

"Good. It won't help you in terms of your sentence, I want to make that clear before I begin. Is that understood?"

Again the nod. The eyes stared into space, fixed on some point behind her.

"Did you have any contact with the drug cartel besides the Ranandan brothers? I'm thinking of a specific name. Chinese."

The eyes swivelled, engaged her for the first time. There was something there now that reminded Charlie of Sheldrake's past as a hard-nosed, 'get the job done' senior officer. "Why do you ask?" His voice was quiet, but steady.

"Because I've received a report that a leading member of an international cartel has been seen locally. I want to know more. Why is he here? What does he want?"

"Chinese?"

"Yes. Name of– "

"Huang Xian Kuai."

Charlie leaned back and smoothed her jacket in a reflexive motion. "Right. Can you describe him?"

Sheldrake laughed, a cracked and humourless sound. "Looks like a Chinaman. Big, though. Tall, I mean, for a chink."

"What can you tell me about him?"

There followed such a long silence that Charlie thought Sheldrake had declined to answer. As she opened her mouth to repeat the question, Sheldrake spoke.

"What can I tell you about him?" Sheldrake made a non-committal face. "He's one of the top men – if not *the* top man, now his brother's dead. If he's in the UK it's for one of two reasons." He paused and scratched his chin.

"Go on," Charlie prompted.

"Either there's a huge deal going down and he wants to be on hand to personally supervise the details, or he's come over to settle a score."

"I see. I can't imagine that any major drug crime operation would risk a big one in Reading, or anywhere near Reading for that matter. After recent events it's too risky, surely?"

Sheldrake leaned forward in a swift movement, catching Charlie unawares. Her chair scraped as she moved back instinctively. The warden took two paces towards them and stopped when he saw Charlie's raised hand. "It's OK."

"Surely. Too risky," Sheldrake said. "I agree with you." He leaned back and studied her expression. "And that being so, you have your answer." Sheldrake stood up and nodded to the warden. "Goodbye, DI Pepper. And good luck. You'll need it."

"Wait. I'm not finished."

"I am," Sheldrake jabbed his finger into his stomach. "I have to catch up with my carpentry project. I've been neglecting it."

"Look, Sheldrake. It's no skin off your nose. Why can't you help me?" Charlie held herself in check for a moment but then thought, *sod it.* "You owe us *some* cooperation at least. After–"

"After what? After you and Moran screwed things up for me? Wrecked my life?"

"*Your* life?" Charlie felt herself losing it and swallowed hard. "What about Helen's life, and Harding's? What about Zoe?"

"The tart?" Sheldrake smirked. "What's one less tart in the world?"

Charlie's hands were trembling. She wouldn't be goaded. "Tell me something about Huang. Anything."

Sheldrake stuck his chin out aggressively. "Anything? OK. If Huang Xian Kuai is here you'd better be on full alert, DI Pepper. I've seen his handiwork, and it's not nice. If he's here for you, you'll know all about it." Sheldrake's lip curled in a sneer. "By god, you will."

"How does he operate? Where is he likely to be?"

"That's all you're getting, Detective Inspector." Sheldrake turned to the warden. "I want to leave. Right now."

Charlie signalled her assent. No point prolonging this;

Sheldrake wasn't going to open up. She was half-way out of the door when Sheldrake seemed to change his mind and called her back. She turned.

"I never thought I'd say this, DI Pepper, but after what you've told me I'm grateful to be here. I wouldn't swap places with you now. Not for any money."

Charlie watched him being led away. She left the room quickly. Her heart was beating like a snare drummer at a military tattoo and she had to lean against the corridor wall to regain her composure. The memory of the night she had been attacked in her flat came back to her vividly. She could see the shadow of the assassin, feel the splinters of glass beneath her feet. A trickle of sweat ran down her forehead as Sheldrake's words echoed inside her skull.

To settle a score…

As Charlie drove back to the station she tried to reassure herself. Why should Kuai single *her* out? Sheldrake was just trying to rattle her. After all, it was the only weapon he had at his disposal. *Don't let it get to you, Charlie girl…*

She jumped as a car behind her beeped. The lights were green and she hadn't even seen them change. Irritated, she ground the car into gear and pulled away. *Report the situation to the Super and leave it to him, Charlie. Fretting about it won't do any good…*

A few minutes later she turned into the station car park and found an empty space. She switched off the ignition and sat quietly. Her flat lease was due for renewal next week. Right now, another six months on her own didn't seem like a great idea. Maybe a flat share would be better.

Charlie checked herself in the mirror. Her mascara was

intact but her eyes looked tired. Hardly surprising, given the current workload – and now, guess what? The case that wouldn't go away was back in her lap. The repercussions from the Ranandan episode were, like the ripples from a heavy stone lobbed into a pond, still spreading far and wide. The death of a police officer always made a splash, but four – five if you counted Mike Airey – had resulted in a national outcry and howling demands from the press and the House of Commons for Sara Stevenson's resignation; by all accounts the Chief Constable was hanging onto her job by the skin of her teeth. Everything about the case had been subjected to the most intense scrutiny, which in turn meant that further developments would also be examined 'with the fine toothcomb of thorough investigative procedure, at the highest possible level', as DCS Higginson, Mike Airey's replacement, had taken pains to point out.

Which was why Charlie needed to speak to Higginson ASAP.

As she waited for the lift she wondered how Moran's holiday was going. It sounded as if the guv had got himself well and truly roped into this misper case. Typical of him, she thought with a wry smile. Charlie entered the lift and nodded a greeting to Sergeant Robinson who was on his way out with a bundle of leaflets.

"Morning, Charlie. Still covering for Brendan?"

"Don't I just know it." She tried for cheerful and failed.

Robinson, one of the station's old lags, picked up on her mood immediately. "Chin up," he said. "BM can't keep away from this place for long," Robinson told her with a knowing look. "He'll be back soon enough, don't you worry."

"I'm counting the days, Sergeant." Charlie forced a laugh.

"One at a time."

"*You* have a room?" Charlie frowned. "Seriously?" She wondered why she had confided in Banner. *Insecurity is bottomless, Charlie. Any port in a storm…*

"Yep. I was going to place an ad today, as a matter of fact."

"What sort of house?"

Banner gave a short laugh. "A normal sort of house. It's a big semi. Four beds, big lounge, diner, conservatory."

"Sounds too grown up for you, Banner."

"Funny. Actually, I inherited it from my parents. Early. They downgraded to Cornwall, so I'm living there, renting out rooms to cover costs."

"Right." Charlie sipped her coffee. She hadn't meant to share her thoughts, least of all with Banner, but hey, maybe it was serendipity. "Who else shares?"

"One guy and a girl so far."

"They OK?"

Banner shrugged. "I don't see much of them. Maybe the odd weekend – when I'm not here. They're fine. She's a student. He's in IT, plays football twice a week. Regular guy."

"You'd really rent me a room?"

"Why not? It's a big place. We can keep out of each other's way. Who knows, we might even get to like each other."

"I don't dislike you, Banner." Charlie finished her coffee. "I have a job to do. Play by my rules and we'll get on fine."

"Whatever," Banner said. "Anyway, it's up to you. Let me know."

"I will."

She watched the Detective Sergeant stroll across the canteen floor, pausing briefly to banter with a young WPC. The WPC giggled and gave Banner a friendly shove. God, what was she thinking? Renting from *Banner*? But it was tempting. It would be nice to socialise a bit, get to know people, share stuff. Charlie pursed her lips. Four in a big house. It was do-able. She didn't have to spend time with Banner, she could get to know the girl, maybe go out together. It was closer to the station, too.

Charlie stacked her tray and left the canteen. She was in a decisive mood. No point procrastinating. What was more, her landlady would be onto her about the lease renewal any day now.

She went after Banner. No time like the present.

Chapter Six

Moran drove up to the iron gates and stopped the car. It was raining, a slow, persistent patter on his windscreen. He got out. There was no lock. He could see the house at the end of the long, curved drive. Or perhaps 'house' was not the best description. *Pile*, his convalescing sergeant, Robert Phelps, would have called it.

Moran swung the gate open on protesting hinges and returned to the car. As he crawled up the drive he wondered how much money was required to maintain a place like this. But even as the thought occurred to him he could see the first evidence of neglect. The gardens were untended, the grass too long and the hedges untrimmed and unkempt. The building itself was half-covered in ivy and creeper and those stone blocks which were visible seemed, even to Moran's untrained eye, to be in urgent need of a mason's expertise. Impressive, nevertheless, he conceded; a once stately home for sure, even allowing for the obvious signs of decline and decay.

His feet crunched on the gravel as he made his way to the

front entrance and climbed the steps to the grand porch. *And why are you here, Brendan?* Moran hesitated on the threshold. *Because you're taking your mam's advice,* he reminded himself. *If you want to know what's going on, be it office politics, consumer complaint or idle curiosity, go straight to the top.*

He raised his hand to knock and paused again. Idle curiosity? No, it was more than that. He pulled the pitted brass knocker towards him and let it go, impressed at the resonant noise it made.

He waited. Nothing. Two further knocks also failed to elicit a response. He stood back. There were outbuildings to the east of the drive and he could hear the sound of hammering. Perhaps an estate worker could tell him where to find the lady of the manor. As he approached the nearest building a door set into an alcove of the main house swung open and a tall woman stepped onto the drive. "Can I help you?"

Moran altered his trajectory and approached the woman with a courteous nod. "I'm not sure, to be truthful. I hope you don't mind my asking, but I'm looking for some information concerning a missing person."

"Ah. The police."

"Well, yes, indirectly. But I'm not here in any official capacity," Moran explained. "Actually, I'm on holiday, but as I was in the vicinity—"

"—You thought you'd do a little recreational sleuthing?"

Moran laughed awkwardly. "I suppose you could put it like that, yes. But a friend of mine is seriously concerned, and I said I'd do what I could."

"A friend?"

"An acquaintance. A local lady. You might know her. Her name is Celine."

"I didn't catch *your* name," the woman said coldly.

"I apologise. Brendan Moran." He held out his hand, which was not taken.

"Irish."

"That's right." Moran dropped his arm. "I take it I'm speaking to the owner...?" Moran waved vaguely towards the house.

"Lady Cernham. Yes."

She was a striking woman, Moran observed. Beautiful, once, he supposed. Her face was still handsome but the onset of middle age had lined her forehead, creased her cheeks and greyed her hair, which she had kept long, but wore piled in an unfashionably high bun. Her bearing was aristocratic and her voice and tone left Moran in little doubt that Lady Cernham was used to being obeyed without question.

"So, you don't know Celine?" Moran kept his voice conversational, pleasant.

"I do not."

"Can I–?"

"And I don't see what business it is of yours, either," Lady Cernham interrupted, "to come here asking questions. Leave it to the local police if there's a problem."

Moran took the hint. "Yes. Well, perhaps I'll do that. Thank you for your time, Lady Cernham."

But she had already turned away and Moran watched her re-enter the house. The door closed and he was alone in the rain.

"Nice to meet you, too," he muttered.

He didn't bother closing the gate.

Parked in his favourite petrol station, Moran waited

impatiently for someone to pick up.

"Avis. Can I help?"

Moran gave Blanche's details. And waited.

"Sorry, sir. No one of that name has hired this week."

He tried another.

"Prestige. Name please."

Moran gave it and waited. Muzak blasted in his ear.

"Due back tomorrow," the call centre operative told him. "Cassidy, yes? Mrs Blanche?"

Good. A match. "That's right," Moran said. "What time tomorrow?"

"Let's see." A pause.

Moran drummed on the steering wheel.

"Already back with us, sir. Is there a problem."

"Back with you? Mrs Cassidy returned the car?"

"One moment." The muzak returned briefly. Moran ground his teeth.

"It was delivered back by a Mr James Clark. Early this morning."

"I see. A relative?"

A pause. "Who am I speaking to?"

"The police."

"Oh, I see. Well, I can't tell you much more, I'm afraid. That's what the records show."

"Can you give me a description of Mr Clark?"

"I can't, but I can try to find out who was on earlies today. Can I call you back?"

"I'd be obliged." Moran gave his number and thanked the operative. As he went into the shop to buy a Coke and a Mars Bar he remembered that he had no signal at the cottage. Hopefully Prestige would leave a message. He was half-way across the forecourt with his purchases when his mobile rang. He answered the call.

"DCI Moran?"

"Yes."

"This is Jane Levitt from Prestige. I understand that you were enquiring about a return?"

"That's right." Moran explained again briefly.

"How do I know you're who you say you are?"

"Call Thames Valley HQ. Ask for DI Charlie Pepper. She'll confirm my ID and number."

A slight pause, then, "That won't be necessary. How can I help you?"

"Can you tell me what time the vehicle was returned; perhaps give me a description of the gentleman in question? Anything he might have told you about the circumstances under which he was returning the vehicle?"

There was a brief silence. "Yes. I booked the vehicle in this morning at about quarter to eight. From a Mr Clark – he told me he was Mrs Cassidy's brother, as a matter of fact. Sorry, Mrs Blanche Cassidy was the name on the rental form – and as she had decided to extend her visit he had offered to lend her a vehicle for the duration of her stay."

"Can you describe Mr Clark?"

"Mmm. Around six and a bit foot. Late forties, early fifties, perhaps. Short, sandy-grey hair. Well dressed. Jacket and slacks, expensive-looking."

"Well spoken?"

"Posh." Jane Levitt laughed. "Very plummy."

"I see. Thank you. You've been most helpful."

"Pleasure."

"One other thing."

"Yes?"

"I want the Lexus quarantined. Until the police have conducted an inspection."

"I'm not sure I–"

"Just do it, Ms Levitt, would you?"

A slight pause. "I'll see what can be done. Can I reach you on this number?"

Moran explained the signal restrictions, gave Jane Levitt the pub's landline number and ended the call. He retrieved his Mars Bar, took a bite and chewed thoughtfully. How was he going to get the Lexus inspected when he had absolutely no jurisdiction in the area, no evidence regarding the suspect, and possibly the biggest hindrance to any possible cooperation with the local force, no body? Moran crumpled the chocolate wrapper and tossed it aside. *More thought required, Brendan…* But in the meantime his next port of call was much clearer.

It was time to pay Mr de Courcy a visit.

"What's on your mind, Charlie?" DCS Higginson invited her to take a seat with a friendly gesture. As she settled into the chair – a quality piece from the latest Staples range, no doubt – she noted with pleasure the other small touches which pointed to Higginson's status as a comfortably married family man: a photo of the kids, a bone-handled letter opener, a brass inkstand. A china mug inscribed with 'Best Dad' above a smiley face resting on a patchily sewn coaster, a remnant of some long-forgotten needlework project. The homely ambience gave her a warm, cuddly feeling, like she was working for her own dad rather than a senior – and very successful – police chief. So far, DCS Higginson's profile ticked all the right boxes and Charlie knew from previous conversations that he was more than happy to provide a listening ear during Moran's temporary absence.

"DS Banner has come up with a name, sir. I thought you should know."

"The Ranandan case?"

"Yes, sir."

Charlie described her visit to Sheldrake and the ex-policeman's assessment of the possible reasons for Huang Xian Kuai's presence in the UK.

"I see." Higginson rested his arms on the desk and interlocked his fingers. Firm, dry hands, Charlie noticed. She admired his meticulously pressed, speck-free uniform, his calm, unhurried manner, and the neatly trimmed fingernails. The Chief gave a small cough and Charlie, realising she'd been gawping like a teenager at a rock concert, launched herself into a flustered, ill-prepared speech.

"I thought perhaps it might too big for us, sir? I mean, with all the press stuff we've had, the fallout from the summer? I thought you might want it referred onto SOCU? They can keep a handle on Huang Xian Kuai, maybe carry it through and bust the whole UK operation while they're at it?"

You're babbling, Charlie. Shut up. Shut up and let the man speak...

"We could." Higginson nodded. "But I'm not keen to get them involved without a little more to go on." His hands toyed with the letter opener, the broad fingers moving up and down the blade, back and forth, back and forth. Charlie found herself mesmerised by the slow, repetitive action and flinched when he rapped the handle on his desk, decision made. "It would be nice for us to start the ball rolling with a little hard evidence, don't you think? Given the history? So, let's keep a weather eye, Charlie. Have a chat with the team; ask them to keep gentle tabs. The man may just be passing through. Watch, wait. Let's be patient. Keep me in touch. Understood?"

"Yes, sir." Charlie got up, smoothed her skirt. Higginson made her feel as if she was ten years old. "Thank you, sir."

"Oh, by the way, Charlie?"

"Sir?" She turned at the door.

"I know how sensitive an issue this is for you and the team, believe me. I worked with DC Harding in Southampton." Higginson paused, a flicker of emotion clouding his face. "He was a good lad."

"Yes, sir." Charlie bit her lip fiercely. Harding had asked her out just minutes before his surveillance van was firebombed. And Helen, gentle, helpful Helen…

"I know, I know." Higginson was on his feet and before Charlie could gather herself had placed a strong, fatherly arm around her shoulder – not threateningly, not creepily, just – just right.

"DI Pepper, listen to me." He spoke gently, made her face him, placed his hands on both her shoulders and engaged her with his confident, grey-blue eyes.

"Sir." *Don't blub, don't blub…*

"Huang Xian Kuai has done himself no favours. We know who he is. We know where he is. We'll get him. The slightest move out of line and we'll get him, all right? He'll make a mistake and you'll be there to nail him."

"Yes, sir."

"You're a good officer, Charlie. And you have a good team out there. Use them."

"Yes, sir. I will. Thank you, sir."

"And how are you sleeping these days?"

"Not too bad, thank you, sir." *Liar.*

"No more amnesia episodes?"

"No, sir. The doctor said it was to be expected, after a trauma, you know. But he was more than happy for me to resume active duty. I'm fine, really."

Higginson nodded and returned to his chair. "That's the spirit. I expect I'll see you before Moran gets back, but in case I don't, have a good couple of days." Higginson picked up the letter opener and reached for a pile of correspondence. The interview was over.

Charlie made it to the toilet door before the tears exploded in a volley of repressed grief as it all came back to her. *Helen, Harding, the van, the fire… Oh God, why did it happen?*

She should have been with them. She should have died too.

But where had she been when the van was being doused in petrol? Getting a fish supper, for God's sake.

A stupid *fish supper.*

Chapter Seven

"Not bad. Not bad at all," Charlie whispered under her breath as she parked her car outside the red-bricked Victorian detached. Number 226. *Dovecote Villa*. Very posh. Banner's parents weren't short of a bob or two by the look of it. Nice road, tree-lined, off the beaten track. OK-looking pub down the lane. *This'll be fine, Charlie girl. You can handle Banner. Won't see much of him anyway, the size of the place.*

Charlie killed the engine and rummaged for her handbag. The car badly needed de-junking; it was amazing how stuff just accumulated, especially when you were flat-out busy all the time...

There was a tap on the side window. Charlie looked up. A girl of around her own age was peering in with a quizzical, half-expectant expression. Charlie opened the door and stepped out. "Hi?"

"Are you Charlie?"

"That's me."

"At last! I have been so looking forward to you coming! Stephen told me we are getting a new house mate and when

I hear you were female – well, I was so happy!" The girl offered her hand. "My name's G."

"G?"

"Yep. Or Gosh, but most people just call me G. I know they both sound like exclamations, but what to do?" She laughed and shrugged.

"Well, you know who I am already." Charlie grinned as they shook hands. "Nice to meet you, G."

G laughed. She had long, thick brown hair, an infectious chuckle and an accent Charlie couldn't quite place. "You too." G said. "Come – let me give you a hand with your stuff."

Charlie followed G along the path. A blackbird sang out a shrill, twittering warning from somewhere deep in the hedge as they approached. Charlie's heart sang along with the bird. Banner or no Banner, she already felt as though she'd made the right move.

"So, what would you like?" G opened the fridge and retrieved a bottle of wine. "White – this is really nice, Spanish. Or I have some red in the cupboard. Or–"

"White sounds great. Thanks." Charlie's eyes roved around the huge kitchen with its granite-topped breakfast bar, beautifully restored Aga range and state-of-the-art coffee machine. The units and cupboards were exquisitely unobtrusive, beautifully presented in a dark, peachy matt finish. Not your standard flat-pack assembly, that's for sure, Charlie thought to herself. She knew just by looking that the drawers would glide open at the lightest touch. Everything in the room had been designed for ease and comfort. She felt a sudden pang of jealousy, thinking of the flat she'd just vacated, her parent's poky little galley kitchen. Dad had always promised mum the kitchen of her dreams. If he won the lottery. Charlie's lips tightened. It wasn't going to happen. And here was Banner, reaping his parents' good fortune, taking it all for granted…

"Hey!"

Charlie snapped out of her reverie. G was offering her a glass, eyes twinkling with amusement. "Oh. Thanks." She accepted the glass, a long-stemmed crystal beauty she felt immediately reluctant to handle. "Sorry. Miles away."

"I know what you're thinking. It is too good for Stephen, all this, yes?"

"It's gorgeous. His parents must be worth a bomb."

"He worked in advertising, I think. TV. Some big job. Come on, let's go through."

Charlie followed G into the living room. Well, one of the living rooms. So far she'd only had a brief tour, a 'quick whiz round' as G had called it. "Before you freshen up, because if you are like me that is the first thing you want to do when you get home from your work. Yes?"

G flumped into the sofa with a sigh and kicked off her shoes. She had gorgeously long legs, Charlie noticed, and a very pretty smile, attributes which would not have escaped Banner's attention. Well, whatever. Charlie picked an armchair and sank into its designer folds. Why should she worry? Banner's love life wasn't her problem and G looked as if she could take care of herself. She raised her glass. "Cheers, G. I feel very welcome."

G grinned and lifted her glass in response. "Salut! Stephen's out with Andreas tonight so we have the place to ourselves."

"Who needs men?" Charlie laughed and sipped her drink. "Mmm. This is *gorgeous* wine."

"Glad you like it – I have a secret supplier. You can't get it at the Tesco." G winked.

"Oh yes? Friends in high places?"

G gave her a mysterious look. "Every girl needs the friends."

"Too true." Charlie grinned. G's accent, which could be Slavik, or perhaps Polish, became more pronounced when she was excited, or when she shared a joke. Charlie found it engaging.

"Do you count Stephen as a friend?" G asked with a half-smile on her lips.

"I'm not sure, honestly. I can't even get used to the 'Stephen'. He's 'Banner' to me." Charlie shook her head. "We've never got on that well, to tell you the truth. I'm still surprised at myself that I took him up on this."

"He's fine," G said. "All right most of the time."

"Try working with him." Charlie made a face. "Nightmare."

"I did think he might have waited for you this evening," G said. "You know, to welcome you to the house."

"Don't worry. I wasn't expecting flowers."

Both girls laughed and Charlie raised her glass again. "Oh well, here's to a girly evening." She sat forward in the voluminous armchair. "So come on. Tell me about Andreas."

By the time they had finished the wine Charlie was ready for bed. The strain of covering for Moran, moving house, worrying about whether it was the right thing to do, had taken its toll. G was good company and Charlie couldn't remember the last time she had laughed so much. She set her glass down and stretched. "I'm knackered, G. I'll have to turn in or I'll pass out on you."

"No problem. I'll send your love to the boys."

"Don't you dare," Charlie giggled. She paused at the lounge door. "G, it's been really nice. Thanks for a great welcome."

"*You're* welcome." G yawned. "I'm going to go up to the bed myself."

"Well, night then. And thanks again."

"I hope your sleep is good."

Charlie went upstairs and pottered around the bathroom; yes, it was small, but it was all hers. Her own en-suite. She hummed happily as she changed into her pyjamas and poured herself a glass of water from the bedside jug. The bed was large and comfortable. She set her alarm and snuggled down. The house was very quiet; Banner and Andreas had yet to return. As she drifted into sleep she found herself thinking about Moran, his mysterious disappearing lady. *The lady vanishes*, she thought sleepily. *Where have I heard that before?*

I am the spirit of the forest. I rule the trees, their leaves and branches, the green moss and the dark earth. I choose who will travel my paths, who will run free with the deer and the fox. I move unseen among them, these earthbound souls of clay, and watch and wait.

When the time is right, I take what belongs to me. When the seasons merge, when the year pauses on the cusp of change, I give back to the earth what the long winter has eroded.

I give to it the blood of new life.

Chapter Eight

The thirst was the hardest to tolerate. She could endure the cold. She could cope with the darkness. But the thirst was what made her despair. Time had lost its meaning. And the pain: in her wrists and ankles where the rope cut, in her neck where the steel fingers had half-strangled her, in her mouth where days of dehydration had turned her tongue and mouth to sandpaper. But she was alive. That much she knew. And while she was alive, there was hope.

You are Linda Harrison. Married, with a house, three dogs and a life. You will be missed. Matt will be searching for you.

She twisted, tried to relieve the pressure on her spine where the walls of her prison dug into her back. She was in a space just large enough to lie in, legs curled. Above her was solid stone, on one side a metal grille of some sort, on the other what felt like hard earth studded with sharp-edged rock. *Like being buried alive...* Linda felt panic rise again and forced her mind onto another subject. She tried to picture herself standing in the open, leaning on Matt for support. Her abductor in police custody, the prospect of warmth, safety, *water…*

It's only a matter of time.

But as she lay cramped and blind in her silent dungeon, some essential part of her, a part she kept desperately trying to suppress, went on whispering the one thing she didn't want to hear.

You haven't much time left, Linda.

"You again."

Moran ignored the look, the tone, the frost in the space between them. "I'm sorry to bother you, but I was wondering if I could have a brief word with Mr de Courcy?"

"What about?" Lady Cernham's eyes narrowed.

"I wanted to clear up a misunderstanding."

"And what possible misunderstanding could you be referring to?"

"I'm sure Mr de Courcy would be happy to—"

"Can I help?"

Moran turned to see de Courcy walking briskly from the direction of the outbuildings, a broken shotgun in the crook of his arm.

"It's perfectly all right, Mother," he said, climbing the steps until he reached their level. "Mr Moran and I have already met."

"He's a policeman."

"Yes, yes, I know he's a policeman. It's all right. What can I do for you, Inspector?"

"Oh, just a little thing. It won't take a moment. You see, I was having a drink in the pub and I got chatting to one or two of the locals. An American lady arrived. She was looking for a friend."

"What on earth has all this to do with us, would you mind telling me?" Lady Cernham had come forward onto the porch as if to shoo Moran away like some disposable door-to-door salesman.

"Mother, please." De Courcy raised his voice a fraction.

His mother gave him a long look. "As you wish," she conceded, and with a disapproving shake of her head she retreated into the house.

"I apologise. My mother doesn't take kindly to strangers."

"Not a problem." Moran smiled, he hoped tolerantly. "You were saying?"

"Yes. This American lady. You see, after I left the pub she was found in her car."

"What do you mean, found?"

"She was dead, Mr de Courcy."

"How extraordinary. Is that what you were telling PC Frobisher about?"

"Yes, as it happens."

"But how can I help you, Inspector? I mean, it's terribly sad, I'm sure, but I can't see–"

"Why did you return her hire car?"

"I'm sorry? I don't understand."

"I think you do. A man answering your description returned a silver Lexus to the car hire company early this morning."

"Ridiculous. You can't prove any of this. Absolute nonsense. Now, clear off before I have you removed from my property."

"*Your* property?" Moran pitched the question with an innocent expression. "I understood that the estate belongs to Lady Cernham."

De Courcy half-raised the broken shotgun. "I'm warning you. Leave now. For your own good."

Moran looked steadily at de Courcy. "Sorry to interrupt your day, Mr de Courcy. I've no further questions – for the moment." He gave de Courcy a pleasant smile, turned and, shoulder blades tingling, crunched back to his waiting car.

"What do you know about the Manor house?"

Celine shuffled a beer mat to and fro on the bar and furrowed her brow. "Not a lot. Lady C's a bit of a recluse. I've only ever seen her once, walking in the woods."

"Never comes into the village?"

Celine shook her head. "Not that I've ever known."

Moran was admiring the way Celine's hair was braided into two long plaits, yet somehow coiled into a style that suited the shape of her face. On anyone else of a similar age it might have looked too young, but Celine pulled it off with aplomb.

"Are you with me?" Celine waved her hand up and down, like a camera shutter.

"Sorry. Didn't mean to stare."

She held his gaze. "That's OK. I'm of that 'certain' age when a man's attention has become a bit of a rarity."

"I can't see why," Moran said, swilling his beer around the half-empty pint jug.

"You old charmer, you." Celine grinned, obviously pleased. "Cork man through and through."

Moran smiled. He enjoyed Celine's company, but he was also wondering how much to tell her. For all he knew she might be a close friend of de Courcy's, although something told him that wasn't the case. "I thought I might visit Mrs

Harrison's husband tomorrow."

Celine raised her eyebrows. "You really can't switch off, can you?" She toyed absently with one of her plaits. "Brendan, you're on holiday. You've reported an incident. Let the local police deal with it. Relax. It's probably nothing."

"A dead woman? Nothing?"

Celine sighed. "Maybe we were wrong. I mean, no one's reported her missing, have they? I'll bet she just had second thoughts about staying over and–"

"I traced her car."

Celine's mouth hung open. "Really? How?"

"It wasn't difficult. I contacted the hire company."

"Oh. I see." Celine's face was a picture of confusion. "Well, I don't actually."

"Whoever returned the car, it wasn't Blanche."

"Curiouser and curiouser."

"So, I was wondering if you knew where I might find Matt Harrison? Maybe his wife has come back from wherever she's been; she may be able to fill in the gaps." He decided not to mention his conversation with de Courcy – nor his intuitive feeling that Linda Harrison would not be at home.

"Sure. It's on the corner, right by the village stores. Crossroads Cottage."

"Great. Thanks."

"Are the police really doing nothing at all?"

"I tried to contact DS Wilmot again. No go – Exeter has been hit by a flu bug. They're short-staffed, flat out busy according to the desk sergeant, and I can't get hold of Wilmot or anyone else. Not that he took any of it seriously anyway."

"Same again?" Terl's broad arm hovered over the glasses.

"A half for me, Terl. Thanks. Celine?"

"Not for now, Terl. Cheers anyway."

Moran reached for his half-pint and felt his heart skip as Celine placed her hand on his. "Brendan. Perhaps it would be better to let all this pass by. The village is … well, it's different here."

"Different? How, exactly?"

"I can't explain. It's just – well, it's just the way things are. Look, Brendan, I really like you. I don't want to see you getting into trouble." She read Moran's blank expression. "I'm not making much sense, am I? Look, I have to go. Why don't we meet up tomorrow lunchtime, maybe drive to the coast, take a look around, have lunch?"

"Sounds like a good idea," Moran nodded. "Come over to mine, say ten o'clock?"

Celine visibly relaxed and treated him to a wide smile. "Great. See you then. Sleep well."

Moran nursed his beer as he pondered Celine's remarks. What was she trying to hide? What sort of trouble was he about to get into? One thing was certain; Celine knew a lot more about what was going on than she was prepared to admit. Ten o'clock. Fine. That still allowed him an hour or so to visit Crossroads Cottage in the morning.

Moran poured himself a nightcap, an oaty malt he had been introduced to by his sergeant, Rob Phelps. He took a sip and grunted appreciatively as the fiery liquid warmed his throat. He wondered how Phelps was getting on. The heart attack had come out of nowhere, as they always did. Phelps had been lucky. Moran grinned as he thought of Phelps' battered features expressing disagreement in his usual forthright way. "*Lucky?*" he would have said. "*Flat on my back for months, a teetotal diet, Chaucer and the Bard for stimulation, daytime TV for relaxation and Mrs P laying down the law 24/7? Lucky? I think not, guv, I think not.*"

Moran slumped into the small sofa. He missed Phelps. Would the DS return? He hoped so, but had his doubts. It was stressful work at the best of times, and Rob always gave his all. He'd need a radical switch of lifestyle, and Moran was doubtful whether Phelps would even want to make such a drastic change. Still, another couple of months of daytime TV might do the trick, or maybe the patient would fail to find solace in his Open University Shakespeare after all.

Moran sat quietly, warming the whisky. Charlie Pepper was a safe pair of hands in his – and Phelps' – absence. No worries there.

Charlie.

Don't even go there, Brendan. Too young. Too close to home. Station romance was always unwise. Nevertheless…

And what about Celine? A very attractive proposition. But she was guarded, keeping her distance. Something to hide, perhaps. Or a bad history of relationships. *I'll drink to that,* his subconscious whispered.

But she had tried to warn him off. Who was she trying to protect? She knew damn well that Blanche Cassidy was dead. She couldn't have faked that. Moran had seen shock before. The pallor, the shakes, the slight incoherence of expression. The questioning. No, she had been sure all right. But now, apparently not. Had someone spoken to her? Warned her off? Moran took another sip and thought about de Courcy.

Leave now. For your own good…

Moran tossed down the remainder of the malt and banged his glass on the table. De Courcy wasn't to know, was he? That, to Moran, an undisguised threat was like a red rag to a bull?

No sign of life at Crossroads Cottage, but a regular, percussive sound from the rear of the property indicated activity of some kind. Moran opened the gate and followed the path around the cottage into the back garden. A man in a red vest was laying rhythmically into a section of tree trunk, swinging a long-handled axe in a wide arc and bringing the head expertly down in precisely the same location as the previous stroke. Splinters flew as the wood shuddered under the blow. The axe lifted again. The man looked up and the axe halted in mid-swing.

"Mr Harrison?"

"Who the hell are you?" Matt Harrison squared his shoulders and hefted the axe before letting it dangle, loose-gripped, at his side. He was a fit-looking young man in his early thirties, short hair with the fashionably flicked tuft at the front which, to the great amusement of the rest of the team, Moran had once tried to adopt. "Bit young for you, sir," one of the WPCs had advised, *sotto voce*, in the canteen queue. Since then Moran had stuck with a regular off-centre parting.

"DCI Brendan Moran. Hope you don't mind my arriving unannounced, but I thought you might be able to help me."

"With what?" Harrison's stance was not aggressive, but neither was it inviting.

"I understand that your wife was expecting a visitor?"

"What's it to you?" Harrison rested the axe against the back wall of the cottage and wiped sweat from his temple with the back of his hand.

"An American lady. An old friend. Perhaps I could have a word with your wife?"

"She's not here."

"I see." Moran watched Harrison's face. It was giving nothing away. "When will she be in?"

"No idea."

"Well, later this morning?" Moran prompted. "This evening?"

"I said I don't know, all right? She's away."

"Away?"

"Away. Not here. Not at home." Harrison picked up the axe and made as if to resume his chopping.

Moran hesitated. Should he push any harder? He wanted something tangible, something to go on, however small. He noticed a roomy kennel near the front door but there was no sign of a canine occupant. "Dog out too?"

"She's probably taken them somewhere. A friend's, maybe. Like I said, I'm not her keeper."

"Perhaps you could ask her to call me. She can leave a message if I don't answer – the signal's bad here. I'll get back to her." He handed Harrison his card.

Harrison glanced at it briefly. "Thames Valley? What are you doing poking around here?"

"I'm helping with a local enquiry." Which was not untrue.

Harrison looked at him. "Really."

"Thanks for your help, sir. Sorry to bother you." Moran walked away but paused at the side gate and turned. "You don't recall anyone looking for your wife the other evening?"

Harrison leaned on the axe. "No. I don't."

"You see, the person in question had arranged to visit."

"I said no."

"I see. Strange, because the lady told me that she'd spoken to you." Moran registered Harrison's expression, a mixture of surprise and outright hostility. "Well, thanks anyway, sir. I'll be in touch."

He felt the eyes bore into his back as he pushed the gate open. Moran glanced at his watch. Ten o'clock. It was nearly time to see a friendlier face. He couldn't help feeling that, all things considered, he was becoming rather unpopular in Cernham.

Chapter Nine

Linda Harrison woke from an exhausted sleep cold, sore, and, as memory washed into her consciousness, absolutely terrified. She knew she was going to die. She wasn't a prisoner; for a prisoner there was always the prospect of release. No, she had been incarcerated, left to rot. No one would find her. She would die here, and her body would dissolve into the earth like so much fertiliser. The thought made her hysterical and she found herself laughing at the absurdity until the laughter broke down into a fresh bout of sobbing. Eventually her breathing calmed and her heart rate slowed. There must be hope; she would *make* there be hope. Blanche would have arrived by now. If she was still as feisty as Linda remembered she would leave no stone unturned. And Matt would be out of his mind with worry. He would search; they would never give up. *Never give up...*

Her leg cramped and she screwed up her face at the agonising pain, unable to straighten or relax the iron-hard muscle. She heard herself whimper like a caged animal as the pain twisted like a knife then very, very slowly receded.

She gasped in relief.

The grey light was fading. Evening had come around again. How many days? Two? Three? What did it matter? She wouldn't have to endure the cold nights for much longer. There was just one thing she wanted to know. Not *who*. No, the question that haunted her was *why*. She couldn't imagine who could hate her this much. She had never made enemies, never had so much as a bad quarrel with anyone…

That was when she heard the footsteps – slow, purposeful footsteps, yet strangely unbalanced, as if the owner had some difficulty walking. A brief, metallic rattle gave way to a low, murmuring chant which found its way into each nook and cranny of her prison like a gust of icy wind.

She closed her eyes.

Chapter Ten

Charlie woke suddenly and spent a good fifteen seconds wondering where she was before her memory kicked in.

Banner's house.

No – wrong.

My new home.

That had a better ring to it. The clock said 9.36am. She was on lates this week. Praise be. She lay back and luxuriated in the big double bed, smiling as she recalled the previous night's girly session and her new friend's irrepressible chatter. Charlie stretched. She had slept like a log. *Woke up in the fireplace...* her brain automatically cued the old Groucho Marx joke.

She swung her legs out of bed and yawned. The house was quiet. No passing traffic to disturb the morning's peace, no buses thundering along the main road. This *was* a good move, Charlie girl.

She congratulated herself again on her way to the en-suite bathroom. As she brushed her teeth and ran a hand through her hair she wondered how she would deal with Banner's questionable wit as she prepared breakfast, or how she would manage to hold her tongue when he started on his lame innuendos. Not Banner – *Stephen*, she reminded herself. Stephen here. Banner at work.

But would it work? Could she live *and* work with him? Time would tell. She dressed quickly – jeans and a Mumford and Sons t-shirt – and skipped down the wide staircase to the kitchen. There was no one there. Perhaps Banner had already left for the day? But he was on lates too… She knew that because she had drawn up the rota herself. Still in bed then. Lazy sod.

Charlie whistled as she made coffee and toast. Should she make something for G? Better not. She mightn't appreciate a wake-up call for tea and toast. Still, Charlie wanted to do something to show her appreciation for being made to feel very much at home. She settled for laying the table, preparing a fresh cafetiere of coffee and scribbling a note. She continued writing as a list of supermarket essentials crowded into her mind.

Ten minutes later she was out the door, coat on, heading for Tesco. She would catch up with G later.

The sun was warm, a perfect spring day in the making. As Charlie clipped her seat belt she wondered how Moran was getting on. She grinned at the thought of the guv abandoning his R and R for a spot of door to door and shook her head. Once a copper…

It was almost two by the time Charlie returned, laden with Tesco bags and dying for a cup of tea. She dumped her bags on the doorstep and spent thirty seconds trying to untangle the front door key which had somehow managed to jam itself in the key ring fob. She freed it with a muttered expletive just as the front door opened.

"Hello. You must be Charlie."

Charlie felt her mouth gaping like a goldfish. The man who had addressed her was possibly – no, *definitely* – the most strikingly handsome man she had ever seen. He was somewhere in his late twenties with dark, collar-length hair which flopped attractively across his forehead. His eyes were green, his chiselled but expressive face topped off with a wide, friendly smile which would have done George Clooney proud.

"Yes. Hi. I wasn't–"

"Let me take those."

Charlie felt her knees weakening as she groped for something coherent to say. "Oh. Thanks." She followed him meekly into the kitchen. "I actually quite enjoy shopping." *Whaaat, Charlie?* She tried again. "So, you're Andreas, then?" *Brilliant…*

"Yes." He leaned against the breakfast bar and folded his arms. The smiling eyes followed her movements. He was wearing chinos and a navy jumper that did little to hide his impressive physique. "And how are you settling in?"

"Fine. I mean, really well. I met G last night. We talked non-stop, had a few glasses of wine, put the world to rights, you know."

Andreas laughed softly. "Sounds like a G evening. G for girls, that is."

"Yes." Charlie felt her face reddening. "Anyway," she babbled on. "Where's Ban– Stephen? I haven't seen him since I got here."

"No?" Andreas frowned. "He must have had a good night

also, I guess."

"I thought he was with you?"

Andreas nodded. "He was. But he went with a friend. Clubbing. I was tired. I have work, so I came home."

Clubbing. On a weekday. She'd have words, for sure. The irritation she felt at Banner's irresponsible attitude helped her defluster. She began to unpack her shopping.

"You are annoyed with him? Ah yes, you work with him? You are his boss?"

"That's right. For the moment, anyway."

Andreas moved silently across the kitchen floor and lifted the kettle. "Tea?"

"You read my mind."

"I wouldn't like to be in Stephen's shoes when you catch up with him," Andreas said with a grin as he filled the kettle.

Charlie paused with her hand in the last Tesco bag. "Seriously. I don't come over that scary, do I?"

Andreas plonked two mugs on the breakfast bar. "Not at all. I'm – what is your word? – yes, teasing."

"That's OK, then." Charlie sat on one of the elegant breakfast bar stools and checked her phone for messages. There was only some rubbish notification from Twitter. She'd been half-expecting something from the guv. No emails. Good; all well then.

"Sugar?"

"No thanks." She took the proffered mug.

"So." Andreas sat on the opposite stool and sipped his drink. "You have a day off today?"

"Nope. Late shift."

"Ah. Then the local bad guys must watch out."

"I hear you're an IT man," Charlie said quickly. Andreas

seemed nice, but a little too familiar for someone she'd only just met. Maybe it was a cultural thing. She tried to remember his nationality. Judging by the accent, Andreas sounded as if he'd learned his English in the States.

"Yes. I specialise in system integration. Middleware. I have a short contract with a company called Oracle."

"We have an Oracle database," Charlie nodded. "And we could do with someone like you onsite. Our systems are always going down."

"Bad support?"

Charlie shrugged. "They talk a good story on the phone. Never seem to fix anything, though."

Andreas laughed. "I'm sure you'd notice if they all went home."

"I'm not sure we would," Charlie said. "Anyway, I shouldn't be telling you this. Confidentiality and so on."

"Of course. No problem."

Charlie glanced at the kitchen clock. Four thirty-five already. Time to get going. "Thanks for the tea. I have to get ready for work. Nice to meet you."

"Sure. You too."

As she left the kitchen Charlie noticed that the cafetiere of coffee she had prepared earlier was still there. Beside it lay her note to G, untouched and, by the look of it, unread.

Charlie went upstairs, hesitated outside G's door. Should she knock? No, better not. G might have company, or still be asleep. She pressed her ear to the door and then felt immediately guilty and embarrassed. What if Andreas caught her eavesdropping? She hurried away along the deeply-carpeted corridor to her own room.

As she changed into her work suit she heard Andreas

clattering around in the kitchen, the sound of a tap running. Domesticated, then. Another plus.

Make up. Phone. Handbag. Deep breath. She looked herself up and down in the full-length mirror. Not bad. She would pass for a DI.

*You **are** a DI, girl. You worked damn hard to get it. Walk tall.*

Keys. A last look around. Tidy room. Good. She closed the door behind her. The house was quiet. No, there was music somewhere – Keane? Yes. Good taste as well, then.

As Charlie let the handbrake off and eased her car into second she found herself humming the tune she had heard as she was leaving: *If you have a minute, why don't we go talk about it, somewhere only we know…*

The small seaside town was reluctantly stirring from a prolonged winter lull, its freshly-opened shop, café and restaurant doors yawning widely to swallow passing tourists, like plankton drifting into the mouth of a whale.

Moran and Celine walked arm in arm among the visitors, exploring the narrow cobbled streets, window-shopping and conversing easily about nothing in particular.

"Coffee?" Celine pointed to an attractive corner café.

"Good idea." Moran allowed himself to be led to a table and sat gratefully, feeling the familiar stiffness in his leg, a constant reminder of Charnford Abbey and the closest brush with death he had experienced in a long, eventful career.

"Are you all right?" Celine let the menu in her hand drop onto the tabletop.

"I'm fine. My leg gets a little stiff after walking. It's nothing."

They ordered, an espresso for Moran and a latte for

Celine, and sat awhile in companiable silence watching the world go by. Moran felt an uneasy contentment. He knew that he was about to spoil the moment. After a moment's consideration, he elected to at least wait until they had finished their drinks. A lone gull circled overhead, side slipping in the breeze, scouring the area for scraps. There was a pleasant tang of salt in the air and the promise of, if not warmth, then at least stability in the mid-afternoon sunshine.

He swallowed the last of his coffee and wondered how to start. No point in beating around the bush. Celine knew something and he needed to find out why she was so reluctant to share it with him.

"You said that Cernham was different. What did you mean by that?"

Celine stiffened. "Nothing, really. It's a typical English village. Everybody knows everyone else. You can't do anything without it being round the whole place in half a day."

"'Typical' isn't 'different'."

She shrugged. "I suppose I meant different to what I was used to before I lived there."

"No, you didn't," Moran said. "Why won't you tell me? Is it something to do with de Courcy?"

"Him? God, no. Why would it be?"

"You tell me."

"Look, Brendan. You've been here a few days. You don't understand village life. You live in a big town near London, so how could you?" She paused, took a sip of her latte. "We get on well. It's nice. I'm not under any illusions here. I know you'll go back to Berkshire, back to your work. Let's just enjoy the time we have, OK?"

"I'd like that," Moran said. "But we both know that a woman died. And I need to know what happened."

"You're like a dog with a bone, aren't you?" Celine gave him a half-smile of – what? Frustration? Maybe a little disappointment?

"I'm sorry. I'm a copper."

"Don't be sorry. You're you, and that's why I like you."

"The feeling is entirely mutual."

She laughed. "Good."

"But I need to know."

"All right. You're very perceptive. De Courcy and I had a little thing going a while back."

"I see."

"No, you don't." Celine fiddled with her cup. Her nails were painted blood red. She looked up. "It's just that … well, I might have seen him in the car."

"De Courcy? In Blanche's car? When?"

Celine sighed. "I couldn't sleep that night, after what had happened, you know. I was standing at the window; I suppose it must have been four or five in the morning. It just drove past, slowly. Maybe the engine was off; it seemed to just roll quietly past. I saw him – at least, I think it was him."

"Driving?"

"Yes."

"Well, that makes sense."

"Does it?"

"Yes. It does."

Moran related his conversation with the car hire company.

Celine had gone pale, was worrying at the tablecloth. "Oh God. Do you think he–" She looked up.

"I don't know, Celine. But he at least knows what happened. Look, I can understand that you want to protect him; if you had a relationship it's only natural that–"

"No. Not a relationship. A nightmare."

"You'd better explain," Moran said softly. "It might be better in the long run, when it all comes out."

"You mean in court, don't you?" Her voice began to quaver. "That can't happen, Brendan. It mustn't happen."

"What are you so frightened of?" Moran took her hand, which was trembling. "Listen, de Courcy isn't above the law. Whatever is going on needs to come out. You'll be fully protected."

"Against *them*? I don't think so."

"Tell me. Tell me what you know, Celine."

"I will. I just need the loo. Excuse me."

"Sure."

Moran waited, deep in thought. Five minutes later he was cursing himself for an idiot. He hurried into the café and accosted a waitress.

"A lady?"

"Yes, she went to the toilet." Moran struggled to keep his cool.

"We don't have a toilet here, sir. I'm sorry."

Moran pushed past and went to the rear of the café where a small patio area had been created to allow the inclusion of four more tables. There was a fence and a back gate, which was open.

Damn.

He spent twenty minutes trawling the streets but eventually gave up and went back to the car park.

The sun was going down as he turned into his petrol

station by the Cernham turnoff. He filled the tank and wondered how else he could have handled Celine and the now thorny issue of extracting any worthwhile information from her. De Courcy clearly had a leading role if not in the death, then certainly in the disappearance of the American woman. As he replaced the petrol cap and walked pensively across the forecourt he realised that he was now resigned to the abandonment of his holiday. He had a duty to follow this to its conclusion, however inconvenient.

"All right, boss?"

Moran looked up to see the familiar smile of the shop attendant. His badge said "Manjit – happy to help".

"Hello again, Manjit." Moran fumbled in his wallet. "Hang on a second. Can't find my blasted wallet."

"All good today?" Manjit asked brightly.

"Not really." Moran checked his other pockets. Nothing. "I won't be a moment," he told Manjit.

His wallet wasn't in the car either. That meant he had left it in the café. Or it had been stolen. He went back to the counter. "I'm terribly sorry, but I seem to have lost my wallet. Look, here's my ID – can I owe you?"

Manjit scrutinised Moran's credentials and returned the card with a grin. "Sure, boss. I can trust a policeman."

"Well, I'm glad someone can."

"No cola today?"

"Not today. Listen, I'll be back tomorrow. I have another credit card in my suitcase."

"No problem. See you then, Chief Inspector Moran."

Moran followed the winding road towards Cernham village. He didn't want to admit to the obvious: that Celine had taken his wallet. But why? Moran racked his brains, tried to recall every conversation. Nothing made sense. His car's shadow danced ahead in the late afternoon sunshine, distorting and jinking with each bump and dip in the narrow road.

Chapter Eleven

The voices were close, very close, as though their owners were huddled just outside, just beyond her field of vision. Linda drew her legs into her body, wrapped her arms about her, wished she could shut the noise out.

"Well? What now?"

"Kill her."

"Why?"

"She'll talk. Make trouble."

"Keep her, then."

"In the house?"

"There are spaces."

A crunch of gravel, someone shuffling their feet. A cough.

Light flooded in. Linda's heart beat a tattoo of fear. Her eyes wouldn't focus. Shadows, faces, stale breath. Something poked her in the side and she stifled a scream.

"Alive."

"That's all we need to know for the present. You can tell him."

"No, you."

The light disappeared. Footsteps receded. Linda breathed again.

When she had regained her composure she made herself stretch, fearful of the terrible cramp which was never far away.

And something rattled. Something loose.

Her heartbeat accelerated. Had they left something open by mistake? She prodded experimentally and felt something give. She pushed again and some unseen part of her prison crashed to the ground. She froze. After a while she felt brave enough to wriggle again, shuffling towards the space she had made. Once, twice she tried to roll, but she was so stiff and cold it was hard to make any progress. *One more, Linda, come on…* She made a huge effort and rolled into space. For a split second she hung as if suspended from a wire, and then she felt herself falling. She hit something solid and the breath was driven out of her.

Linda writhed, badly winded, willing her lungs to take in air. After thirty seconds of torture she was able to take a ragged breath, then another, and another, until her breathing had returned to near normal. She was scared to move her arms or legs, sure that she must have broken something in the fall, but the ground she was lying on had a soft, earthy quality. She flexed her legs experimentally. There was no agony of fractured bone, just aches and pains – bruising for sure, but at least she could move without restraint.

But where to? It was dark and she could vaguely make out that she was in some kind of building, but she couldn't tell whether square or round. Was there an exit? Very slowly she sat up, groaning at the stiffness and soreness in her spine. Hope fluttered in her stomach. She would get out of here, somehow.

On all fours she began a cautious exploration. The air smelled musty and damp. Perhaps she was in some kind of storehouse? And then she saw it – a ramp of raised earth.

The way out.

The thought made her dizzy. She was so close. She crawled on, her senses vibrating like antennae, ears straining for any noise that would indicate the return of her captors. In her weakened state the effort to crawl up the ramp almost defeated her, but she screwed up every last ounce of strength and used her legs and feet to push herself to the top.

And there was the door. Partially ajar.

A long, dusty beam of moonlight picked out the wooden struts and contours of the building. The door creaked as a gust of wind blew an eddy of dead leaves along the floor and made the hinges complain. Linda lay flat, hardly daring to breathe. Silence returned. She moved forward, scraping her knee on something sharp, an old nail or splinter of wood; she didn't stop to check. Now she was at the door to the outside; she pulled herself upright, leaned on the rough wall for support. Taking a deep breath she put her head through the opening and looked out.

Bright moonlight illuminated a large garden, tinting the extremities of its bushes and trees a dull silver like some Victorian daguerreotype. Linda felt a sudden wave of nausea and held onto the door for support.

Keep calm. Listen. Watch.

Nothing moved. To the left a line of trees provided good cover. If she could make it that far, it would be just a question of finding a road, flagging someone down.

One thing at a time… Let's get out of here first…

She eased herself through the opening and took a tentative step outside. The urge to run, to just make a break for it, was almost overpowering, but Linda waited, checking the shadows. When she was sure she was not being observed she limped stiffly to the nearest cover, a laurel hedge, feeling the waxy leaves brush her skin as she pressed herself against them. Her heart was racing. Ahead of her was an expanse of lawn, the flat contours only broken by a sundial, or maybe a fountain of some kind? It would provide little cover. She had no choice but to cross the moonlit expanse if she were to have any hope of making cover. Linda looked up. There were few clouds, but none were anywhere near enough to the moon to offer her the critical twenty seconds she needed.

Now or never, Lin, come on...

She broke cover, hobbling as fast as her cold limbs would allow. Half way across she heard it: a shambling, thumping sound of pursuit. She choked back a scream and threw herself at the line of trees, so close, so close... Fear lent her wings and she crashed into the woodland at full sprint. Behind her came the noise she remembered, the deep, heavy breathing, the oddly spaced footfalls, uneven yet powerful and fast.

She felt branches in her face, tangling her hair, the breath heaving in her chest. A stitch was forming around her midriff, crippling her so that she was running almost bent double. The moonlight, her recent enemy, now befriended her, filtering through the woodland's burgeoning foliage and showing her the beaten path ahead. But her muscles, weakened by hunger and thirst, had little energy left and she felt control slipping away. The realisation made her panic and she tripped on a root, fell full length. Her head connected with something hard and she saw stars.

As she lay stunned, something stood over her. It wasn't until the ice-cold grip clamped around her arm that she finally gave voice to her terror and let out an agonised, primal scream of despair.

To her surprise the pressure eased and her pursuer straightened, stepped back.

What?

She was on all fours now. The figure was silent, watching her. She glanced to her left – she could see the way through. There was a path, maybe even one she had walked the dogs along in some previous existence. She knew what was happening, and the realisation filled her with a hopeless dread.

He's playing with me...

Linda bolted, bullying her legs into action. She flew along the path, not daring to turn, waiting for the awful sound of footsteps behind.

Nothing.

She stopped, turned, fell again, got up, stumbled on. The ground was getting muddier, wetter, sucking at her feet. She slowed to a standstill, clutched at a sapling, retched bile, wiped her mouth and staggered on. Two metres later she realised her mistake: she was no longer running on solid ground. Her feet were catching – no, *sinking* – into the earth.

The bog...

She was up to her knees in soft, sucking moistness. With a cry she tried to pull a leg out, to backtrack. It was no use. She only succeeded in sinking even further.

No, no, no, no...

It was up to her thighs, the weight of peat and

decomposition which formed the body of the great bog squeezing against her like some living thing, pulling, drawing her down.

And he was there, at the edge. Watching.

Watching me die...

She couldn't believe it was all going to end like this, with no answers, no reason given ...

Very quickly her own weight drew her inexorably down. She took a final, despairing gulp of air and the bog closed gently over her head. Two small bubbles rose and were replaced by three more, before they also popped and were gone. The murky water swirled once, twice, and was still.

A figure detached itself from the shadows and hovered, head bowed, at the edge of the bog, as though mourning the passing of some noble beast. A long time later it moved away, almost sorrowful in its gait, until it too was absorbed by the darkness.

Chapter Twelve

"Seen the Banner man, Charlie?"

Charlie looked up from the mound of paperwork which, despite her best efforts, had accumulated on Moran's desk. "I wish," she told the detective sergeant, a likeable lad from Braintree with the unlikely name of Toby Glascock, better known throughout TVP as 'Brit', an abbreviation of 'Brittledick'. However, as his senior officer, Charlie had thought it wise to stick with plain 'Toby' .

"He is on tonight, isn't he?" Toby scratched his chin absently. "According to the rota."

"He is. Do me a favour, Toby, would you? Give his mobile a call and tell him if he doesn't haul his arse in here by seven at the latest there'll be trouble."

Toby grinned. "Pleasure."

Charlie bit her lip. It wasn't like Banner to be quite so irresponsible. Stupid, yes. Stubborn, yes, occasionally. But a no-show was unusual. Banner liked his work, she knew that. He enjoyed being a detective. Sometimes he was even quite good at it. Trouble was, he was also pretty good at partying.

She remembered the conversation with Andreas, the look he had given her when he had told her about Banner's friend and their clubbing intentions. But her mind was also reaching back to another scenario – the time when Banner had been clobbered at the Zodiac, the club frequented by the late Ranandan brothers, two of Huang Xian Kuai's deputy drug pushers. Banner had been found half-comatose, trousers around his ankles and his bloodstream swimming not with alcohol but with a dangerous dose of Ketamine. It had been a warning. *Back off…*

But the Ranandans were dead. The Zodiac was clean – well, cleaner, at any rate. And who knows where Banner had intended to go? Maybe he had mentioned the club to Andreas. Should she call him at the house? No, not yet. Banner was a big boy, he could look after himself. Charlie chewed her biro, only dimly aware of the buzz of conversation filtering in from the open plan office as the rest of her team arrived for their shift.

Enough.

There was no point worrying about something that probably hadn't happened. Whatever, Banner had better have a damn good excuse.

The phone rang. She picked it up reluctantly. For some reason she had forebodings of bad news.

"Charlie?"

"Guv! Nice to hear your dulcet tones again. How's things in the wild west?"

"Unsettling, to be honest."

Moran sounded decidedly unholiday-like. Something in his tone…

"How can I help? Did you find the awol woman?"

"Not yet. This is a wild shot, Charlie. I don't want to waste your time."

"Come on, guv. Out with it."

"OK. Can you have a nose around any old unsolveds in the Cernham area? Get someone to check back through any media coverage, anything at all on the area. Whatever it is, just drop me a line anyway."

"Why not Exeter?" Charlie asked. Strictly speaking it was their patch, but obviously there was a reason.

"Forget it," Moran told her. "Undermanned and fighting flu. I've given up."

"Ah. But what are we looking for?"

"I don't know. Misper, maybe. Suspicious death? Something's being hidden here. Something somebody doesn't want me to know."

"OK. I'll get someone on it."

"Banner will be delighted."

"Uh huh." Charlie hesitated. Should she say something?

"Uh huh what?"

She could sense Moran's antennae twitching. "Guv, you know I said I was going to move?"

"Yes. Sooner the better, I believe I suggested."

"You did. Well … I've taken your advice. I've moved in with Banner."

"You've *what*?"

Charlie laughed out loud, drawing surprised looks from the desks immediately outside Moran's office. "No, not like that. He mentioned that he had a spare room, you know. And there's two other people sharing. It sounded great, actually. And it is. The house is amazing."

There was a brief silence at the other end, then: "Well,

good. I don't know what to say. I mean, you and Banner…"

"I know. But we won't get in each other's way. It's a big house."

"It'll need to be."

Charlie smiled as Moran expressed his surprise down the wire.

"You'll probably end up an item," Moran said.

Charlie snorted in derision. "I think not."

"Mark my words."

"*Guv!*"

"Well, I'm glad you're in a safe place, Charlie. Seriously. After what happened I wasn't happy with you staying put."

"I know. I'm fine now. Sorted."

"Good. Anyway, see what you can do about Cernham. It's not a priority, but…"

"But it is really. Got it."

"Bye, Charlie."

"Bye."

Charlie put the receiver down with a smile. Now, which officer would best be suited to Moran's request? Not Toby. She needed him on other stuff. Maybe George…

"Evening, Charlie."

Charlie looked up as DCS Higginson came in.

The Chief surveyed the office. "News, views?"

"That was DCI Moran, sir." Charlie offered Higginson a seat, which he declined with a regretful gesture.

"Meeting with the CC this evening. Have to be punctual. Anyway, what's Moran doing calling you from afar? Keeping a weather eye open?"

"It was nothing, sir. He's enjoying his leave."

"Glad to hear it. What about this Chinese fellow?"

"No recent sightings, sir. We're keeping all likely venues under obs."

"Great. Well, have a good night. Let me know if I can help with anything."

"Sir."

"Oh, and Charlie?"

"Sir?"

"You're going to take some time off when Brendan gets back, OK?"

"But–"

"Some time off," Higginson interrupted with another of his fatherly looks which almost made Charlie fill up again. "No arguing. You didn't take a break after the Ranandan case, did you? Not even a day to recover from what I understand was a very serious assault?"

"No, sir," Charlie said quietly. And she hadn't. What would have been the point? She would only have stayed at home, front door barred (*replacement* front door), waiting for her next duty day to come round. Fretting. Watching every passer-by.

"Well then." Higginson nodded briskly. "No arguing." He grinned. "See you later."

After Higginson had left Charlie wondered whether she should have mentioned Banner's unexplained absence. No. Not yet. She wanted to know for herself what the Banner man had been up to. The phone rang. Charlie sighed, and pushing the paperwork to one side she reached for the beeping instrument. She listened to the caller, one of the patrol car lads suspicious that a town centre assault might be drug-related. Charlie had asked to be first on the call list for any sniff of drug-related crime, and the officer had thought it prudent that she should know. Good man. Charlie made a note of the name. After Sheldrake's warning it wasn't worth taking any chances.

She bumped into DC George McConnell on her way out. The wiry Scot had accepted her instructions without question, as she'd known he would. That was why she'd chosen him. Banner would have moaned loudly, Toby would certainly have pointed out that Cernham was a tad beyond TVP's normal jurisdiction, and the new DC, Tessa Martin – well, she was new. And although George's rather peculiar end-of-shift habit of having to collar an audience to summarize the events of his working day grated a little, he was nevertheless a good, solid copper. George simply did what he was asked, and very efficiently too.

"Boss. I have a few bits. Nothing too meaty, though."

"Oh, thanks George. Look, I know it's a little off track, but–"

"The thing is," George interrupted, "I'm actually quite interested in this historical stuff. It's not the first they've found in the UK, either. I must say, I didn't realise they'd dug one up in Somerset."

"George, you've lost me."

"Sorry. A bog body. You know, preserved in peat."

"Right." Charlie frowned. She was tired and running low on patience.

Undeterred by Charlie's weary expression, George went on. "There was a big archaeological hoo ha in '78 – guess where? Yep, Cernham. Some local yokel found a hand sticking out of the bog. Turned out to be four thousand years old."

"George—"

"I'm getting there. Now, the thing is that this wasn't the only body in the bog; a search turned up another one, but it was a lot younger. By this time they had a pukka archaeologist on site and local press coverage to boot."

"Go on."

"It was thought that it might be the body of a missing girl, name of Rachel O'Neill." George paused. "So the press conjectured, anyhow."

"And? Was it?"

"That's the thing. The body disappeared before it could be positively identified."

"And where exactly did this disappearance occur? Coroner's office? Path lab?"

George delivered his punch line with evident pleasure. "Neither, boss. It disappeared way before it got to that stage, according to the local rag. But here's the thing – the archaeologist was interviewed by the same reporter a few days later but by then he'd changed his tune – said he couldn't be sure if the second body *was* recent after all. Said how he had acted too hastily, jumped to conclusions before a proper analysis could be performed and so on."

"Interesting. So what happened then?"

"Not a lot by the look of it." George gnawed his fingernail. "It all went quiet."

"What about this archaeologist, though? Is he still alive? You could try contacting him."

"Nah," said George. "A week later the local paper carried a ten liner about him."

"Don't tell me. He died?"

George shrugged. "No one knows for sure by the look of it

but he and his wife disappeared. They never returned to the site."

Just after six, Charlie climbed wearily into the driver's seat of her blue Kia Picanto. The dawn sun, promising a warm day, highlighted the deep shadows beneath her eyes as she checked herself briefly in the mirror. *What a state. Zippy breakfast then bed for you, girl…*

She guided the car along the empty but soon to be bustling roads towards the leafier suburbs of the University area and her new home. The shift had been busy, but routine. The drug-related assault had turned out not to be, which was a relief. Higginson's suggestion of time off was becoming more and more appealing. She could shop, maybe buy some pictures for her bedroom to replace the musty old portraits of Banner's parents' tenure. And maybe even a day or two in Cov? She could catch up with a few mates. Get away, recharge the batteries.

But not yet. Not till the guv was back. She'd have to call Moran tomorrow with news of George's bog body. Strange one, that. Probably no connection, but you never knew.

The house was quiet. Charlie dumped her bag on the breakfast bar and checked the coffee machine. Her note to G was still there. And the coffee. *So what?* G had probably had to rush out somewhere. She made toast, filled her customary glass of water and headed upstairs. Which was Banner's room? Should she check? He was probably still sleeping it off. By god, he'd be sorry this evening…

Her bedroom was warm and cosy. She drew the heavy curtains, changed into a light onesie, read a few pages of a paperback until her eyes grew heavy, flopped onto the bed and was asleep within seconds.

Sixteen minutes later her bedroom door slowly opened and closed again with a muffled *click*. Charlie slept on.

I wait, and watch, and hunt – I move in harmony with the earth goddess and she in turn soaks up the life I offer – you see, men who are truly men possess this instinctive knowledge, a deep awareness of what is needed.

Of what **she** *needs...*

And now she has shared her secrets with me.

And now I know.

I know that she is not yet satisfied.

Chapter Thirteen

Moran looked at his watch and pondered his next move. He'd had a solitary meal at the pub and Terl hadn't been particularly forthcoming. Celine was nowhere to be found. Not for the first time he found himself wishing he was back at work; he missed the banter of the station, the cut and thrust of station politics, the constant pressure of keeping a dozen or more issues spinning like plates at the forefront of his mind. He missed Charlie. He missed Shona. He hadn't yet plucked up the courage to call her since the Ranandan case had come to its chaotic conclusion. Moran sighed deeply. *You don't know what you want, Brendan, do you?*

He poured himself a large malt and cast his eyes around the cottage interior. Should he pay Matt Harrison another visit? Or should he just leave the whole damn thing alone and go home, dumping it all in Exeter's lap on the way?

He collapsed into the armchair and closed his eyes. *No, not until I know exactly what's going on. Not until I'm sure about Blanche. And not until I get my wallet back, either...*

*

It had seemed an instant, but when he opened his eyes again the first thing that Moran noticed was that darkness had fallen. He had dozed off. But something had disturbed him, jolted him awake. He rubbed his eyes, yawned.

And a face appeared at the window.

Before he could gather his wits, it was gone.

Moran sprang up and threw the front door open. The road was clear on either side but he caught a movement beyond the church, at the edge of the cemetery where the churchyard met the dark line of the woods. A figure was moving quickly, darting between the tombstones with odd, loping strides. It hesitated briefly at the cemetery gate before turning away and, at a more leisurely pace, vanished into the shadows.

He closed the door and found his whisky, downing the dregs in one. What had he seen? He wasn't sure. Moran wasn't easily rattled, but his hands were unsteady as he held the glass. Some local tramp or vagrant? Of one thing he was sure: whatever it had been, it hadn't come to his door by accident. He had seen the intent, some gleam of recognition in the eyes – as if they'd found what they were looking for.

The next day brought a damp morning; a ceiling of low, flat cloud had replaced yesterday's unbroken blue sky. It wasn't cold but Moran shivered as he made his way through a steady drizzle towards Matt Harrison's cottage. He had no plan except to follow his instinct.

There was no one about as he approached the cottage. The curtains were drawn and silence hung around the building like a shroud. He knocked.

And waited.

He knocked again, waited again, and after while turned away.

Half-way down the path he heard the front door open. He turned back.

Celine stood on the doorstep. She half-raised her arm, tried to smile but only succeeded in looking drawn and weary. "Hello, Brendan." She hovered awkwardly on the threshold of Harrison's cottage, half in, half out. "I was just on my way to see you."

"OK." With his elbows on the table Moran pressed the heels of his hands into his eyes for a second or two before resting his chin on them and squaring up to Celine's frankly sheepish expression. "So let me get this right. You took my wallet because you wanted to protect me from something. To cast some kind of spell? I mean, seriously? You expect me to believe that?"

Celine sighed. "I needed something of yours. Something that was close to you."

"You could have asked."

"You would have laughed at me."

A fair point, Moran conceded, although he didn't voice this thought. "I would have been a little taken aback, I suppose. I don't hold much with all this white witchery stuff."

"See? Exactly. You wouldn't have understood."

"I still don't. Why did you run away?"

Celine got up and went to the cottage window. Moran watched her tinker with an ornament on the ledge, a wooden carving of a hunter mounted on a rearing horse. Through the window he could see part of the church and the darker line of trees into which the figure he had seen the night before had disappeared. Celine replaced the ornament and turned to face him. "I had a panic attack. I get them occasionally. Ever since I was a little girl. I'm sorry, it was so rude of me."

"What were you panicking about?"

Celine looked down at her feet. Her hair fell across her face, hiding her expression. "I suppose it was because of what we were talking about."

"De Courcy?"

She nodded.

"I'm sorry," Moran said. "I didn't mean to be heavy-handed. It sounded as if you wanted to tell me something important."

"I did. I mean, I do."

"Well then. Tell me."

There was a silence while Celine played with her amber necklace until, apparently having made up her mind, she came and sat again at the table.

"Maybe you can start with the reason you were at Matt Harrison's house this morning?" Moran prompted.

"Oh, that's nothing really," Celine said. "He's a friend. I only popped in to see him about something. A bit of work he was going to do for me."

"I see. Has his wife come back yet?"

"His wife? Oh, I don't know. I mean, I didn't ask."

"You didn't *ask*? Why ever not?"

Celine shrugged. "I suppose we tend not to pry too much in Cernham. They might have fallen out. I didn't want to go there. You know, cause any embarrassment."

"Did he seem worried at all to you?"

"Maybe a bit distracted. He wasn't quite himself. Brendan,

I feel as if I'm being cross-examined."

"Sorry. Force of habit." He decided to change tack. He'd get to Harrison later. "So, anyway. De Courcy."

"What about him?"

"Celine, there's no point in being coy. I've been around a bit. I'm not easily shockable."

Celine ran her fingers across the table surface and sighed. When she looked up her eyes were both beautiful and sad. "We had a grand affair," she said, a faint smile raising the corners of her mouth at the memory. "Unexpected. *Completely* unexpected, actually, and not at all what I was looking for when I came here."

Moran just nodded, said nothing. At last she was talking.

"I'd had a string of unfortunate relationships, Brendan. I suppose I was trying to put it all behind me, coming to Cernham. I'd settled for singleness, a quiet life."

"Understandable."

"Is it? Brendan, I wonder if you could ever truly understand me. I've asked myself that question since I first saw you in the pub. I think I asked the question because I thought to myself, 'Here I go again…'"

"I can relate to that one, for sure," Moran said quietly.

Celine met his eyes briefly. "I saw it in you. The damage. I knew I had found a kindred spirit."

"But we're talking about de Courcy."

"Yes. Sorry."

"It's all right. Go on."

"It wasn't like that with him. He was rugged, assertive. Not really my type, but I suppose I was flattered. I went along with it."

"And?"

Celine gave a little tap on the table and sat back. "For a while it was fine. We kept it all very hush-hush. You know what village rumours are like. We fell into an easy rhythm, but then, of course, the spectre of long-term commitment reared its head."

"And who introduced that old chestnut?"

"I did, of course. I'd been through too much to be mucked about again."

"And what happened?"

Celine fell silent. Moran waited. The tick of the antique carriage clock filled the space. Outside, a gust of wind rattled a shutter.

"He changed," Celine said eventually. "Became very shifty. Didn't want us seen out and about together. I felt like an actor in some war film, a French resistance spy, flitting here and there, ducking and diving, keeping undercover. After a few months of that I woke up one morning and thought, 'What am I doing?'"

"Understandably," Moran said.

"So I decided to adopt a little assertiveness myself. I went up to the manor and called for him."

"And that was unusual?"

Celine snorted. "Unusual? Forbidden, more like. He'd made me swear not to visit, not to come anywhere near the manor house."

"Didn't that strike you as rather an odd thing to ask?"

"I suppose. But I was caught up in the romance of it at the time. I thought, well, if he doesn't want to introduce me to the family for a while, that's fine. Plenty of time for all that cosy stuff later."

"He spoke to you about the family?"

"Guardedly. I knew he had a mother, and a brother somewhere, but that's all really. When I asked him about either of them he would just look at me and shake his head."

"So you called for him. What happened?"

"His mother answered the door."

"Ah, yes. I've met her."

"She looked me up and down as if I were some local gypsy selling lavender sprigs and tried to close the door in my face."

Moran remembered Lady Cernham's expression of disdain, her aloofness bordering on downright hostility. And de Courcy himself, shotgun raised.

Celine was in full flow now. "I put my foot in the door to stop her. I said I only wanted to say hello, to introduce myself, but she completely blew a fuse. She called me every name under the sun. I told her we were an item, her son and me, and she gave me such a look of hatred and contempt I was scared stiff – and I'm not easily rattled. And then she said, 'So, you're the latest, are you? You'll go the way of the others, believe me. I'll make sure of that.' She said it in a very quiet voice, which was somehow worse than when she'd been ranting and raving."

Moran noticed Celine's hands beginning to shake a little as she spoke. He rested his hand briefly on her arm. "Can I get you a drink? A little whisky, perhaps?"

"Thanks." Her eyes smiled. "I'd like that."

As Moran poured two measures of malt he imagined a difficult time ahead trying to forget those eyes, the way they seemed to pierce him. He gave Celine her glass and raised his own. "May you have warm words on a cold evening–"

"–a full moon on a dark night, and the road downhill all

the way to your door." Celine raised her glass and clinked it against Moran's. "Cheers."

They drank and Celine coughed at the malt's sting.

"Slowly. Savour it."

The colour soon returned to Celine's cheeks. Moran cradled his malt and sat back, wordlessly prompting Celine to continue in her own time.

"There was something in the way she said it. I don't know, it was creepy. And as I said, I'm not one to scare easily. Anyway, I beat a retreat, tail between my legs. And that evening he came and found me and it was all different; he was like a stranger. Cold, as cold as ice."

"Did he threaten you?"

"Not in so many words. It was just the way he was. It was weird."

"An Oedipus complex?" Moran suggested. Such things were not unknown. "The overbearing mother?"

"Who knows? His relationship with Lady Cernham is far from normal, that's all I can say. Anyway, after that it began."

"It?"

"My paranoia. Or maybe some kind of persecution complex. Even now I don't know if it's just me, or… anyway, after a pretty heavy scene a few days later in which I told him in no uncertain terms that as far as I was concerned it was over, he told me that, no, I *belonged* to him; I was never to leave Cernham. He said it with such assurance, such – I don't know, conviction, that now I actually feel like some kind of prisoner. Ever since that final scene I've always felt as though I'm being spied on. I know it sounds crazy, but whenever I'm out and about I'm sure someone is following me, just out of sight."

"Do you think it's him?"

"I don't know." Celine finished her malt and shrugged. "Like I said, I'm probably paranoid."

"You could cast a spell on him." It was out before he could stop himself.

"Now you're making fun." Celine said reproachfully. "I'm disappointed in you, Brendan."

Moran spread his hands in supplication. "I'm teasing. I'm a policeman, Celine. I don't go for all this new age stuff. And by the way, you haven't told me yet why you think I need protection."

"You've met Lady Cernham. That's reason enough."

"And do I get my wallet back?"

"Of course. Sorry. Here, it's in my bag." She retrieved the wallet and gave it to him. "You can check it if you like. I don't mind."

"It was enough just to have it with you for a while, was it?"

"Yes."

"You don't need one of my socks, or maybe a used handkerchief?"

"I shan't dignify that with a reply."

Moran elected not to pursue the hocus-pocus line of enquiry. He could see that for Celine it was a serious and sensitive issue, and he decided to hold himself in check, at least for now. "So," he said. "Joking aside, let's summarise where we are. Firstly, you and I both know that a woman has disappeared. There's also the possibility that Matt Harrison's wife has gone the same way. You've told me that you have good reason to believe de Courcy is harassing you, albeit subtly. We've both experienced Lady Cernham's 'hospitality'.

She talked about 'others'. That sounds a little sinister, agreed? We both know that de Courcy has something to do with Blanche's disappearance."

"Am I attending a briefing here?"

Moran grunted. "Sorry. I'm used to bouncing ideas off the team. But look." He paused, suddenly exasperated. "You found Blanche's body, for goodness' sake. Surely you want to get to the bottom of what happened?"

Celine shrugged. "I just want a quiet life, Brendan. That's why I came here. I know that something happened, but…"

"Tell me why I shouldn't just drive to Exeter now and bring back the cavalry," Moran cut in.

"Because you're on holiday. Because you can't prove anything. And because you've just drunk a large malt whisky."

"Yes, all right. Point taken."

Celine got up. "I have to go, Brendan. I have a music practice and I'm late already." She leaned across and kissed him on the cheek. "We'll talk more later."

"Fine. I'll be in the usual place. Here, let me." Moran helped her on with her coat and shawl.

"See you later." She smiled. "Thanks for the drink."

Moran closed the cottage door and toyed with the idea of another malt. No. Best not. Instead he made a coffee and went over the last hour, dissecting and evaluating. It had been enlightening in some respects, less so in others. However, there was one thing about which he could be absolutely sure. One thing that hurt more than he could have expected.

And that was the certainty that Celine was lying.

Chapter Fourteen

Charlie wasn't sure what had wakened her so she lay still, warm and comfortable under the enormous duvet. She didn't want to check the time; it would only tell her that the next shift was coming up sooner than she wanted. Eventually she had to look. Quarter to four. Mid-afternoon; too early. But she was wide awake and knew from experience that she'd never get back to sleep. Her mind had already kicked in, prioritising the tasks ahead.

She had planned to go for a run before breakfast so she threw on a pair of tracksuit bottoms and a baggy t-shirt. Downstairs it was clear that she had the house to herself again. *So much for company...* Still, as soon as she was off nights it would be better. She made a quick slice of toast and downed an orange juice.

Keys, iPod – ready. Charlie opened the front door and set off at a brisk pace along the tree-lined avenue. The sun was out and the apple trees blossomed pink in the passing gardens. She enjoy running and it was always a good way to get to know your neighbourhood. She took a detour through the University campus, surprised and pleased to find a large lake, alongside which ran a pleasant pathway with a picturesque bridge up ahead. She passed groups of students, recently returned for the summer term, strolling and conversing in groups of two and three. It was such a pleasure to find this on her doorstep, another tick in the box confirming that she had made the right move. Her iPod cued another song – *Postcards from a Young Man*, a favourite Manics track. She hummed along as she completed a final circuit of the lake and made her way back to the road, maintaining a steady pace until the house came into view.

A quick shower followed by a well-practised makeup routine – eyeliner, a touch of pale lip gloss subtly applied, minimal foundation – followed by four fingertips of hair gel and she was ready. Mirror check. Not bad. She closed her bedroom door. The big question: would Banner turn up this evening? She *had* to check his room. At least she'd know if he'd come home or not. It was time for some answers.

She made her way along the landing corridor and put her head around the first door after a brief knock elicited no reply. Girl's room – G's, obviously. Next, a room with the bare essentials. A pair of running shoes on the floor, a bookcase filled with complicated-looking IT manuals. A couple of magazines on the neatly made bed, a faint smell of aftershave she recognized from their brief meeting the day before. So, Andreas' room.

The next bedroom was just past the main bathroom. She knocked, loudly. No response. She opened the door. The curtains were drawn and the room was in semi-darkness. She squinted, trying to discern the layout. There was an odd smell, as though some chemical had been spilled; its taint hung in the stuffy atmosphere of the room making Charlie put a hand reflexively over her mouth. She took a few steps and the shape of a bed materialised, curtained like an old four-poster. The master bedroom, Banner's parents' old room. The end of the bed was open, though, and she could see the shape of crumpled sheets inside.

A creeping dread filled her stomach. She didn't want to see any more. She went to the window and pulled the curtain cord. Sunlight pooled across the floor, lighting the bed as if it had been caught in a stage spotlight. Charlie stood beside it and, heart pounding, slowly drew back the drapes.

And stepped back, hand to her mouth, bile rising in her throat.

Banner lay curled in a foetal position, his face a grotesque mask of agony. Around his neck she could see traces of the thin wire which had garrotted him, squeezed into the swollen flesh like a tramline sunk into wet tarmac. His hands were at his throat, one bloody finger caught beneath the deadly wire in a reflexive but futile attempt to stop it choking the life out of him.

Charlie backed away slowly, her eyes automatically scanning the room, shockingly aware of her own vulnerability. She made it to the door, staggered shakily along the corridor to the bathroom, shouldered the door open, doubled up over the gold-tapped sink and emptied the contents of her stomach into the enamel bowl.

She sat on the toilet and took a gulping breath. Her mobile was in her pocket. She took it out with trembling hands and dialled the station. Message delivered, she ran in a limping half-stumble back to her room, expecting to be confronted by the killer at any moment. She banged the door hard behind her and felt for the key. It wasn't there. She heard a whimper of fear escape from her throat as she grabbed a chair and jammed it under the door handle.

She waited, shivering, on the edge of her bed until she heard the faint ululation of the sirens rising and falling, carving their way through the rush hour traffic. Only when she heard the urgent knocking on the front door and saw the flashing blue lights in the road outside was she able to kick the chair away with a sob and flee her bedroom, taking the stairs two at a time.

DC Tessa Martin placed a steaming mug of tea on the breakfast bar, just under Charlie's nose. "Hey. Come on. Drink it. You'll feel better." Tessa sat on the opposite stool and rested her hand briefly on Charlie's forearm.

"Will I?" Charlie smiled weakly. How would she ever?

"Course," Tess grinned. "Tea solves the world's problems, y'know. Can't remember who said that, but there's some truth in it."

"Thanks, Tess." Charlie wrapped her hands around the warm mug and tried to return the smile. The house was a turmoil of activity: SOCOs, forensics, and Moran's old buddy, Sandy Taylor, the doctor, buzzing to and fro, in and out of the tape-encircled front drive like worker ants supporting the queen – the queen on this occasion being DCI Suzanne Wilder, a senior officer Charlie had heard of but hadn't met. Wilder now appeared in the kitchen grim-faced, a little shaken perhaps, but with an aura of purposeful intent still very much in place. She took the stool next to Tess and accepted the DC's offer of tea.

Wilder was an attractive woman in her late forties with a

complexion indicative of her recently relinquished Australian citizenship, shoulder-length auburn hair and a no-nonsense approach some had interpreted as being a little on the matronly side; nevertheless, over the comparatively short period since her arrival in the UK she had won her colleagues' grudging respect. Rumours abounded about her marital, and even orientational, status but as far as Charlie was concerned they were just that: rumours. In any case, Charlie's philosophy had always been to allow fellow officers' private lives to be just that. As far as she was concerned, what went on in Wilder's free time was her own business.

Wilder didn't beat around the bush. "DI Pepper," she spoke firmly, "I know it's early days, but I need to ask you a few questions."

"Of course. Sure."

"When did you last see DC Banner alive? Did you see him today?"

Charlie shook her head. "No. He didn't turn up for his shift last night. I thought he was ill. I didn't check to see. If only I had checked, I might—"

"Ah, ah," Wilder shook her head. "Let's leave the 'if onlys' out of this."

Charlie bit her lip. Banner was dead. It didn't seem possible. All those times she had quarrelled with him, all those frosty encounters. Now she could never put things right between them.

"So, when?" Wilder prompted. "Yesterday morning?"

"No. I haven't seen him at all since I moved in." Charlie took Wilder through the last forty-eight hours, her conversations with G and Andreas and his mention of Banner's nightclub intentions.

"Right. So where are this G and Andreas?"

Charlie shrugged. "I have no idea. Andreas is in IT. Maybe he has an office phone number in his room. G's a student. I guess she's up at the Uni?"

"Ma'am?" One of the forensics, a bespectacled and rather geeky looking girl, interrupted. In her gloved hand she was holding a clear plastic bag in which coiled what appeared to be a length of looped wire. "We found this in one of the bedrooms. Under the carpet by the window."

"Ah. Thank you, Monica." Wilder held the bagged item up for inspection. "Which bedroom?"

"Second along."

Charlie froze, horrified. *My room...*

"Covering all eventualities, DI Pepper, it seems." Wilder pursed her lips and raised her painstakingly sculpted eyebrows a fraction. "I've heard through the grapevine that you're a thorough person. Which is why you made sure you had a spare to hand. Right?"

Chapter Fifteen

Charlie waited restlessly under Tess' watchful eye as the house was slowly disassembled by the forensics team. As the evening wore on she gradually began to feel more and more detached from what was happening around her. Wilder was here, there and everywhere, asking questions, jollying the team along, probably getting their backs up.

Leaving her till last…

She needed an ally and it didn't take a lot of guesswork to predict that Wilder wouldn't fall into that category. Moran was the man she needed right now. She could at least try to reach him. She appealed to her new DC.

"Tess, can I just make one call?"

"Under orders, I'm afraid, boss." Tess cocked her head in a gesture of regret. "Ma'am says you're to stay put for the moment. She'll be with you shortly." The DC looked sympathetic but it was too early in their relationship to be sure what she was really thinking. Keeping her nose clean and following orders, which was fair enough; Charlie couldn't blame her for that.

A uniform was at the kitchen door. He looked at Charlie with a kind of horrified fascination before turning his attention to Tess. "DC Martin? Young lady outside. Says she lives here."

A moment later G burst into the room. Instinctively, Charlie got to her feet.

"What's going on? Is everything OK? They said it was a serious incident–" G's face was white with shock.

Tess' voice had an edge to it which G picked up on immediately. "You'd better sit down, Miss. And you too, boss. Sorry."

G shot Charlie a bewildered look as Tess gestured to the row of mugs aligned neatly on the shelf above the drainer. "Tea?"

"All right. Thank you."

DCI Wilder's voice could be heard rising above the general hubbub elsewhere in the house, issuing orders and requesting updates until she eventually appeared in the hallway. Wilder paused on the threshold, her expression smug with certainty. She'd already made her mind up, that was obvious. Already Charlie felt vilified and dirty.

The DCI's voice reached a new level of brusqueness. "DC Martin, please take the young lady into the lounge and establish her recent whereabouts."

"Ma'am."

G looked over her shoulder as she left the kitchen and Charlie gave her a nod of encouragement. Wearing an undisguised expression of distaste, DCI Wilder settled herself into the chair G had just vacated and steepled her hands beneath her chin. "Now then, DI Pepper. Let's start at the beginning."

"Ma'am, let me assure you–"

"I'm not assured about anything yet, DI Pepper. I just want to establish the facts."

"You really think I killed Stephen Banner?"

Wilder let the question hang for a few seconds before replying. "I don't know. Did you?"

"No I damn well didn't. Why would I?"

"You didn't get on. That much I do know."

Charlie shook her head vehemently. "No, we weren't best mates, but we'd come to an understanding."

"Had you?" Wilder toyed with her bracelet, stroking its contours affectionately. It looked expensive and featured a plain, rectangular section embossed with an ornate letter or marking Charlie didn't recognise. She found herself wondering if it had been a gift from an admirer, and if so what sort of person would have been attracted to this handsome, yet hard-nosed woman. Maybe she was different off duty, but looking at her again Charlie decided no, probably not. Wilder gave her bracelet a final jangle before switching focus back to Charlie. The grey-green eyes prompted.

Charlie leaned forward. "We had a chat. I told him that as long as he did his job well it didn't matter that we didn't see eye to eye socially."

"You didn't see eye to eye socially, so you moved in with him?"

"It's not like that. I needed a place to stay. I didn't feel safe in my old flat on my own–"

"Ah yes, the break-in." Wilder tapped her nails on the breakfast bar.

"It wasn't a break-in." Charlie struggled to keep her cool.

"Someone tried to kill me."

"But he was no match for you, was he, DI Pepper? You're quite the little fighter, I understand. Would you say you had an aggressive nature?"

"*Aggressive?* No. Absolutely not. What are you implying? I resent that remark."

"Maybe you moved in here so that you had a better opportunity to fix Banner for good?"

"Ridiculous." Charlie was fuming now. She folded her arms. "I want to talk to the DCS. I don't have to put up with this."

"No?" Wilder leaned forward. "You're in a lot of trouble, missy. There's a dead policeman upstairs. I have a plastic wallet containing a garrotte. Maybe it'll have your prints on it, maybe not – we'll see. In the meantime, I suggest you start talking."

"Look, Wilder, someone's fitted me up." Charlie felt herself close to tears and mentally gritted her teeth. This woman would not get to her. "I don't know why or who, but it's obvious. Check my records. I'd never do anything like this, never. Can't you see that? And the killer is walking further away with every passing minute. I–"

"It's ma'am to you," Wilder said coolly. "And nothing is *obvious*, as you put it, until proven. Your record cuts no ice with me, love. Understood?"

"Yes."

"Yes, ma'am."

Charlie felt hatred burn in her gut. She fought the impulse to lash out, run, flee the house. Instead, with a huge effort she made herself say it. "Yes, ma'am."

There was a pregnant pause during which Charlie could

hear a continuous banging and scraping from upstairs. Floorboards were coming up. Incongruously, someone began to whistle.

Wilder's eyes gleamed. She looked almost happy. "That's much better. Now, shall we go over everything from the start? I want detail, mind. All of it."

DC George McConnell wasn't thinking about work when the phone rang. He was thinking about the end of his shift and how he was going to get through the evening without a drink. The worry of his regular indulgences had begun to prey on his mind a while back. He was young, true. Well, young-ish – if late thirties counted as such. But he'd noticed a growing reliance on his daily alcohol intake which had begun to ring alarm bells in McConnell's Celtic and very ordered mind. His mother had been an alcoholic, his father had died young for the same reason, and now, if he wasn't careful, he might also begin to slide down the helter-skelter of no return which led to pancreatitis, liver calcification, stomach ulcers and who knew what else. McConnell actually knew very well what else because, in his usual precise way, he had researched all the signs, symptoms and likely outcomes of alcohol abuse. And having completed his investigation he had to admit that he didn't much like what he had discovered. Trouble was, he had a reputation for being a bit of an entertainer, a 'good laugh down the pub'. The truth of the matter was that without a few drinks inside him his natural shyness and lack of self-esteem formed a barrier so impenetrable that he was barely able to converse, far less assume the 'life and soul' persona anticipated by his peers.

The magic formula was two swift pints and a whisky

chaser. From that point on McConnell became the true life and soul. Nothing was beyond him: jokes, impressions, anecdotes; they tumbled out at a rate of knots which always surprised newcomers and delighted the old hands. And that had been fine, for a long, long time. Until the morning he had woken up with shaking hands and an overwhelming desire for a large scotch. He hadn't told anyone. No one seemed to notice anything amiss, so he comforted himself with the thought that he probably just had some 'habitual' issue with drink. It was part of the routine, part of the job. He could stop if he wanted to. No problem, right?

Wrong.

It had got steadily worse, and now he was struggling to go cold turkey. What he needed was distraction. Work, in other words; preferably lots of it. He wasn't one for corporate misery-sharing, which ruled out the local AA meeting. No way was he going to carry *that* membership card. He was going to handle this one himself. He could do it; it was just a question of will power and bloody-mindedness. That and avoiding the dreaded social gatherings altogether. But that was asking a lot. He couldn't just become a recluse. Or could he?

"George, are you going to pick up that phone or just let the poor sod at the other end hang on till Christmas?"

McConnell looked up, startled, to see DC Bola Odunsi grinning at him like a Cheshire cat from across the office. "I've got it, Bola, keep your brakes on, OK? Hello?" He glowered across the desk at Odunsi, who was shaking his shorn head and chuckling loudly.

As McConnell listened he forgot his colleague's amusement and his mouth gaped. "Steve *Banner*? Are you

sure? You've got to be kidding. I mean, Steve *Banner*?"
McConnell had never warmed to Banner but he was
thoroughly shocked.

"I know," DC Martin said through the earpiece. "But
there's worse to come."

McConnell fell silent as Tess updated him.

"Bloody hell," McConnell said. It felt less than adequate.

"Wilder's giving Charlie the third degree right now. She's
bringing her in. Thought I'd warn you."

"Charlie's no killer," McConnell said.

"I know that. You know that. But Wilder—"

"Yeah. I've heard about her. Stickler."

Tess Martin's voice was terse. "That's what I heard too.
And now I've seen her in action, let me tell you 'stickler'
doesn't cover the half of it. George, I haven't worked with
Charlie for long, but any fool can see that she's been stitched
up."

"Aye. I'd have to agree."

Sensing something of interest, Odunsi had sidled over and
was now perched on the edge of McConnell's desk, trying to
follow the conversation.

"But," McConnell said to Martin, rolling his chair back as
Odunsi's invasion of his personal space gained another
couple of centimetres, "it's no secret that Steve Banner and
Charlie didn't get on."

"That's neither here nor there," Tess' voice had adopted a
more covert tone. Either someone had come into the room,
or was earwigging what was being communicated. "Anyway,
look, I have to go now. DI Pepper asked me to remind you to
deliver that message to the guv."

"Message?"

"Yes. Something about bogs?"

"Ah, right. Sure. Will do."

"His contact number is on her desk. She wants you to tell him everything you know."

The emphasis on the last few words needed no further explanation. Charlie needed Moran here. And fast.

Chapter Sixteen

"Any messages, Terl?" Moran made for his usual stool, aware that he was falling into a comfortable routine. Same pub, same area of the bar, same beer. Well, why not? Surely he could salvage something from his break, even if it was only a regular pint or two?

"Nope. Nothing, I'm afraid." Terl selected a fresh wineglass from a full tray and set about polishing it with gusto.

"Are you sure?" Odd; Charlie was usually pretty quick off the mark, even if she'd drawn a blank.

"Aye, positive." Terl held up his latest glass for inspection. Satisfied, he bent to place it on some unseen shelf below bar level and rose stiffly to his full height with a groan. "Back's killing me today. Getting too old for this caper. Now then." He clapped his hands. "Usual, is it?"

"Yes, please."

"Back to the real world soon, then?" Terl said as he pulled the pint.

"I may stay on a day or so," Moran remarked casually. "I

want to be sure the missing lady is accounted for. Or should I say 'ladies'?"

"It's a storm in a teacup, Brendan. Marital tiff at the Harrisons'. Visitor given the usual Matthew treatment. Nothing to worry about, if you want my opinion. Folk sort themselves out around here." Terl gave a gruff laugh.

"Well, just to be on the safe side, you know. I'd hate to think I left someone in trouble. Or danger."

"Danger?" Terl accepted Moran's five pound note and rattled the till open. "You've been watching too many movies, Brendan. Cernham's about as dangerous as a Labrador puppy."

"You think?" Moran smiled benignly. "In my experience the most innocuous surroundings can sometimes be home to the most unpleasant goings-on."

Terl shook his head. "Well, not here they're not. I wouldn't worry myself over nothing. Especially as you're on holiday." Terl gave him a look which, to Moran, seemed rather more than friendly advice. He watched as Terl went to the other end of the bar to serve another customer. Perhaps it was his imagination, but the landlord's body language seemed tense, uneasy, giving the lie to his forced bonhomie. Moran sipped his pint. He'd hit a nerve.

Half an hour later Moran looked at his watch. "What time do they finish music practice, Terl?" Celine had told him half past eight. It was now after nine.

Terl sauntered over, glanced at the grandfather clock by the entrance and shrugged. "Any time. You know what musicians are like. They'll be gasping by now."

Another five minutes passed and Moran wondered whether he shouldn't just go ahead and order food for himself. As he reached for the menu the door opened and a group of men came in, clearly in high spirits. The musicians; Moran felt a sudden lightness. He wasn't going to be stood up after all. But then the door closed and there was no Celine. He waited politely until the band had placed their orders before questioning the fiddle player.

"Excuse me, but was Celine with you this evening?"

The man turned in surprise, as though unused to being spoken to by an outsider. "Celine? No. Not tonight. We was expectin' her, but she never showed." Information delivered, he turned away to accept a pint and showed Moran his back.

All thoughts of food abandoned, Moran finished his pint and quickly left the pub. Could be nothing.

Could be something…

He paced up and down, wondering what to do. Foolishly he had neglected to ask Celine for her address – or maybe he had thought that asking for it would have been interpreted as being too pushy. He had no idea where to find her. But the band would know her house, surely? He reached for the pub door handle then quickly stepped away, something telling him that it might be unwise to make his intentions too clear. He walked slowly in the direction of his cottage, thinking hard. Matt Harrison would know where Celine lived.

Or maybe that's where she is…

Moran halted and leaned on the churchyard wall, observing the way the sharp curve of the moon silhouetted the church tower against its backdrop of inky-blue sky. He was struck once again by the stillness; there was not a sound from the village nor its environs, not even a chirrup of birdsong.

Matt Harrison.

He took a deep breath.

All right, then. Just a quick look.

Moran stood in the narrow lane by the crossroads, feeling foolish. The cottage was in darkness. He was about to turn away, go back to his static-fuzzing TV and a glass of malt before bed. *Before you make a complete prat of yourself, Brendan. And it wouldn't be the first time...*

But then the front door opened and a crack of light appeared. Moran retreated into the hedgerow and waited. Low voices, Harrison's large build blocking out the light. The man stood on the threshold for a few moments, as though satisfying himself that there was no one around. He went inside. A minute later he reappeared, this time bent over as if dragging some heavy object. He backed carefully down the steps and Moran saw that he was being assisted by someone else. A voice was raised in a terse whisper.

De Courcy.

The two men carried their burden the short distance to Harrison's car and dumped it roughly in the driveway while keys were produced and the boot hauled open.

Moran's mind raced. What should he do? Challenge them? No, together they would easily overpower him.

De Courcy got into the car and started the engine. Any second now he would flick the headlights and Moran had nowhere to go. He pressed himself deeper into the hedge, feeling the tight clusters of twigs and branches cut into his neck. De Courcy rolled out of the driveway and turned left, leaving his headlamps off. The car disappeared round the corner. Harrison paused briefly on the doorstep before softly shutting the door, but by then Moran was walking quickly in the opposite direction, back to his cottage and his waiting car.

He wanted to be there when de Courcy unloaded at the other end, and he had no doubt at all where that was going to be.

Terl was tidying the last glasses away when he noticed the scrap of paper on the floor by the phone. Gina the barmaid's writing, soft rounded letters like her large, obtrusive bosom. Terl chuckled to himself. Thick as two short planks, Gina, but worth the occasional fondle in the cellar. He read the note and his face darkened.

Attn. DCI Moran. Archaeological dig 1974. Cernham. Bog body found, male. Dated at 3–4000BC. Also another, female, initially thought to be contemp., well preserved. Never identified. Body missing. Follow up unknown. Checking misper records. Nothing so far.

DI Pepper in need of assistance. Incident at residence. In police custody. Please contact DC George McConnell urgently.

G.M.

Terl frowned and crumpled the paper in his brawny hand. The dig. That's when it had almost unravelled. He remembered as if it were yesterday. But he didn't *want* to remember. It was in the past, gone. Nothing could change what had happened that day. Everything was all right now. Everything had a balance. Nothing must upset that.

Especially not DCI Moran.

Terl picked up the phone, dialled a number and waited.

1974. He could see it all now. Bright sunshine, mid-July, a semi-circle of goggle-eyed onlookers watching the second body's exhumation from the mire. He remembered her face, serene, skin glistening with water and mud, the swell of her breasts, as yet untainted by decay, preserved for their guilty, curious eyes. And Rufus at a distance, watching, stirred by something primal.

That had been the start of it. That look, that connection. That girl.

Moran turned the ignition key. *Click*. And again.
Whirrrrr.

He thumped the dashboard. Flat battery? No. He knew the battery was good. So be it. He got out, slammed the door and began walking in the direction of Cernham manor.

Chapter Seventeen

"What do you know about the Ranandan case?" Tess asked George McConnell as she threw her bag onto the floor and herself into the chair.

George McConnell looked up. "You're back then." He adjusted his NHS-like non-designer glasses. "Had a bit of a scrappy afternoon, really. First there was–"

"Save it, George. This is important."

"The Ranandan case? I know what everyone knows about it. Unacceptable loss of police life, biggest drug ring in the UK exposed. Media overdrive. Chief Constable bricking it."

"She's the last one, George. Her and the guv."

"What?" McConnell fought off irritation. He'd been toying with the idea of a quick pint on the way home. Just a quiet one, to calm his nerves. "The last what?"

"Charlie. She's the last officer to work directly on the case who is still on the force. They tried to kill her before, George."

McConnell glowered. "So? Where are you going with this?"

Tess' fingers flew across her keyboard as she spoke. "I don't know, but it doesn't feel right. Banner dead, Charlie implicated. It's all too neat. Like a total set up."

"So you're saying Banner was targeted by the druggies? And part of the remit was to nail Charlie Pepper at the same time? Stretching it a bit, don't you think?"

"No, I don't think. Charlie was talking to me about this Chinese guy. The big man. He's been seen in Reading, George. You were at the briefing, too. Charlie was frightened. I know she was. She never said, but–"

She broke off, bit her nail, grimaced and inspected the damage. "We need some tangible evidence that she *couldn't* have had anything to do with Banner's murder. And then we need to find out who did."

"And how do you propose we do that with forensics crawling all over the property and SOCU in charge? If there's anything to find, they'll find it. Wilder'll work by the book, in triplicate with a gold ribbon tied round it."

"Yeah, no stone left unturned." Tess worried her nail thoughtfully. "But I don't know, George. I don't like it. Something's not right."

"Too bloody true something's not right. Steve Banner was a colleague. OK, I didn't like him much, but that doesn't mean I don't want to nail the bastard who did for him. Whoever it was."

"You can't believe that Charlie had anything to do–"

"I don't know yet, Tess. And neither do you. Let Diva deal with it. She's a safe pair of hands."

"And what about the guv?"

McConnell scratched his chin. "He'll be back on Friday. Up to him, then. I'm betting he won't get this one, though.

He's too close to Charlie."

Tess considered McConnell's assertion. "Maybe. But why should the guv be in any safer a position than Banner or Charlie?"

"Don't turn this into some kind of Hollywood revenge trip, Tess. It's probably got nothing to do with the Ranandans, or the Chinese guy. It could just be random. A break-in."

"You don't believe that any more than I do, George."

"I don't know *what* to believe at the moment, OK?"

Tess turned back to her keyboard and began typing. A few moments later she tapped the screen. "Got it. Sheldrake. He was the insider. Charlie visited him a couple of days ago. She told me he said something about the Chinese. That he was *glad* to be inside. He told her he felt safer. That sounds to me as if Sheldrake knew what was going down. Like this Chinese guy takes no prisoners. Moran and Charlie wrecked his operation, so he's come over here in person to sort them out."

"Welcome to CSI, Reading." McConnell shook his head.

Tess coloured. "Well, if you're not going to bloody support me on this I'll do it myself."

"All right, all right. Calm down. Where do you want to start?"

"The usual place – neighbours, passers-by. Any security cams around the local shops?"

"Diva will be covering all that."

"And we're going to cover it too. But tactfully."

"If Wilder finds out we're sneaking around behind her back there'll be hell to pay."

Tess sighed. "I have the feeling that there'll be hell to pay anyway by the time this is over. You've always wanted to be on covert ops, George. Now's your big chance."

The numbness and shock was beginning to wear off. From the rear window of the squad car Charlie watched the houses flicker past and wondered when Moran would return. George would surely have made contact by now and she couldn't see Moran dragging his feet once he found out what had happened. In the meantime she was pinning her hopes on DCS Higginson. He would take her side, wouldn't he? DCI Wilder had temporarily released Charlie into her sergeant's care and DS Maggs was at the wheel, driving silently and efficiently. He was an ascetic looking guy in his late thirties who looked like he spent too much time working and too little time relaxing; the bags under his eyes seemed out of place, almost as if Maggs had them on loan from someone a lot older.

They were en route to the station, where Wilder would no doubt instigate a further debriefing in one of the station's interview rooms. Charlie wrinkled her nose in dread anticipation. No matter how much aerosol was sprayed, rooms A1, B1 and C1 perennially stank of disinfectant and stale sweat. Debriefing? *That's a laugh*, Charlie muttered under her breath. *Interrogation, more like*. Wilder had it in for her big time. But the evidence was so obviously rigged. Charlie's mind whirled. The question was, by whom? It had to be this Huang Xian Kuai bastard. Revenge, pure and simple. But how? And who else was involved? How did they find Banner? Had he known his killer? She bit her lip hard as a more frightening thought occurred to her…

Did *she* know Banner's murderer?

I remember it. That long, endless summer. But when you're young summers are always endless, aren't they? Ha! One of Mother's favourite expressions. "You only remember the good days, Rufus – the blazing sun, the woods vibrant with greenery and the buzz of insect life, the bog dry and cracked in the dog day heat."

She always spoke like a poet. But not any more, not these days. And now the green months are full of damp, and drizzle, and greyness. But still I remember those long, hot bygone days. I remember the music, the pop songs blasting out of old Mackenzie's transistor radio as he tended the gardens. 'All you need is love' and one song I used to hum all the time, 'See Emily play'.

When the bog was dry and cracked.

When it gave up its secrets…

But that didn't matter, because Mother was in control. She always knew what to do.

I hurt. If I hold my head just so, it will be better. I know what to do. Mother told me how to reduce the hurting. The headaches are the worst of it. Sometimes I feel I can't endure them any longer and I walk to the edge of the bog, and stand there, and wonder.

I remember the fat man, the bearded digger, and his skinny wife. I forget their names but I recall their matching gold teeth – an odd substitute for an exchange of rings, I thought, but perhaps that's just what archaeologists are like. Maybe it was their way of remembering to smile at one another, I can't be sure. Anyway, they slipped through Mother's net, unusually, perhaps because she was still preoccupied at the time with what had happened. I only wanted to make things right for her. It was only fair. He never wanted that. How could he have, the way he treated her?

The girl. The hippy. The child of the earth. She wasn't the first one.

But she was the last. I saw to that. I never expected to see her again but the fat man found her. It was meant to be. She came up out of the soil, out of the wetness and she was beautiful. Terl was there. I saw the fear in his eyes, but I knew it would be all right. There was nothing to fear. And, as the fat man and his skinny wife fussed around the body, it was as if I heard the girl speak.

Now I am of the earth and water, Rufus. I am one with it all... thank you...

I remember the way they stepped back when they found the watch on her wrist, the sweat running down the fat man's forehead, gathering in a band of moisture above his bushy eyebrows. It's recent, he told his skinny wife. And she put her hand over her mouth, turned away. I heard her retching into her handkerchief. A dainty cotton handkerchief, not the sort of thing you would expect an archaeologist's wife to own. I had imagined archaeologists to be tough and sturdy, careless of their own comforts and eschewing material possessions. But the skinny wife had a little lacy handkerchief! Odd how I still remember, how it sticks in my head like...

Like an arrow.

She arrived in the village like a waif from another world, carried in on the breath of Scott Mackenzie's lyrics – "If you're going to San Fran Cisco..." – like a creature from some exotic city, a city basking in the haze of marijuana and sunshine. The summer of love. Not that, as a couple of fourteen-year-olds, we knew much about love. But we were old enough to recognise beauty, sensuality, sex appeal. When we saw her in the woods that first time she told us she was going to Glastonbury. Me and Terl had never heard of it, but she said it was a magical place. We imagined it must be something like San Fran Cisco, the way she spoke of it. There was a hill, a tor, King Arthur, and so much else, she said. But she liked Cernham, she told us. She had met some interesting folk and was going to stay awhile. I knew who she'd met. She'd met him.

And she had already fallen under his spell. I was old enough to get that. I never told her he was my father. I suppose she just thought we were a couple of local kids. Which of course we were, but she seemed – I don't know, interested in us. Adults usually ignored us, but she, this girl-woman, sat cross-legged under the oaks by the cemetery and spoke about life, and peace, and love, and the change that was coming upon the world.

It's all going to be different, she told us, and our hearts fluttered. The times, they sure are a-changin'. If she'd had a guitar I expect she would have played it, but she just sang unaccompanied, and the sweetness of her voice held us in thrall.

I suppose we both had a crush on her. I know I did. Well, what else would you expect from a fourteen-year-old boy? She was pretty, and I was besotted. I knew I was too young for her, but to me it didn't matter.

One day, when I found her alone in her usual spot by the cemetery, I told her how I felt. I didn't do it very well. I was embarrassed, awkward. But I got it out anyway. I knew I had to grab the opportunity while Terl was busy with his chores at the pub. I told her everything I felt. And then I just looked down at my jeans, picked at a loose thread, waiting for her words to lift me up, to tell me she felt the same. But when I did look up, when the words I so wanted to hear never came, she was smiling – no, grinning. Trying not to laugh. "Silly boy," she said, giving my shoulder a push. "I'm a grown woman. I need a man, not a boy."

And I fled from her, with her laughter chasing me as I pelted through the green tunnels. Silly boy... what a silly, silly boy...

I never told Terl what had happened. But he could see I had changed, that I felt differently about her. I think he was pleased. He mistook my indifference for a sign that he could pursue her himself without compromising our friendship. Terl was a few months older, a bit taller, and he had started shaving. I didn't care if he pursued her or not. I didn't care about her at all any more. Until the day I found her with my father in the study.

"Oh," she said, "so you live here too?" That was all. And he had his arm around her shoulder, a look in his eye I knew well. It didn't seem possible that they were here, in the house. Together.

"Where's mother?" I asked. And he told me he didn't care. Told me to clear off. Close the door behind me.

I walked into the salon in a daze. Not her. Not here. I knew there had been others, but her…

I found Mother in her bedroom. Her eyes were red. I knew the signs. She told me she was all right, asked me where Terl was today. Her hand was shaking as she brushed her hair in front of the full-length mirror with wide, sweeping motions of her delicate, prettily sculpted arm. I told her she was beautiful and she tried to smile.

"Thank you, Rufus. You're a blessing to me. Always a blessing." That, I think, was the moment I made my decision. I knew what I had to do.

It was a very simple plan. The woods were my domain, and I was a skilled hunter. Time and again my mother had praised me for the variety of game I brought home from a day's stalking. Rabbit, pigeon, partridge; all had fallen prey to my skill with a sling and my favourite weapon of all, the one I identified with the most, the glory of Crécy.

The longbow.

Chapter Eighteen

By the time Moran reached the manor gates the sky had cleared and the grounds were silver with moonlight. The house itself was in darkness, squatting silently like a sleeping wolf. De Courcy's car was parked in front of the porch.

Moran skirted the outbuildings to the right of the main house and worried about cameras. Although he considered a surveillance system unlikely, it was best not to make assumptions; as he skirted the side of a low stable block he comforted himself with the thought that he'd seen nothing to overturn his initial impression of neglect. If there was money here it wasn't being invested in property maintenance, far less security. He closed his eyes briefly and reopened them. His night vision wasn't going to get any better. At the outermost edge of the expansive, wall-enclosed lawn the shadow of a smaller building loomed, a different shape to the rectangular, low-roofed outbuildings; its contours were rounded, suggesting a low tower with a conical roof. Moran made a note to explore it later. In the centre of the lawn there was a stone table, possibly a sundial Otherwise there was nothing in the expanse of silvery green to mar the even carpeting of recently mown grass. Someone had at least made an effort on the horticultural front.

He came to the last L-shaped outbuilding, this one connected to the main house. A door beckoned. Moran tried the handle and felt no resistance.

A musty smell made his nostrils flare. He dared not use his torch so he edged forward, testing the floor before committing his weight, stretching his arm in front of him like a sleepwalker. His scalp prickled. This was trespass and no mistake. If he was wrong then his behaviour would take some explaining – and not just to the de Courcys. But Moran had grown used to trusting his instincts; much of the time it was all he had to go on, and now his internal radar was telling him that Celine's life was in danger. To the accompaniment of his drumming heartbeat he felt his way forward until his hand touched wood. This door, judging by its location, would lead him directly into the main body of the house.

The door knob turned easily. Moran took another breath and stepped into Cernham Manor.

A narrow corridor, no lights. Threadbare carpet.

Careful, Brendan…

He came presently to an open space, dimly lit from above. The main hallway. Nothing stirred. He decided to risk a shielded beam from his torch. In its narrow V he could make out the grandeur of a sweeping staircase and, spread out before him, a flat plain of worn marble. A grandfather clock stood sentinel-like by the far wall and beside it the dark recess of an arched doorway. He traversed the beam. To his left was the main entrance, twin elevations of oak locked and

143

bolted top and bottom. The manor appeared deserted but Moran knew this to be an illusion, perhaps even a carefully prepared illusion for his benefit. But how could the de Courcys know he was here?

He made for the grandfather clock, hugging the wall and creeping quickly past the staircase. That was when he heard it – a thumping, writhing noise, as if someone or something was rolling, or being rolled on the floor. The noise was accompanied by a low murmuring, an indistinct monologue. Moran reached the shadow of the arch and pressed himself into it. Whatever was making the noise was directly behind this door. He turned the iron handle gently and applied pressure but the door wouldn't budge. He pressed his ear to the wood; the thumping and muttering had stopped.

Moran was torn between continuing his exploration and forcing an entry. Was it Celine? Moran cursed under his breath. Perhaps there was another way in, an internal window, maybe…

Moran turned to find the twin barrels of de Courcy's shotgun pointing at his head.

"Wrong room," de Courcy said.

And oh, yes, it was an easy shot for me. The way she fell, I knew she was dead before she hit the ground. I can always tell. I'm used to it. I always shoot to kill. And I never miss. But I'm getting ahead of myself. I hadn't seen her for a while. Something was amiss, I knew that much. She disappeared for a couple of weeks; I thought she'd gone for good. Stupid – I should have known. She was a skinny girl, didn't show much. Apparently you don't when you're thin and fit like she was. Don't have all that blubber like the fat bints on TV, stuffing their faces with cake and all sorts of crap in the name of 'eating for two'.

*So by the time I saw her again it was all over. She'd had it. A boy –
my half-brother. I heard him bawling up at the house – she'd brought
him to my father but he didn't want to know. I heard the shouting, the
recriminations. How could she have done that – brought the boy into my
mother's house? Mother was gracious, she would have taken him in, but
father said no. He sent the brat away screaming his head off. I suppose
she'd left him in the village later that morning, gone walking like she
used to, to think, clear her head, wonder what had happened to her hippy
dream. Anyway, there she was, walking in the woods – my rejecter, my
mother's nemesis, the evidence of her crime abandoned to some willing
wet nurse for a few precious hours so she could think, plan, figure out
what to do with the rest of her life.*

*Had she named it by then? Did I care? I'm not sure I did. I know
him now, of course. He's very useful to me. But then he was just an
unwanted embarrassment.*

The sins made flesh…

My little brother.

Matthew.

Chapter Nineteen

"There. Pull over." Tess was out of the car before McConnell had applied the handbrake. The girl was hurrying away with quick, nervous strides. And who could blame her? DCI Diva was enough to put the wind up anyone.

"Excuse me?" Tess called out and G spun in alarm, her face relaxing as she recognised Tess.

"It's OK. I just want a quick word."

The girl's shoulders slumped. "They've only just let me go."

"Sorry. I wanted to check something."

"Is Charlie under the arrest? They don't think she did this terrible thing, do they?"

McConnell sauntered up and Tess saw him run his gaze appreciatively up and down G's legs then try to pretend he hadn't as G gave him a reproachful look.

"It doesn't look good," Tess said. "That's why I want to talk to you."

"She is such a nice girl. I only just met her, and now—"

Tess nodded. "I know. We all feel the same. Thing is, if she didn't do it – and none of us think she did – then we need to prove it as quickly as possible."

"But I have told DCI Wilder everything." G shook her head. Her eye make-up had smudged a little and her cheeks were pale. Wilder wasn't much fun to spend time with.

"I'm sure." Tess glanced at McConnell. "You see, G, Charlie's one of us. Wilder's on another team. She doesn't know her."

"Sure. I see. What else can I say?" G shrugged, reached into her handbag for a tissue. "I go to stay with a friend. She is expecting me soon."

"It's all right, G. Look, just have a think. Is there anything you might have forgotten? Anything you might have seen between ten this morning and four this afternoon?"

"I go out in morning. Maybe at half past ten. I wait for a bus to town."

"Hang on," McConnell said. "Where did you wait? The number seventeen stop across from the house?"

G nodded.

"Did anything happen while you were at the bus stop, G? Think hard." Tess gave her a smile of encouragement. The girl looked knackered. Probably best to come back to her tomorrow after she'd had a night's sleep.

G shrugged again. "I wait. Cars go by. No one else is waiting. A motorbike goes past. I remember him because he looks at me and drives slowly, then he speeds up."

McConnell had a pen and pad out. "Describe," he said, rolling the r.

"He has on black leather. Helmet, of course. I don't see his face."

"What kind of bike, G?" Tess asked. "Try and picture it."

G sighed. "I don't know bikes. It is black and metal. It has the bars like this." She stretched her arms out and towards her.

"Harley?" McConnell muttered.

"I don't know. It was just a bike. Then I get on the bus. Then I come home, and—" G's face twitched as she tried to fight back tears.

"Did you tell DCI Wilder about the bike, G?" Tess asked. G was dabbing at her eyes with a tissue. The girl was really shaken up.

G sniffed. "Sure, but she wasn't that interested."

"Oh?" McConnell was jotting furiously. "Why was that, do you think?"

"I don't know," G said flatly. "I am not police. She asks me again about Charlie, what we do on Monday night, what time I leave the house. That's all."

Tess exchanged a glance with McConnell. "All right, G. Get some rest. If you remember anything else, give me a call," Tess said. "Here's my number."

"Bike worth following up?" Tess was driving. She needed something mechanical to do with her limbs.

"May as well," McConnell said. "Let's see now. G caught the bus, she says, at half ten-ish, right?" He studied his notes.

"Right. Traffic cams?"

"Nearest would be top of Whitley Street."

"So." Tess tapped the steering wheel. "If he came through town, there's a chance."

McConnell grunted. "Maybe. If we can weed out the other bikes as well."

"It's a short time frame."

"Top of Whitley Street to Banner's would take how long?"

"Let's time it." Tess swung the wheel.

As they edged through the rush hour traffic McConnell began to wonder when, if ever, he'd get to that beer he'd promised himself earlier..

Charlie was stiff, sore, tired and angry. She'd spent the night in a cell on Wilder's orders and her pleas to see DCS Higginson had been ignored. She had tried several times to get a message through to her team but so far Wilder had blocked all attempts. At least Tess knew what was going down. Charlie paced the small room and fretted. Tess seemed pretty sharp, and Moran was a good judge. He wouldn't have got her on board if he hadn't been impressed, and Moran wasn't easily impressed. But what could Tess do? Maybe she thought the same as Wilder and co. Guilty as hell. *Hated Banner. Found a way to get in close. Killed him. Then left a spare garrotte under her carpet?* Ridiculous. It screamed 'stitch up' – but not, apparently, to Wilder. Why not? What did Wilder have against her? Charlie had had no previous contact with the woman. Heard of her, yes. Heard she was well respected down under; heard she'd started at regional SOCU in Bristol before being drafted into the recently formed National Crime Agency, the Home Secretary-instigated successor to the National Serious Crime Unit.

Charlie sat on the edge of the cell's narrow bunk. That meant Banner's murder had gone straight to the top. A senior DCI and forensic team conjured up at a moment's notice. Hardly surprising, after the Ranandan episode: police corruption, international drug cartels, unprecedented loss of police life. And now this. Charlie didn't hold out much hope for the Chief Constable's future career once the news reached Whitehall, but that wasn't her problem. She needed to know someone was on her side. She rubbed her aching eyes. A sleepless night and the prospect of a morning's interrogation on the wrong side of the table lay ahead. She jumped as the lock rattled and the door swung open.

"Morning, boss."

Charlie exhaled with relief. "Toby. Thank God for a friendly face."

DS Glascock dumped the tray he was carrying on the bunk beside her. Coffee, a croissant, cereal. "Thought you might appreciate some breakfast."

"Are you a detective sergeant or an angel?" Charlie seized the coffee and took a grateful sip. "Thanks, Toby. How did you get it past Rosa Klebb?"

Toby's face broke into a grin. "Easy. When that miserable sod Maggs challenged me I said I was following DCS Higginson's orders and if he had a problem with that he should take it upstairs."

"Genius." Charlie munched the croissant.

"The gruppenfuhrer isn't in yet anyway. She's been diverted to sort some other problem out. Or so I'm told."

"A reprieve."

"Boss, I need to ask–"

"I know." Charlie put the mug down and smoothed flakes of croissant off her skirt. "Did I or didn't I. So, what do you think?"

Toby cocked his head to one side, a mannerism she had noticed before when something important was being discussed. "What you tell me now is what happened. That's it."

"Toby. I didn't kill Banner. That's all I'm sure of. I woke up. I went to look for him, and there he was. I thought I'd be next."

"It must have been terrifying."

"It was. But Wilder's scarier."

"Tess told me they found something in your room."

"And that," Charlie leaned back and felt the coldness of the wall, "is the sole basis of Wilder's case against me."

"Someone planted the garrotte."

"Yes."

"What about the flatmates?" Toby was hovering by the cell door, clearly uncomfortable. "She grilled them yet?"

"I expect so." Charlie thought about G, her bubbly evening. G wasn't an assassin, not by any stretch. And Andreas? What did she know about him? Charming, good-looking. Worked in IT. Maybe.

Footsteps rang along the corridor. Maggs, coming to check them out.

"I'll talk to Tess," Toby said in a low voice. "She and McConnell are digging for you. We'll do what we can."

Charlie squeezed a smile from somewhere. "Thanks, Toby. I'll hold onto that."

She had to. That's all there was.

Chapter Twenty

Moran felt the barrel of de Courcy's shotgun burrow into the small of his back. "Sit down."

He settled himself slowly into the nearest vacant armchair. De Courcy had led him along a chandelier-lit passageway into what appeared to be the main drawing room. Wide and expansive, it was furnished like a salon in an Agatha Christie play. Velvet drapes, plush carpet, fine antiques, gilt-framed portraits, a grand piano. Sitting alone on the six-seater settee was Lady Cernham, hands folded on her lap and a glass of sherry perched beside her on a spindly occasional table.

"Good evening, Inspector Moran." She nodded imperceptibly and de Courcy joined her on the settee, shotgun cradled in the crook of his arm.

"You want answers, evidently." Lady Cernham took a sip of her sherry. "Well, now you shall have them, for all the good they will do you."

"Where's the woman?" Moran elected for an equally direct approach.

"I think I had better start at the beginning." Lady

Cernham smiled sadly. There was no trace of her earlier coldness and Moran had the impression that she was looking forward to what she had to say. De Courcy was silent, watching him.

Lady Cernham replaced her glass on its lace doily. She was about to speak again when the silence was broken by what sounded at first like muffled laughter; the noise quickly rose to a howling crescendo before tapering off in a breathless, echoing chuckle that made Moran's hair stand on end. A heartbeat's pause, and then, through the closed salon door, the passageway outside rang with the reflected sound of intense conversation as if two parties were locked in some fierce dispute. The de Courcys exchanged glances but seemed unfazed by the interruption. A low thumping began, as if someone was beating on a calf-skin drum to attract attention.

"Rufus." Lady Cernham said simply. "My youngest son. He… talks to himself."

"Where is Celine?" Moran thought there was no harm in being specific as well as direct. "Why have you abducted her?"

"Abducted that woman?" Lady Cernham laughed thinly. "Don't be absurd. She's not worth the time of day, let alone going to the trouble of an abduction."

"All right," Moran said. "But the American – Blanche Cassidy?"

"Gone, I'm afraid." Lady Cernham reached for her sherry again. "Too many questions. Unfortunate timing."

The drum beat recommenced, slower this time, each report rumbling through the manor like distant thunder.

"Richard here is my eldest," Lady Cernham said. "Rufus

153

was born eighteen months later. He was a difficult child at first, but as he grew up we became very close. He always wanted to help me, to be with me. It was very rewarding."

De Courcy frowned.

"His father," Lady Cernham continued, "was inclined to travel." She sipped the sherry. "The boys didn't see eye to eye. They had no role model, no male mentor to guide them."

"He doesn't need to know all this." De Courcy tapped the barrel of the shotgun lightly with one hand while the other reached into his pocket.

"I shall tell Inspector Moran what he wishes to know," Lady Cernham said coldly.

De Courcy lit a small cigar and grunted. The shotgun lay against his thigh.

"The boys played in the woods, of course," Lady Cernham went on. "Rufus used to go off on his own. He became very good at hunting, didn't he, Richard?" When de Courcy's only response was to let a narrow stream of smoke escape from his clenched mouth she continued.

"Richard was more his father's son," she said. "Always inclined to defend him, were you not?" She cast de Courcy a frosty glance. "Even the indefensible."

"What's done is done." The cigar glowed as de Courcy took another puff.

Moran was weighing his chances of getting across the room before de Courcy could lift the shotgun. He calculated that he'd make about half the distance before de Courcy shot him dead.

"My late husband was not the most discreet man. Nor the most loyal husband, Inspector. His greatest indiscretion was the impregnation of a young girl who had become infatuated with him."

Moran listened. He had no option. The drum beats had, for the time being, fallen silent.

"The fruit of this indiscretion was brought into my house. By this ... this *girl*. The barefaced nerve of it." Lady Cernham made small, agitated movements with her hands. "*My* house, Inspector."

Moran nodded. "Go on."

"Rufus was here. He became very angry. He knew, you see, what had been going on. How his father had hurt me. Humiliated me. He argued with his father. It wasn't the first time she had brought the child here – to ask for money, of course. She had no family, nothing."

Moran began to work out the story. He had already guessed what was coming – or part of it, at least.

"There was a great deal of shouting. The girl was told to go, to take the baby with her and never come back. She went, after a lot of screaming. And Rufus followed her. He ... well, he–"

"He took matters into his own hands?" Moran finished for her.

"Quite so." Lady Cernham nodded vigorously. "He was beside himself. He was young – just a teenage lad. He did it for me, you see. To protect my honour…"

"Did what exactly?"

"He was an – *is* – an expert hunter. With the longbow," De Courcy explained.

"I see."

"And then he came back," Lady Cernham blurted. "His face was flushed. I knew what he'd done. I could understand it, but—".

"The police," Moran said gently. "Why didn't you call the police?"

"Oh no. We couldn't possibly. The scandal. Imagine! You see, it would only have been an argument, only words, if – if only…"

"If only I hadn't come back from a shoot," de Courcy interrupted. "With a loaded shotgun under my arm. By then Rufus was back from wherever he'd been and he was very agitated."

"So he turned on you?" Moran prompted. "Wrested the gun off you when you wouldn't rally round and support your mother?"

"My father tried to intervene," de Courcy said quietly. Lady Cernham had fallen silent, running her finger up and down the stem of her glass.

De Courcy shrugged. "It was an accident. The gun went off. The first barrel shot my father through the heart. The second hit Rufus in the head."

"A murdered girl, a dead man, and a badly injured teenager. And you still didn't call the police?"

"As I've explained, Inspector, that would have been quite impossible." Lady Cernham had recovered some of her composure. "We look after our own affairs here."

De Courcy ground out his cigar in a cut-glass ashtray. "I think you've heard enough. Shall I fetch the medication?" he asked his mother.

That didn't sound good. Moran thought it best to keep talking. "So Rufus lived," he said quietly. "But he was damaged? Disfigured?" Moran thought of the face at his window.

"He's still my son." Lady Cernham stood and drew herself up to her full height. "He's still a de Courcy."

"And you let him run wild? Indulge him?" Moran felt his face giving away the horror he felt. "To kill? To murder? Why?"

"We look after our own .This is our village. Our estate. What happens here is our business," Lady Cernham said. "I shall fetch the medication, Richard."

She left the room. Moran watched her go and tried not to think about what 'medication' might entail. "Linda Harrison?" he asked de Courcy. "Is she dead?"

"You'll have to ask Rufus," de Courcy replied with a twisted smile. "He might tell you. Then again–" He shrugged. "My guess? Probably."

Lady Cernham reappeared carrying what looked like an enamel syringe tray. Moran braced himself. If he could get to Lady Cernham before de Courcy got a shot in...

"I say we let him spend a little time with Rufus first," de Courcy said. "Let him decide."

Lady Cernham considered the proposition and Moran held himself in check. After a moment she nodded. "Very well."

"Come on, on your feet." De Courcy's eyes narrowed. "I'll introduce you."

I can hear them. They are bringing someone to meet me and I think I know who.

It was my brothers who came for me earlier. They often do. They call it 'curbing my appetite'. They tie me up, 'restrain' me, make me sleep. Think it'll calm me, keep me in check.

But it doesn't. Hear my fists on the door? See this knife? I'll gut with

it tonight. GUT WITH IT. They can hear me. Of course they can.
I need to RUN, to HUNT.

Running, hunting, stalking, fear in their eyes, the noise they make. Oh, the noise they make!

So bring the next one to me, dear brothers. Bring him now. Now. Now. Now. Now.

Chapter Twenty-one

"How is she?" Tess asked Toby before he'd sat down. All eyes of the gathered team were on him.

"As you'd expect," Toby told them. "Pissed off. Tired. Angry. Grateful for breakfast."

"Right. Listen up," Tess said. "You all know the score. Charlie's been fitted up big time and we're going to find out why. Better than that, we're going to find the killer before Wilder does and send her off with a flea in her ear." Tess looked at each officer in turn, still worried that DCS Higginson's memo, which briefly stated that with Moran away and DI Pepper under suspicion she was now acting senior officer, would not have gone down too well with more senior members like Bola and Toby. After all, she'd only been here a few weeks. But ... circumstances aside, she had to admit that Acting DC Tess Martin had a nice ring to it. *No time for congrats now, Tess. Just get the job done.*

"What about Wilder?" Bola Odunsi asked. "How we goin' to work under her nose, but keep her out of the loop at the same time?"

"Good question. George and I discussed this earlier. Yes, Wilder and the NCA team are 'in charge'. Yes, she is the SIO. But Charlie's one of us. Something smells very wrong. We have a duty to make sure we do all we can – yes, support Wilder's team, but also do a little sub-investigating ourselves."

"Which," George McConnell added, "we've already started." He raised a bushy eyebrow and Tess gave him the nod.

"OK. We spoke to the housemate, G. She remembered a bike slowing down as it passed the bus stop, right opposite Banner's property. We checked the camera at the top of Whitley Street. And guess what?"

"Hundreds of bikes," Odunsi said.

"Right. But only one with buckhorns."

"Buck *what*?" Toby made a face and cocked his head to one side, spaniel-like.

"Buckhorn handlebars. Mini-apes," Tess said. "Like a chopper."

Odunsi giggled and Tess tried not to colour when she realised what she'd said. "All right, Bola. You know what I meant."

The tension in the room lifted. Tess went on, more confidently. "G described the bike in terms of its handlebars. It's what stood out for her. And, like George said, the only bike which was headed in that direction in that time frame was this one." She motioned to McConnell to switch on the projector. The laptop bleeped and a picture appeared on the screen, slightly blurred. The buckhorns were clearly visible, as was the rider. Black leathers, black open-face helmet. Shades obscuring most of the face.

160

"Cool dude," Odunsi said. "Easy rider."

"You old enough to remember that, Bola?" Toby enquired with a wry grin and George guffawed.

"Bola, can you run an ANPR check asap?" Tess got up and tapped the screen. "I'm betting you won't find that reg."

"Now?"

"That'd be good."

"On it," Odunsi said with a dismissive gesture. He waggled a warning finger on his way out. "Wilder hears 'bout this, she's gonna kill us."

"What else we got?" Toby returned his attention to George and Tess.

"So far," Tess replied quietly, "that's it."

"And the guv's back when?" George was fiddling with the laptop, moving it back and forth in a futile attempt to improve the picture quality.

"Should be tomorrow, but we have to factor in a possible delay," Tess said. "He's only got himself tied up in some misper case."

"You're kidding." Toby grinned. "Sounds like the guv, though."

Tess frowned, remembering Charlie's request. "You phoned that message through all right, George?"

"Yep."

"Can you call again? See if the guv's available?" At least she could ask for some advice, Tess thought. And it would be a comfort to know that Moran would soon be back.

"Aye, can do," George said.

"He'll soon sort this out – not that you won't, ma'am, er boss, I mean –" Toby flustered to a halt.

Tess forced a smile "It's OK, Toby, I know what you

meant."

Chapter Twenty-two

Moran heard the key turn in the lock behind him. The room was in semi-darkness but he could make out detail enough to momentarily forget his situation and simply gape in wonder. The space in which he found himself was huge, like an ex-banqueting hall or refectory. Looking up he could see that the high ceiling had been painted in an artful representation of the sky at night; rather like the London Planetarium he remembered visiting in his youth, except that this seemed warmer, truer somehow, as if the artist in some instinctive moment of clarity had captured a special moment in the planetary movements and frozen it forever.

The walls were no less extraordinary; covered in elaborate artwork, the pervading theme of woodland – dark, leafy arbours, mossy river banks, ancient oaks presiding over moonlit clearings – gave the hall a gloomy yet somehow strangely evocative atmosphere of times long gone by. Moran was so captivated that he almost forgot his predicament.

Moving cautiously into the room his foot tripped on what

appeared to be a discarded sack and several lengths of knotted cord. The sack was slashed and torn and as Moran bent to examine it, his fingers found traces of moisture on and around the thick hessian. He had smelt blood enough times not to require visual confirmation. The question was whose? Celine's?

Moran rose from his haunches. Some sixth sense told him that he had company. He strained his eyes but could see nothing except a long, empty space. There was a slight movement in his peripheral vision; what he had assumed to be the inanimate subject of a forestry scene had shifted subtly from one arboreal shadow to another.

"Rufus." Moran's heard his voice bounce back from the unseen far end of the hall.

Another movement.

"You know my name?"

The accent was similar to de Courcy's, slightly deeper but with an edgy quality about it. Moran could sense the psychosis; it was almost palpable.

"Yes. I've been talking to your mother and brother."

A low laugh. "Them? My keepers. So they believe, anyway."

Moran could make him out now, whether it was his eyes adjusting to the lighting or Rufus moving closer it was hard to say. There was something about the shape of the head, something displaced or perhaps contrived. "I know the truth, Rufus. I know what happened."

"Ah, you can't know it all, Brendan. Not all."

First name terms, then, Moran thought. Was that significant?

"They've given you to me, Brendan," Rufus de Courcy

said. "But what will I do with you? How shall I proceed?"

"I can help you. You know you need help, don't you, Rufus?"

A long pause.

How far? Moran tried to assess the odds. Ten, fifteen feet? Could he rush him?

"Help," Rufus repeated. "*Help*?"

The laughter Moran had heard from the salon was more disturbing at close quarters. He raised his voice a fraction. "I'd just like to know why, Rufus. I understand what happened when you were younger. But why kill again? You did kill Linda Harrison, didn't you? And Blanche Cassidy, the American?"

The laughter ceased abruptly. "I killed my father. And *her*, the beautiful one. She who is still alive, alive in all her kind."

The penny dropped. This young girl, Lord Cernham's plaything – she had been the subject not only of an older man's philandering desire, but also of deep adolescent longing. "You loved her, didn't you, Rufus?"

There was another long silence.

"I did," Rufus said eventually in a low whisper. "But she had to die. She always has to die. Every year she has to die. Do you see?"

"You were under a lot of strain, Rufus. I can't condone what you did, but now I understand why, and I can help, believe me. It's time to put the past where it belongs. These other women – they were innocent. No one else has to suffer."

"They must." The voice was stronger now, more threatening. "Their blood goes into the soil. For her. She *needs* the blood. How else will she be renewed, remain one

165

with the earth?"

A warped cycle of murder, guilt and repetitive sacrifice. It didn't take a degree in psychology to work it out. Maybe it was the shotgun blast that had damaged Rufus de Courcy's brain; it was either that or the mental agony of knowing that he had killed something infinitely precious to him for the sake of an overarching, oedipal love for his mother.

"Come with me, Rufus. Let me help you. Please."

Rufus' voice took on a distant, unfocused cadence as he began a conversation with himself. "What shall we do? A man. A man who knows. *Everything*, he says. If we let him go, he might tell. He wants to *help*. But he can't *help*. We don't *need* any help."

Moran began to edge away. Perhaps Rufus would forget that he was not alone.

Head bowed, Rufus' muttering continued. "No. No. It won't do. Call them. They can put him away for a bit. Yes. And then we'll run. Then we'll hunt. *Then* we'll kill."

Moran tensed as Rufus darted to the wall and reached for something above his head. In the distance came the sound of a tolling bell. He was calling the de Courcys.

Now or never, Brendan.

The door through which he had entered was locked, but what about the far end? There would be another exit, surely? Moran made his decision and ran for it.

He had only gained a few metres when Rufus battered into him like a rugby flanker. Moran had an impression of great, tensile strength, a panther-like grip on his neck and he was down, flat on the floor, face crushed into the heavily piled carpet. He heard a door slam, de Courcy's voice, a padding, cautious approach. A word of command? No, a guarded request…

…Hold him…

Helpless, Moran felt his sleeve dragged up. As the needle slid into his flesh he consoled himself with the thought that sedation was preferable to death by gunshot wounds, or worse. But the question remained: sedation pending what? He felt consciousness sliding away, rough hands turning him, de Courcy's eyes on him, Lady Cernham just visible behind her eldest son, hands clasped, watching. As his vision faded he thought he saw Matt Harrison behind his mother, arms folded, shifting uneasily from foot to foot.

He's not happy with this…

Moran held on to the thought.

Lady Cernham's voice, distant now. *Enough, Rufus. Enough.*

The room wobbled like a badly engineered TV set, darkened, then went out.

His head ached and he felt nauseous. What had happened? Where–? It took a good thirty seconds for Moran to remember. He flexed his arms experimentally. No problems there. Legs. Check. He opened his eyes. Darkness. He reached out and felt metal against his fingertips. He tried to get up and banged his head hard on a low roof. He was in some kind of cavity – a small cell, or…

For a brief, terror-filled moment he thought he'd been buried alive, but he soon realised that he could feel air circulating; he sensed a wider space just beyond the bars of his prison. *A cage.* That's what it felt like; a cage just slightly larger than his body. He could move, but not freely. Already he could feel cramp tightening his leg muscles. How long had he been unconscious? And, more importantly, what would the de Courcys do with him? Moran remembered a fragment of Rufus' monologue, something he'd rather not have overheard: *then we'll hunt...*

They meant to keep him alive.

For now.

Chapter Twenty-three

DS Maggs looked even more unsavoury in daylight. His hooded eyes, bleary from lack of sleep, regarded her condescendingly. The sweat stains beneath his armpits almost made Charlie gag as the detective sergeant leaned back in his chair, stretched both arms vertically and yawned with practiced, uninhibited satisfaction.

Next to Maggs and looking much fresher than she should have been, DCI Wilder reached over and clicked a button on the ancient tape recorder. "DCI Wilder, DS Maggs interviewing DI Charlie Pepper. Thursday fifteenth of May, 10.45am."

"I want to see DCS Higginson." Charlie tried not to sound as if she were pleading.

"No deal. We've been through this. Higginson's busy."

Was he? Did he even *know* what was going on here? Surely he must – but then why hadn't he made an appearance? Charlie remembered their chat, his office, the avuncular reassurances...

"Let's go over it from the beginning, DI Pepper."

There was no point objecting, Charlie knew. Once more, then. Maybe it would clarify things for her, too. *Keep positive…*

Charlie sighed. "I got in from my shift. Made coffee. I went to my room. I was tired. I went straight to bed."

"You didn't think to check on Banner?"

"No."

"Why not? You said yourself that you were concerned that he hadn't turned up for duty." Maggs spoke slowly, almost lackadaisically.

"I was tired," Charlie repeated. "I had no reason to think there was any problem."

"But Banner's no-show was unusual." Wilder jutted her chin. Her make-up, Charlie noticed, was understated but perfectly applied.

"Yes."

"Then surely a quick check, a knock on his door at the very least?"

"I went nowhere near his room until the afternoon."

"After you'd woken up?" Maggs scratched his stubble and took a swig of water from a plastic cup.

"Correct."

"You heard nothing? You didn't hear your flat mate, G, downstairs in the morning?"

"I was asleep," Charlie said. Already her patience was evaporating. "I heard nothing."

Maggs leaned forward. "I understand from your medical report that you've been using sleeping tablets."

"Yes."

"And there have been occasions," Maggs continued, "where you found yourself sleepwalking?" The DS consulted some papers on the table. "In fact, it says here you woke up once in front of the bathroom mirror. No recollection of how you made that trip from your bed to the bathroom."

There was little point denying it. The medical report was thorough. A condition of her return to work had been regular meetings with the medics. Dr Keefe, *the shrink...*

"I know where you're taking this," Charlie said. "That was a one-off. It hasn't happened since. I've been off the knock-out drops for a month now. It was just a side effect."

"But it may have reoccurred without your knowledge, DI Pepper," Wilder said. "How can you be sure it hasn't?"

"I'd know," Charlie said. *God, how weak it sounds.* "I'd just know."

"Tell me about your relationship with Stephen Banner. When did you realise the full extent of your dislike of the late officer?" Wilder folded her arms.

"Now, hold *on.*" Charlie tried not to raise her voice. "If I'd hated Ban– Stephen that much, do you think I'd have moved in with him? Into his parents' house, for God's sake?"

Maggs shrugged. "Maybe. Depends what you were intending."

"I wasn't intending anything. I was frightened of living on my own, OK? Do you get that? Someone tried to kill me and I wanted to have people around, people I could trust. I felt vulnerable, Maggs. Is that so hard to understand?"

"You're a tough lady," Maggs sniffed. "You certainly proved that you can look after yourself."

"If you are referring to the incident at my flat when a man attempted to break in and murder me–"

"Who you killed with a piece of glass, I understand?" Wilder interrupted.

"He smashed his way into my flat. He broke the glass. I

had to fight for my life. Why don't you get that?"

"I get that perfectly well," Wilder said. "We are simply trying to establish the level of your aggression."

"I am not aggressive. It was self-defence. You'd have done the same."

"But you killed him," Maggs said.

"I didn't intend to kill him. It was over so quickly. I though *I* was going to be killed." This was harder than she'd imagined. She was beginning to realise how much she'd been suppressing. *Just like Dr Keefe said…*

"Your prints are all over this. Explain." Wilder tossed a plastic wallet onto the table.

"I can't explain it. Whoever set me up got my prints somehow."

"Wouldn't you know if someone borrowed your fingers for a while?" Maggs was picking his teeth with a match.

"Funny." Charlie grimaced, but felt a sudden chill. *That's exactly it. Someone was in my room. While I was asleep…*

"What's the matter, DI Pepper?" Wilder widened her eyes a fraction. "Remembered something?"

"No. There's nothing to remember."

Maggs gave up with the match, tossed it towards the bin and missed. "The thing is, DI Pepper, there aren't any other suspects. Both flatmates have an alibi. They were nowhere near the house at the official time of death. You were the only one there."

"I've told you. I was asleep. I didn't hear *anything*."

"Explain this." Another wallet hit the table.

Charlie peered at it. It was empty. No, wait…

A hair.

"Well?" Wilder drummed on the table. "It's yours. We had

it checked."

"When I found the body, maybe—"

Maggs made a negative gesture with his finger. "No. It was *under* the body."

"So. Were you two an item?" Wilder asked.

"Are you crazy?" Charlie's heart was thumping. Someone had gone to a lot of trouble.

"Well? Were you, DI Pepper? All this 'couldn't stand him' stuff is just a cover, isn't it? What happened? Lovers' tiff? Temper get the better of you? Again?"

"Do you honestly think I could overpower someone like Stephen Banner and throttle him on my own?" Charlie sat on her hands. She wouldn't let them see how rattled she was. "Are you charging me? Seriously?"

"What would you do?"

It was rhetorical. Charlie chewed her lip. This was as bad as it got. "I want to call a lawyer."

Wilder and Maggs exchanged satisfied glances.

"No problem," Wilder said. "DS Maggs will arrange a telephone for you. Interview suspended at 11.01am."

Chapter Twenty-four

"Message from Bola, boss. Plates are dodgy." Toby's head poked round Moran's office door. Tess looked up and felt a brief wash of elation. "Right. Thanks."

"And I can't get the guv on his mobile." Toby came in. "So I rang the pub."

"And?"

"Landlord reckons the guv's left town."

"Well, that's something." She tapped the screen with her knuckle. It showed the motorbike image, frozen at the Whitley Street pedestrian crossing. "See this?"

"See what?"

"Look. The boots."

"What about them?" Toby squinted.

"Look carefully."

"Black. Single strap. Cuban heel."

"What about the size?"

Light dawned on Toby's face. The eyes behind his round rimless specs brightened. "A girl."

"I reckon."

"Yeah, now you mention it. Body size. Could be a small bloke, though."

"With that footwear? They're ladies' boots, Toby."

Toby brought his face closer to the screen. "Right. So, maybe the polsky girl's lying."

Tess shook her head. "I don't think so. G doesn't look like a biker to me. And if she is, then why would she even mention a bike? It would only draw us to her if she was spinning us one."

"True."

"Toby, how does Wilder come over to you?"

Toby scratched his chin. "Efficient. Ambitious. Focused."

"Right. Focused. Entirely on Charlie. If it were me I'd be doing all I could to prove that Charlie had nothing to do with it."

"And you think Wilder's doing the opposite?"

"Don't you?"

"I must admit she does seem to have pounced with alacrity."

"Good. We're agreed then. So, I want you and Bola to make a few enquiries in Bristol. Discreetly."

"Is that wise? I mean—"

"Like I said, discreet. Apart from her professional reputation as a grafting high flyer, nobody seems to know much about her. See if you can get to the person underneath. I mean, she must have *some* friends."

"Plenty of enemies, I'd say."

Tess shrugged. "It's all information. Whatever it takes to get a quick profile." She consulted her mobile. "It's only eleven. You could be there by lunchtime."

"If we can get out of the building," Toby said.

"That bad?"

"Siege conditions at the front door. The DCS is banged up somewhere with the Chief."

"Trying to figure out what statement they can make without being eaten alive," Tess muttered. Once the press smelled blood, that was it – and this news would go up the seniority ladder like an Apollo launch. Another policeman killed. Chief suspect: a senior officer. How much worse could it get?

"Rumour has it the Home Secretary is on her way," Toby added morosely. "They'll probably shut us down."

"Let's leave that to the CC. Close the door after you, Toby. I can't concentrate with all that jabber going on out there. And keep me posted, OK?"

Tess sat quietly for a few minutes, thinking hard. Finally she roused herself and went out into the open plan. Heads looked up. Conversation faded.

"George?"

George followed her into the office along with a buzz of resumed conversation.

Tess stood at the window with her finger between one of the blind's vanes. Outside she could see a gaggle of press and four uniforms doing their best to maintain a clear path to the front door. Traffic crawled up to the roundabout, motorists slowing to look. Horns blared. "George, how many bike shops in the immediate area?"

George furrowed his brow. "Three, maybe four. But we don't even know if the rider is Reading-based."

"I know. But we have to try. We know the bike's dodgy. Ask around. There's the buckhorns, and the boots. Go with that."

George sighed. "You're the boss."

Tess watched George leave with a concerned expression. She liked him. He was a hard-working, solid copper, but Tess had been brought up in the same household as an alcoholic – her father. She knew the signs. She'd had plenty of opportunity to study them. Maybe no one else had noticed the slight tremors in George's hands, but she had. Should she say something? She knew George's reputation; everyone did. Life and soul. But at what price?

Tess forced it to the back of her mind. Right now she needed a chat with the CSM – before Wilder and Maggs finished with Charlie and came looking for her. They'd have plenty of mundane procedures ready to keep her occupied, out of the way and too busy to ask questions.

What a nasty, suspicious mind you have, Tess Martin. But that's why you're a damn good detective.

Tess found Dom Jensen, the CSM, doing what he did best: managing the scene. She'd worked with Jensen before and they'd always got on, but he also liked to follow the rules and Tess wasn't sure he'd be willing to go along with her request.

Jensen met Tess outside the house, shrugged back the hood of his coverall and, in his usual brisk, businesslike fashion, came straight to the point. "Couldn't this wait, Tess? I'm up to here." He waved a gloved hand over his head.

"Sorry, Dom. I know. But I need to find out where you're at. Wilder's going to book Charlie."

"Not surprised," Jensen said. "Given what we've found so far," he added.

"Charlie is innocent, Dom." Tess stepped aside to allow a member of the forensic team by. "How much more do you have to do?"

Jenson peeled off his rubber gloves and scratched his nose. "We've still got to finish the bedroom carpets. After that I'll be collating our findings. It takes as long as it takes."

"Any objection if I suit up and give you a hand?"

"You've cleared it with Wilder?"

"She'll be fine. More hands on deck and so on."

Dom gave Tess a knowing look. "You've got something."

"Maybe. I don't know, Dom. There was a motorbike nearby at the time, that's all. Could be relevant."

"And Wilder is aware?"

Tess made a non-committal gesture. "Sure. So, traces from footwear? Oil? What's likely if our biker entered the premises?"

"Depends how careful they were."

"Every contact leaves a–"

"–Granny, eggs, suck. If there's anything to find we'll find it."

"So that's a yes? I'm acting DI by the way, until DCI Moran's back."

Jensen shook his head. "I don't know, Tess. I have four officers in there already."

"Come on, Dom. I'll tread lightly."

Jensen groaned. "I thought you were borderline pushy before."

"I've had lots of practice."

Jensen's face split into a grin of resignation. "Go on then. You'll find a suit in the back of the van. Just be *careful*."

Tess had attended murder scenes before but that didn't mean she was comfortable standing in the place where someone's life had been brutally terminated. Jensen's team had finished in here, the primary site. What they'd collected from the bed was what they'd use to charge Charlie: a hair. Tess hadn't known Banner or Charlie very long, but she knew the difference between light friction and outright hostility. Charlie was a professional. She had dealt with Banner fairly and pleasantly, and Banner hadn't been easy; always a not-so-well-disguised streak of chauvinism and male superiority in his manner. He'd tried it on with her, of course, but she'd been warned and anyway she was used to deflecting unwanted advances without repercussions.

Tess stood at the foot of the four-poster and tried to imagine what had happened. Banner, asleep. The intruder, the garrotte around Banner's neck before he knew what was going on. And once that wire was firmly in place... He'd managed to slide a finger under the wire but the digit had been almost severed by the relentless pressure of the garrotte.

Tess moved to the head of the bed. Dried blood on the wall, on the woodwork. And something else: a mark above the bed on the wall. She leaned in closer. A slight dent? Yes. A depression in the paintwork, a hairline crack. Banner's head, banging against the wall in his death throes? Or something harder?

Like a motorcycle helmet.

Tess left the room and went into Charlie's. Jensen had ticked it off but she wanted to check for herself. The bed was as Charlie had left it when she'd got up that afternoon, duvet thrown back, pillow indented. The bedside cabinet was bare except for a lamp and an empty glass. Beside the oval coaster a few droplets of water still adhered to the polished wood like a scattering of tiny pearls. Tess took a clean handkerchief from her pocket, picked up the glass and sniffed. Nothing.

She went looking for Jensen but before she could locate him her mobile bleeped.

"Tess Martin."

"It's George. Guess what?"

"I'm all ears."

"Traffic's just been to see me. Heard we were interested in the bike. So are they. It was the subject of a high-speed pursuit on the M4, Wednesday evening."

"And?"

"They found the bike dumped near the council tip. It's garaged here if we want a look."

"Tell them no touch, no move. Dare I ask about the rider?"

George clucked. "Nah. No sign."

"OK. I'll be right over."

Tess stripped off her suit, and only pausing to tell one of the SOCOs to get Jensen to call her, raced to her car for some high-speed driving of her own.

Chapter Twenty-five

In the silence something scraped. A foot against stone, or the movement of some small animal? With a jolt Moran realised he'd been out again; whatever they'd pumped into him wasn't going to be shaken off easily. His head throbbed and his limbs were ice. The sound came again, this time closer and accompanied by an exhalation of breath. Human breath.

"Brendan? Are you here?"

Celine? He opened his mouth and managed a groan.

He felt her beside him. She rattled the lock once, twice, pulled impotently at the cage and banged the bars in frustration. "Oh God. I'm so sorry. I should have warned you."

"Just get me out."

"I haven't much time. They'll be back."

Moran turned his head and wished he hadn't. Lights danced before him, sparkly, painful lights. Eventually they faded and he could see Celine's face pressed anxiously against the iron struts of his prison.

"Is there anything you can use as a crowbar? Have a look."

"I already have. There's nothing."

"I thought they'd taken you." Moran made a full-body turn so that he was facing out.

"I need to tell you something."

"Save it for later, maybe?"

"You know, don't you? They've told you about Rufus, and what happened?"

"Yes."

"You need to know, so you understand. The girl – the girl he killed."

"Which one?" Moran stretched his legs as far as they would go. It wasn't far enough and he could feel his muscles beginning to stiffen and contract.

"The young girl. Her name was Rachel O'Neill."

"You knew her? How–"

"Of course I knew her. That's why I came here. That's what I want you to understand."

"Understand what, exactly?"

"She was my sister, Brendan. My big sister."

Moran took a moment to digest this. "But if you knew–"

"–Why didn't I go to the police? Because I needed proof. I had no proof at all. I still have no proof. I came here because this was the last place Rachel visited. I knew something terrible had happened to her, but I had to be careful. Over time I built up a picture, about the de Courcys, about how things were here. People knew what had happened, I could tell, but they wouldn't say anything, wouldn't put themselves at risk."

"And that's why you started the affair with Richard de

Courcy?"

"Yes. And that's when I found out about Matt."

"What about Matt?" Moran shifted again, massaging his leg. His Charnford leg, as he called it.

"Matt is my sister's child, Brendan. But he's under the control of the de Courcys. They... They use him."

Moran felt a cold thrill run through his body which had nothing to do with his physical situation. "Don't tell me. To supply the annual offering? He travels. Meets a girl. Spins some yarn about the idyllic country life. Brings them here. Marries them. And then–"

"They have to be ... the right sort." Celine whispered. "I mean, no ties. No family, no baggage."

Moran was silent. This was unprecedented. Feudal, dark ages barbaric. For a moment he forgot his own predicament.

"I have to go." Celine moved away.

"You can't leave me here, for God's sake," Moran hissed. "And while I'm on the subject, where *is* 'here'?"

"It's the ice house. In the grounds at the far end of the lawn. They've ... adapted it."

Moran remembered the low shape he had seen earlier. *Ice house*. Appropriately named...

"I have to finish this tonight, Brendan. It's been too long. It's time for it to stop."

"Celine! Wait!"

Moran heard her footsteps recede, then the clunk of wood against wood. He spent the next ten minutes throwing his body weight against the metalwork before exhaustion finally overcame him.

Moran was suddenly alert. Something felt different. He

turned his head very slowly, wary of the consequences after the last time. The lights danced again, but not as wildly. He prodded the cage door. To his amazement it gave immediately and fell, soundlessly at first, until it met the floor somewhere beneath him with a rattling crash.

Moran needed no further encouragement. He rolled over and let his legs dangle. It hadn't sounded that far to the ground, but when he made contact with the compressed earth of the ice house floor his legs buckled and he felt something give in his knee. He lay still for a heartbeat then rose, groaning, to his feet. A brief experiment with weight distribution confirmed two things. First, it hurt. A lot. Second, he could still walk.

Putting aside the puzzle concerning the identity of the cage unlocker for the time being, Moran limped towards the faint outline of the ice house door. He was still drowsy from the de Courcys' anaesthesia, still arguably at a considerable disadvantage, and still in great danger. *But, Brendan*, he muttered under his breath. *you're also still alive.*

"This is nuts," Toby said as Bola Odunsi manoeuvred the car into a narrow parking space in the over-subscribed Bristol police station car park. "We should have waited for Moran."

They'd spent an age on the M4, or more accurately participating in the lorry-fire-inspired M4 tailback between Newbury and Swindon. There'd been plenty of discussion while they waited, the bulk of which had centred on the route their investigation was taking, or rather the direction in which both men felt it had been steered.

"Damn right we should've. The guv wouldn't have sent us

on a career suicide mission," Bola said as he killed the engine and leaned back with a groan. "I don't know what else to call this."

"Goodness," Toby chuckled. "You mean we actually agree on something?"

"Maybe. But who's to say what we do while we're here?" Bola let the question hang between them. When Toby declined to reply, Bola went on. "So this is the scam." Bola undid his seatbelt and half-opened the door. "We sign in. Find the canteen. Have a brew. Wait half an hour and head back."

Toby frowned. "What's the point? We may as well ask around while we're here. What harm can it do?"

"Harm? All it takes is one of Wilder's mates to call her up and tell her we've been poking around and Diva'll plaster the walls with us."

"Tess' orders, though. Can't just ignore them. And Diva doesn't have any mates, right?" Toby took off his specs and began polishing them with his tie, a compulsive habit he invariably succumbed to when uncomfortable. There was no benefit to the lenses; Toby never cleaned his ties.

Bola jigged with exasperation. "Come on, man. No way is Wilder bent. This whole damn biker thing is just Martin trying to make a splash. You can tell what she's like. Pushy, ambitious. She wants to make a mark."

"What if she's right?"

"What if she ain't?" Bola shrugged. "I don't like the idea that Charlie Pepper is guilty any more than you do, but you know as well as I do that she hasn't been the same since the Ranandans. She's a bag of nerves."

"It doesn't make her a killer, Bola."

Bola's expression became thoughtful. After a moment he said, "What if she did it without knowing?"

Toby looked at Bola and puckered his brow. "Are you kidding? How could you throttle someone and not know?"

"That's the angle they're going for, man. Maggs told me. She's been on these pills, right? They've affected her bad – like, she's been sleepwalking. Her med report has it all down."

Toby fiddled with his tie. "So did she sleepwalk to the garrotte shop as well? You don't normally include covert and deadly weapons on your Tesco list. It's the mark of a pro, an assassin's weapon. And Charlie Pepper is no assassin. She's a great copper. Always straight with you. Nice girl, too."

"Aw, come on, Brit. I know you've had a thing for her in the past. Don't let that get in the way. Look, for me, it's way more plausible that she did it under meds than, like, some random biker just happened to break in and throttle someone they didn't even know."

"The housemates' alibis could be false."

"The alibis check out. That much is deffo."

Toby pressed on. "And Wilder does seem to be suffering from serious tunnel vision. And what about the Huang Xian Kuai alert? This could be a Huang hit. That's what Charlie reckoned. She spoke to DCS Higginson about it. Why isn't Wilder following it up? She's from NCA – they've got all the gen on Huang. Come on, Bola, it sucks. Maybe Wilder *is* dodgy."

Bola gave a dismissive tut. "You've got some serious imagination, Brit, I'll give you that. But I'll tell you one thing for sure – I for one ain't going down with *this* sinking ship."

"No one's asking you to. Come on, Bola. We're here. Let's

just ask around. Low profile."

"Fine. Don't say I didn't warn you." Bola got out and slammed the door.

Toby followed suit, blinking as a shaft of sunlight glanced off the car mirror, highlighting his preoccupied expression and the egg stains on his tie.

Chapter Twenty-six

"Prints, provenance? *Anything?*" Tess could see by the expression on the traffic cop's face that the questions were wasted. He glanced at his colleague who shrugged and patted the padded seat.

"We've been over it like a rash, ma'am."

"And you were both involved in the pursuit?"

Nods.

"So, did you get *any* impression of the rider? Size, sex, riding style?"

"Good rider. Fast, took a lot of risks," the first policeman said, and his mate nodded agreement. Small-ish build."

"A female?"

"Could've been. We didn't get close enough to be sure."

"Traffic cams?"

"We have some images, but as the plates are false–" He shrugged.

Tess sighed. "OK. You lost the rider where? A33?"

"That's right. May have turned into an industrial estate and got out round the back somewhere. We found the bike at the waste recycling centre."

"The tip?"

"Yup."

"And did you check to see if the rider dumped anything else at the tip before doing a Houdini on you?"

The officers exchanges sheepish glances. "Our remit was to track down the bike and question the rider, ma'am."

"Right. Great." Tess paused to take a quick photo of the bike as the traffic officers watched with awkward embarrassment. "Well, thanks anyway."

On her way back to her car she called George McConnell.

"George? Time for some treasure hunting. Waste recycling centre, forty-five minutes."

She hung up before McConnell could conclude his long groan of dismay.

"Brew's worse here than back home." Bola Odunsi settled himself in the hard plastic chair. Rain gusted in sheets onto the grimy plate windows. The room was laced with the lingering smell of the morning's overcooked bacon and the temperature was uncomfortably warm. "I'm not hanging around here long, you can bet on it." Bola folded his arms.

"I don't recognise anyone," Toby said, stirring his lukewarm brew with a knife handle. "Any ideas?"

"Yeah. Let's get out of here." Bola knocked back his tea, grimaced and reunited the cup with its saucer with a theatrical clatter. Heads turned. Someone held up a hand, waved.

"Friend of yours?" Toby asked with a jerk of his head.

Recognition dawned in Bola's eyes. "All*right*! Ken Bantu, my man! What's *he* doing here?" Bola's face split into a huge grin.

Toby noted the transformation of his colleague's mood with relief. Better a happy Bola than a miserable one, especially with a wet journey home in prospect. Ken Bantu. He'd heard Bola mention the guy before. An athlete? A runner, was it? As Ken Bantu made his way to their table Toby tried to recall what else Bola had told him.

"Well, looky here what the cat brought in!" Bantu grabbed a chair and scraped it up to their table. He was a big man, six foot four or five, Toby estimated, wiry and muscular. Big-framed for a runner – sprinter probably…

Bola was introducing him. "Ken, this is DS Toby Glascock. Also known as Brittledick to his mates."

Toby felt his hand seized and pumped like a crank handle. "Brittledick? Love it! Nice to meet you." Ken settled himself down and launched into a stream of news updates, much of which was lost on Toby although he noticed that Ken made an effort to include him by means of eye contact and frequent soliciting of his opinion on various topics ranging from last week's Chelsea-Leeds match to the future of policing in inner cities. Toby found himself warming to Ken Bantu as they chatted, but eventually the small talk petered out, shortly after which came the inevitable question.

"So, what are you guys doing in these parts? Thames Valley too dull these days?"

Toby and Bola looked at each other. What would it be? Flannel or fess up?

"Oho. Hush hush, eh? I get it. You guys have joined special ops, right?" Bantu grinned.

"Um, not quite." Toby toyed with his tie.

"Look," Bola leaned forward and lowered his voice. "You

ever heard of a DCI Suzanne Wilder?"

Toby dropped his tie and shot a wide-eyed glance at Bola. What had caused this abrupt *volte face*? Oh well, he obviously felt he could trust Ken Bantu, and so far Toby hadn't noticed anything about the man to suggest even the smallest degree of untrustworthiness. He was one of those blokes you clicked with straight away, who wouldn't let you down. You could just tell. Toby relaxed a fraction.

Bantu frowned. "Sure. She came from down under, right? Not that long ago, neither."

Toby leaned in closer.

Bantu continued: "She wouldn't be my choice of guv'nor. Works her team to the bone. Small on praise, big on criticism. That's how it is in Oz, so they say. Shall I go on?"

"But she's all right, yeah? People say she's ambitious, but hey, why not?" Bola prompted. "Some people are."

For the first time Ken Bantu looked uncomfortable. "What's all this about, guys? What's Wilder been up to? I'm not one for dropping people in it."

"Sure. Understood," Bola said. "We're only after a bit of background, that's all – just making sure Wilder's cool. She's leading an investigation on our patch and she hasn't made many friends so far."

Ken nodded. "Right. She's not known for social stuff. She joined NCA, didn't she? Suit her, I reckon. They call her 'The Diva', apparently."

"So would you describe her as a driven person?" Toby chipped in.

"Oh yeah," Ken said without hesitation. "Big time driven. Especially since her brother went down. She took that real bad, so I heard."

"Brother?" Bola and Toby spoke simultaneously.

"I'm not surprised you're in the dark, guys. She's kept it real schtum. Well, you would, wouldn't you? *I* only found out 'cause I worked a case with a DCS who knew her."

"Kept what schtum?" Toby's heart skipped a beat. Whatever it was, it sounded bad.

Ken Bantu shook his head in disbelief. "Her brother is DCS Alan Sheldrake. *Ex*-DCS, I should say. She transferred to the UK after the trial. Probably wanted to move closer so she could visit. Yeah, Alan Sheldrake. Man, that was a screw-up, huh? Used to be your boss, remember? Or don't you guys read the papers?"

On her way out Tess made a snap decision to pay Charlie a quick visit. Surprisingly, they let her in; Wilder wasn't around and Maggs seemed unusually accommodating, perhaps because they'd already gone through the formal processes and now weren't so concerned about outside influences intruding on their desire to get Charlie banged up.

Tess was shocked by Charlie's appearance. She tried not to show it but her boss looked as though she'd been put through the mill backwards, sideways and once more for good measure.

"Hi." Tess' attempted note of cheeriness fell flat in the stale air of the interview room.

Charlie looked up. Her face was white. Not pale – white. There were dark shadows of fatigue under her eyes. When she replied her voice was emotionless, mechanical. "Hi, Tess."

Charlie was sitting at the plain table, an untouched glass of water in front of her. Maggs hovered by the door, a gaunt, oppressive presence in an ill-fitting grey suit. Tess turned to the DS. "Give us five minutes?"

Maggs made a face. "Three. Max." He closed the door behind him with a bang.

"So," Charlie said in a low murmur. "How's it going?"

Tess came straight to it. She was here to provide hope, something to hang on to. Her heart went out to the efficient, bubbly DI Charlie Pepper she knew, reduced to this grey despair by Wilder and Maggs. "Charlie, we're trying to trace a bike rider seen near the property the same day. It's a long shot, but, well, we're trying."

"I appreciate it." A weak smile.

"I just wanted to say, you know, we're rooting for you. We're on your side."

"That means a lot." Charlie's lip quivered minutely and she reached for her glass. "Is Brendan back yet?"

"No. Tomorrow, we hope."

"They won't let me talk to Higginson. Or anyone above DI."

"There's a bit of a hoo haa going on," Tess said. "Home Secretary's been here. Press all over."

"Fame at last," Charlie said quietly.

"I know you didn't do it, boss," Tess said. "Just hang on."

"They're going to remand me." Charlie looked up. "You know what happens to police officers on remand."

Tess did. "I'm on it, boss. I promise." It sounded horribly inadequate.

Maggs came back into the room sipping from a plastic cup, reeking of cigarette smoke.

"Time up."

Impulsively Tess reached over and squeezed Charlie's arm.

"It'll be OK. I promise."

Tess waited in the corridor. She toyed with the idea of seeking out DCS Higginson. No, not yet. First she needed evidence, and if she had to rake through rubbish to get to it, so be it.

George McConnell had already made a start. His face told her all she needed to know about the scale of the task.

"Do you know how much rubbish comes in here every day?" His face was scarlet.

"No, but I'm guessing you're about to appraise me of that very statistic."

"Two hundred and nineteen tons, on average."

"Better get my gloves on then." Tess ignored George's exasperated explitive and called his team of reluctant recruits to her side where they formed a cautious semi-circle. The noise around them continued unabated as cars drew up alongside the various bays to unload their waste and pulled out again, only to be replaced by another.

Tess raised her voice above the hubbub. "OK, we're looking for anything bike-related. Gloves, helmet, visor, straps, whatever. I'm hoping that our rider dumped his or her costumery here after parking up and before scooting off, either on foot or maybe in a car – we don't know. Just remember, a DI's future might hang on what you do or don't spot. I know it's unpleasant. I know it stinks, but so does the whole damn thing. I'm sure George has given you as much information as he is able. Questions?"

A general shaking of heads.

"OK, let's crack on."

"We've identified the areas to sift for the period in

question," George told her as they walked. "Obviously those bins are today's intake." He waved at the car bays which gave direct access to containers labelled metals, woods, and general household waste. "Over there," he pointed, "my kind friends in Reading's municipal waste employ have indicated where we might find items deposited between Wednesday and Thursday morning."

Tess followed George's pointing finger. The pile of metal debris rose into the air like a slagheap. She blew out her cheeks.

It was going to be a long night.

"Come on, Bola," Toby insisted. "Make the call."

"So she's Sheldrake's sister, so what?" Bola, a passenger this time, drummed his fingers on the glove box. His face was like the Wiltshire sky, dark and brooding.

Undeterred, Toby pressed on. "So *what*? So it gives her a big fat motive, that's what."

"It's just a coincidence. She's a senior officer. No way would she take that line."

"No? Her brother did."

"You really want to go for this?" Bola turned in his seat and the belt strained across his chest. "Count me out. *You* make the call."

"Sometimes, Bola, I wonder whose side you're on." Toby found a police observation lay-by and pulled in.

As Toby dialled through to Tess Martin's mobile Bola's reply came, half-mumbled under his breath: "I'm on my own side, man. My own side."

Chapter Twenty-seven

Moran waited, watched and listened. He had the ice house door open a crack and could see the lawn stretching out like a freshly rolled carpet. All he had to do was start walking, which was exactly why he didn't. After all, why would anyone release his lock? It couldn't have been Celine; she would have freed him earlier if she'd been able. No, this was premeditated, and Moran concluded that, like it or not, he had been nominated as a key player in some bizarre game of chess of the de Courcys' devising.

He weighed his options. One, he could make a run for it. Two, he could stay put and surprise his next visitor. But they'd know that, wouldn't they? It was all part of the game, and Moran's disadvantage was that he didn't know the rules. God knows, from what he'd discovered about the de Courcy set up, anything was possible. Of course, the complication was Celine; if what she'd told him was true he had to act quickly to prevent her taking matters into her own hands.

So, locks undone – they'd expect him to make a break for it, to try to get away. Rule one: never do the expected.

Moran stuck his head out into the open, looked one way then the other. All clear. He exited the ice house, and, hugging the laurels at the lawn's perimeter, made for the main house.

The police constable's expression said it all. Five hours of digging, sorting and sifting, and nothing to show for it. Tess suppressed her disappointment and tried to look encouraging. "OK, no worries, let's keep at it."

The shift was changing at the waste centre and familiar faces were being replaced by new ones. By and large they were a pretty helpful and cheerful bunch, which, given the nature of their job, was quite something. Tess went to the office to find the night shift manager. "Make friends, smooth the path ahead," her father had always told her. She had one hand on the portakabin door handle when her mobile bleeped.

"Tess Martin."

"Boss, it's Toby."

"Aha. How's Bristol?"

"Interesting." Toby's voice had a compressed quality about it, like a spring under extreme tension.

"Well?"

"Wilder is Sheldrake's sister."

Tess took a moment to process what she had just heard. "Toby, say that again."

"Wilder. She's his sister. Word is she took it very badly when he went down. Worshipped the ground he walked on, apparently."

"Well, well, well," Tess said slowly. Her heart was thumping in an erratic, adrenaline-flushed tattoo. "That puts a rather different slant on events, doesn't it? Keep your phone on, Toby; I might need you later."

Tess took a breath to steady herself. She couldn't afford to feel elated at this stage, but Toby's call was a shot in the arm nevertheless. Now she had a motive which made sense, but would Wilder really have gone that far? It was reckless, crazy even, to throw away life and career for the sake of revenge. *Come on, Tess, let's get to the proof and worry about the rest later...*

The portakabin was a simply furnished affair: a desk, a sofa, a sports calendar nailed crookedly to the wall. A cheap heater, fridge, a kettle, a few chipped mugs. A coffee table piled with lads' mags and some old copies of the Sun. The guy getting into his overalls looked up as she knocked.

"DI Tess Martin? Yep. JW's told me what you're up to. No problem. If you need any help, give me a shout. Coffee?"

"I'd love one," Tess told him. He was young, thirties, with a closely cropped beard and blue eyes. Nice. Too nice for this place.

"I'm Chris." He reached over and offered his hand.

"Nice to meet you." Tess took it and felt a light pressure.

"Any joy?" Chris rattled mugs and spooned in Nescafé. "What is it you're after exactly?"

"Bike accessories. Clothing, boots, helmet."

"Not the machine itself?"

"We've got a Harley in custody, but we think the rider stopped by and disposed of their clothing before making a run for it."

"It's a long shot," Chris said, "but I remember one of the night team taking a shine to a helmet the other day."

"Really?" Tess' heart leaped.

"Yep. Seconds are risky, as every rider knows – a helmet is

dangerous once it's been dropped or impacted – but this was a pretty cool one for all that, black and white with graphics. I can ask. He might have let it go, but he might just have put it aside. Hang on a mo, I'll check."

Tess stood at the portakabin door and sipped coffee. *Please*, she whispered. *Please.*

Chris was chatting to a short man in similar overalls. After a moment he returned. "You're in luck. Dave's still got it in his boot – he was keeping it for his lad. I've asked him to fetch it."

Two minutes later Tess and George were heading for forensics with a female's slightly scuffed, custom-painted crash helmet.

"It's not your bog standard Biker's World lid," PC Bill Howlett said, turning the helmet over. "I'm not even sure if you can get these in the UK. Off the internet, maybe?"

Tess had sent George to knock up Dom Jensen while she got the lowdown on their find from the nearest bike-centric experts she could think of – the local traffic bike team in the bowels of the station's underground garage. The air was heavy with the stink of fuel and oil and somewhere in the far corner a vehicle was repeatedly misfiring as a police mechanic hunched over the engine to minister some badly needed TLC.

Howlett's colleague, PC Stuart Rigsby, shook his head. "Nah. I've seen these in Barry's."

"Come again?" Tess looked at each in turn. "Barry who?"

PC Howlett grinned. "Barry's Bikes, Bath road," he explained. "They do limited custom ranges, graphics too. Imported mostly."

"Yeah, right. Look." Rigsby held the helmet up for Tess' inspection. "See the label? VHR – vhrhelmet.com. Chinese. Or Korean, maybe."

The lift pinged and George McConnell emerged, blinking owlishly in the fluorescent lighting. He made a beeline for them. "Dom's opened FSU for us," he said. "And he's called someone in to do the test."

"Good work, George. Thanks, you two." Tess dismissed the officers with a wave.

"Come on then, DC McConnell," Tess thumped the bagged helmet into George's chest. "Let's see if we can nail this bitch."

George followed in Tess' wake, dismissing the bike cops' complicit grins with a tried and tested Anglo-Saxon gesture involving two fingers and an upward flick of the wrist.

DCI Wilder looked up as Bola came in. The temporary office Wilder had commandeered was dimly lit, a desk lamp pooling a yellow circle onto an A4 pad half-filled with precise, evenly lettered handwriting. Wilder was alone, her shady familiar for once absent on other business – or more likely, Bola thought, down the pub. No, a bit late now, thinking about it – unless Maggs had managed to winkle out a local lock-in in the short time he'd been in Reading, which, from what he'd seen of Maggs so far, seemed more than likely.

"DC Odunsi. What can I do for you?" Wilder put down her pen and indicated the vacant chair.

Bola squeezed his large frame into the chair and accepted Wilder's offer of water. It didn't take long to get everything off his chest – in fact, he found that the more he ventured, the more pleased Wilder seemed to be. When he'd finished Wilder steepled her fingers and nodded with satisfaction.

"Thank you, DC Odunsi," the DCI purred. "You've done well. I like people I can trust."

Chapter Twenty-eight

It's getting near dawn. And lights close their tired eyes… Tess reached over and flicked off the radio. She was knackered but buzzing with adrenaline. The marks on Banner's bedroom wall contained traces of lacquer which matched the scuff on the helmet's ridge. And if that wasn't enough, the late-night CSI had also produced a fragment of hair from the helmet's interior which was currently being run through DNA database checks. Tess had arranged to meet George at Barry's Bikes first thing in the hope that the helmet had been a local purchase. It seemed unlikely, but you never knew. If the DNA wasn't on record she needed something else that would stick. Barry's opened at nine. That would give her … she consulted the clock on her car's dashboard … about three hours sleep. Tess parked up and killed the engine. She doubted whether she'd sleep anyway.

Tess rented a maisonette at the western tip of the sprawl of the eighties housing development known as Lower Earley. It was a one-bed, kitchen-diner arrangement with parking space nestled among a myriad of larger houses and flats of similar design. There was a local centre with pub and gym, and the neighbourhood was generally peaceful and family-oriented. Ideal for a young single female working irregular hours – which was precisely why Tess had chosen it two months earlier. She turned the key in the lock and reached for the light switch.

A young Chinese girl in black leather was sitting on her sofa. In the girl's gloved hand a stiletto blade glinted.

The girl smiled.

Tess took a step back. The front door was still ajar, the car keys in her hand. She spun around but a hand closed over her mouth, strong and unrelenting. Tess jabbed both elbows hard but made no contact. The grip tightened and her head was jerked back; now she couldn't breathe. She felt herself lifted off the floor, feet kicking. Without warning her assailant released her so that, balance awry, she staggered and pitched forward, cracking her head hard against the edge of the kitchenette wall.

For a second or two she saw stars, then nothing.

The clock above the bar said half past four, but George McConnell wasn't paying too much attention to the time. It had been a long, hard day and they had unearthed positive circumstantial evidence which happily seemed to be corroborated by the FSU. There was a way to go, for sure – nothing so far had even remotely implicated Wilder – but George nevertheless felt that the successes of the past twenty-four hours merited some small acknowledgement. And as he had been, by his own standards, impressively abstemious for the last couple of weeks, what better way to 'acknowledge' than by taking up DS Maggs on his offer of a late night sup or two at 'a little place he had found' in town? Besides, Maggs might cough up something useful.

"So, George," Maggs said with no trace of a slur, although by George's reckoning the DS had put back at least four pints and a whisky chaser in the last couple of hours, "plenty for your press officer to deal with over the next few days, am I right?"

"Aye," George nodded. "I'm not sure the Chief'll survive this one."

"Bloody circus," Maggs observed morosely. "Did you see 'em out front, like a flock of bloody gannets?"

George finished his pint. The beer was going down exceptionally well and he was feeling rather pleased with himself. "They have a job to do as well, I suppose. Can't hold it against them."

"Well, I do," Maggs said. "They want blood. Anyone's. Another?"

George held out his glass. "Why not?"

The club was sparsely populated, just two or three groups of earnest drinkers huddled here and there in low and heavy-eyed conversation, the air sullied by drifting blue smoke more reminiscent of a bygone age than the twenty-first century.

"'Blind-eye bar' they call this place." Maggs handed him another brimming pint. "Works for me."

"So." George supped his beer, enjoying the warm, blanketing sensation as the alcohol re-established its familiar byways through his bloodstream. "How long have you been with Wilder?"

Maggs' expression tightened. "Couple of months."

"Good guv'nor?"

"She'll do me." Maggs cradled his scotch, nursing it in a large blue-veined hand. "No complaints so far."

"Hard-nosed cow, though, isn't she?" George said. "From what I've seen?"

"It's her way. She's a results woman. They're tough down under, so she had to be too."

George resigned himself to the fact that Maggs wasn't going to be drawn easily. He shrugged. Time to let go, enjoy a bit of R & R, a couple of hours' kip then over to the boss for half eight. A single man with no ties, George didn't need a lot of sleep; when he was knackered he caught up at weekends or off shift. Besides, he'd just remembered a great joke and Maggs certainly looked as though he could do with cheering up. He felt himself breaking into an anticipatory grin. "So, did I ever tell you the one about the copper and the traffic warden?"

"Rise and shine," the voice said again. "Time to be upwardly mobile. Your new suite awaits."

Charlie dragged herself into an upright position. Her back ached and her leg was numb. Two nights in a police cell hadn't done a lot for her musculo-skeletal flexibility. This was it then. Remand beckoned and she felt sick to her stomach.

"Tea? Cappuccino? Glass of arsenic?" Maggs' voice boomed in the confined space like some hideous parody of a Costa coffee barista.

"You're all heart, Maggs."

"And you're a cop-killing bitch who's about to get what she deserves. Ten minutes to get ready."

The cell shutter was closed with a snap that made her jump. Charlie held her head in her hands. So much for her solicitor's optimism. No bail. No mercy.

She wasn't surprised. Given the Thames Valley's recent history she couldn't expect leniency. They'd make an example of her – lock her up and throw away the key. *Stop it. Feeling sorry for yourself isn't going to help…*

As she was led out of the cell and up through the station to the rear car park she was met with hostile stares and whispered comments. A new DC she'd met the previous week following a successful interview shouldered past her leaving one word behind. *Rot.*

That single comment did more to unsettle Charlie than anything which had gone before. She could feel herself breaking down, piece by piece, molecule by molecule; surrendering to the role she had been cast in.

A commotion behind made her turn, involuntarily cowering to protect herself. She straightened up. It was only Toby, demanding an audience.

"I insist on talking to DI Pepper. It's important." Toby's voice betrayed his agitation. Wilder was there, between them, barring his path.

"No go, sergeant. DI Pepper is being taken into custody."

"Two minutes. That's all."

A small crowd had gathered to witness the exchange. Maggs hesitated at the lift. Wilder motioned him on.

"Come on. It won't hurt."

"Watch your tone, DS Glascock. It's DCI Wilder to you. Or ma'am, if you prefer."

Toby apparently didn't. "DCI Wilder, I respectfully request a short audience with DI Pepper."

A semicircle of silent faces waited for Wilder's decision. Someone sniggered. The lift arrived. The doors slid apart.

Charlie felt Maggs' fist in the small of her back. "Get in."

"I'm acting on behalf of DCI Moran," she heard Toby say. "He would want me to communicate with DI Pepper in view of the circumstances."

A murmur of agreement passed through the assembled onlookers. Wilder looked around and realised she was beaten. "All right. Two minutes. No longer."

"Boss, would you step this way, please?" Toby pushed past Maggs and invited Charlie to follow. He ushered her into an empty office near the lift and closed the door. Maggs leaned against the glass from the outside, blocking the light.

"What is it, Toby? Have you heard from Brendan?"

"Not exactly. I wanted to update you."

He quickly briefed Charlie on George and Tess' forensic results. A tiny spark of hope warmed her stomach as she listened.

"You haven't heard the best bit yet," Toby went on. "Wilder and Sheldrake are siblings."

"Oh my God. Are you sure?"

"As eggs is eggs," Toby said with a nervous grin. "But what I also wanted to tell you is that Tess hasn't turned up for shift."

Charlie felt a seeping dread swap places with the warmth she had felt a moment ago. "She's always in on the dot. George?"

Toby shook his head. "Not yet, but he was late last night. He'll be here, don't worry. Boss, can I ask you something?"

"Sure."

"Did Wilder ask about BM? Where he is, I mean?"

"Yes, actually." Charlie's stomach was now doing its best to imitate an icebox and was making a pretty good job of it. "As my senior officer she wanted to let Brendan know that I was being remanded in custody. Protocol and all that."

"Did you tell her?" Toby's voice tried to avoid a pleading tone and failed.

"Yes," Charlie said quietly. "I gave her his holiday address. Car reg, the lot."

They looked at each other in silence.

Maggs banged on the glass and made her jump again.

"Leave it with me," Toby said. "I'll talk to you later. Keep it together, boss, OK?"

"I'll try. Toby, you and Bola get over to Tess' place pronto. And please – be careful."

Toby opened the door and she stepped into the corridor. Maggs took her arm, guided her through the press of hostility. The lift door closed and shut them out.

They went down.

Chapter Twenty-nine

By the time he reached the front steps Moran knew for sure he was being watched. Hopefully by doing the unexpected he would be able to gain some small advantage, although at present he had no idea what that might turn out to be. Off to his right a shadow moved against the lighter stone of the house, paused, came on again. Moran went left, skirted the corner of the building and found himself on a high terrace overlooking the landscaped gardens of Cernham Manor.

He cast about for a weapon. A pile of logs was stacked against the side wall between a drain and a low window. He selected and hefted one of the smaller off-cuts. It would do.

Gravel crunched, getting closer. Moran found a set of stone steps and descended into the wilderness of the gardens. He headed for a tall elevation of hawthorn and waited to see if he could catch a glimpse of his pursuer. A figure appeared on the terrace; moving cautiously but with a measure of athletic grace it went swiftly to the steps, paused as if scanning the darkness, and descended into the garden.

Moran followed the contours of the hedge and came

presently to a ninety-degree dead end. No, wait, there was a gap to the right. He followed it and came to another abrupt turn. With a jolt of panic he realised what he had done.

It's a maze, Brendan, you Irish tosser. You've blundered into the maze…

He limped quickly to the next right angle, trying to remember everything he'd read about mazes. There was a formula; every maze was designed with one. Absurdly the Hampton Court maze anecdote from 'Three Men in a Boat' came to mind. In this story, the unfortunate subject had confidently gathered a selection of lost individuals within the maze and promised to deliver them safely back to the entrance. The theory was that you just had to keep turning right and eventually you'd find yourself at the beginning. Moran couldn't remember how it had turned out but had a strong suspicion that the theory had failed. He took the next right anyway, trying to suppress the unnerving thought that whoever was following him might know their way around the maze with their eyes closed. Someone, for instance, who had lived here all their lives.

Someone like Rufus de Courcy.

Moran froze as furtive footsteps approached. Grasping his makeshift club he waited at the next right angle. The footsteps came closer until, as they were almost upon him, Moran realised that his pursuer was negotiating a parallel path on the other side of the hedge. He held his breath as the footfalls came to a halt and the feral sound of something sniffing the air made the hairs on his neck stand to attention. Moran felt a bead of sweat trickle down his neck as he was scented and prayed that the light coastal breeze continued to blow towards him, in his favour…

The maze grew thicker, untended, so that it became harder to pass quietly through the barriers of foliage without giving his position away. Moran's plan was simple: find the centre and wait for his shadow to join him. He turned right.

And right again.

Stopped, listened.

Silence.

He crept on, bent low. The maze turned left and Moran went with it. A long straight section, one more right turn and he found himself at the edge of a broad, roughly circular open space. But he wasn't the first to get here. Directly in the centre and seated at a long trestle table two figures rested at ease, heads bowed towards each other as if engaged in deep and companionable conversation.

Moran waited to see if the couple had noticed his arrival but they seemed so intent on each other that it he judged it unlikely. As he walked towards the table a sick anticipatory dread in the pit of his stomach told him that the two seated figures had long lost the ability to converse with each other – or anybody else, for that matter.

His assessment was soon confirmed. One of the skeletons, the incongruously fedora-wearing tweed-jacketed male, rested its bony fingers on the female's wrist. She, in turn, was arranged in such a way that she seemed to be gazing rapturously into her partner's empty eye sockets. In one hand she was holding a strip of lacy cloth – a handkerchief, perhaps? Another detail struck Moran immediately: the dental layout of both skulls featured a single gold tooth on the upper set. Whoever they were, they obviously belonged together.

He was jolted from his examination by the sound of

foliage impatiently thrust aside. Moran thought quickly; after making a careful note of the posture it took him only a few seconds to move the male skeleton to a new location under an overgrown section of hedge and take its former place at the table. Moran slipped on the damp jacket, placed the fedora gingerly on his head and let his hand rest lightly on his attentive partner's wrist.

He sensed another presence nearby. It took all Moran's willpower to remain still, not turn his head. He had positioned his woodpile club within easy reach alongside him on the bench. His peripheral vision caught a movement; someone was slowly quartering the circle. Moran prayed that he had sufficiently camouflaged the male skeleton and that the borrowed hat would hide his face for the precious few seconds he needed.

The newcomer backed towards the table with a relaxed and confident ease. Moran's spirits lifted. His hunch had been correct; to the de Courcy family the seated couple were a familiar feature, so familiar that they would hardly be given a second glance. Moran held his breath. He was sure that his pursuer meant to sit quietly and wait for Moran to stumble into the centre, and that being the case, the plan might work. The table creaked as it took the additional weight. Moran's partner jiggled at the movement, her jaw flapping loosely like some ghastly Halloween boogieman. Even now Moran hesitated; he wasn't one of nature's naturally violent men, but then he caught sight of the axe dangling loosely in Matt Harrison's grip and all doubts were quashed. He'd created the advantage, now he had to act on it.

His free hand closed around the club. He saw Harrison stiffen as he sensed something, but by then Moran had brought the club around in a wide, swinging arc and smashed it into the side of Harrison's unprotected head. He collapsed like a felled tree and the axe slipped from his grip, dropping onto the turf with a wet thud.

Moran shed his disguise with a shudder and got straight to work anchoring his pursuer's hands and feet to the table using the flex which had held his skeletal alter ego in place. The cord was tough and Moran doubted that, even if he came round over the next half hour, the youngest de Courcy would be able to free himself without assistance. A quick examination satisfied Moran that his victim was breathing normally. He'd have a cracking headache when he woke up but that would be all.

Moran took a deep breath. Now all he had to do was find his way out.

He caught sight of the axe beneath the table and retrieved it. Hoping he wouldn't be called upon to use it Moran set off once again into the maze. It took him longer to find his way out but eventually he took a final, cautious left turn and found himself a free man.

As he pondered his next move the recheat of a hunting horn rang out, a rapid, repetitive burst of triplets which, Moran recalled from his scanty knowledge of hunting, signified a find.

Somewhere in or near the woods the quarry was at bay, and as it wasn't him, that left just one other possibility.

Celine.

Chapter Thirty

The woods surrounding Cernham Manor pre-dated the eleventh century Domesday survey in which the family de Courcy, closely associated as they were with the Conqueror King and his Norman aristocracy, were noted as wealthy landowners. Before the conquest such woodland would have covered much of the island: oak, hornbeam, ash and then, as areas were gradually cleared for farmland, secondary forests of willow, birch, alder and spruce. With the introduction of feudalism the de Courcys thrived, and due primarily to the fearsome reputation of Guillaume de Courcy and his close relationship with the new king, their land was left untouched and unmolested. The woodland remained as it had done for centuries, as dense and mysterious as the Mirkwood of Tolkien's imagination.

It was into this tangle of antiquity that Moran's feet reluctantly carried him. Although a rational man, his Irish upbringing had been informed by deep superstition and – for his mother, if not his father – the forest had always been a place of magic and haunted spirits. Moran tried to put such thoughts aside but couldn't help but recall his recent dream of the *fidnemed*, the forest shrine. As if in response a sudden rattling gust of wind prompted him to find cover until he was sure it was safe to rejoin the path.

He was painfully aware of the odds against him; Rufus de Courcy was not only a skilled and deadly hunter but also a long-term serial killer. Whether you took his mental instability into account or not made no material difference; Rufus had the advantage. This was his patch, his neck of the woods, his hunting ground. But what were the alternatives? As he crept on his rational mind obligingly provided a solution.

Back to the car. Get to Exeter. Request reinforcements. Bring the gun boys in.

But the car had been immobilised, and even if he could get it started, by the time he returned with the cavalry in tow Celine would have become the latest statistic in Rufus de Courcy's long record of female homicide. And that, Moran promised himself, wasn't going to happen. But strangely, now that he knew the circumstances which had tipped the boy over the edge he found himself in two minds. Sure, Rufus was a killer, but how culpable? Surely the responsibility rested with the two people Moran considered to be the real villains: Richard de Courcy and his mother. Or should that be *villeins*? No, that title belonged to the cowed Cernham villagers, locked as they were in some archaic bond of servitude with the manor's controlling family. Blame could be levelled there, too. If only someone had had the courage to speak up years ago…

He came to a halt at the edge of a clearing. Moonlight played over the remains of an ancient, storm-damaged beech, roots pointing heavenwards like pale, beckoning fingers. Moran hesitated. He felt as though he had been transported back to his childhood to find himself lost and alone in a fairytale world of ghosts and monsters. The shiver of fear which ran down his spine was caused not by Rufus and the threat of physical harm but rather by the unseen world of runes, three-way-meets and flitting spirits which the forest seemed so graphically to invoke.

Keep moving, Brendan, old son. Keep moving…

He distanced himself from the beech, skirting the clearing's perimeter and soon he was swallowed up once more in the density of Cernham's ancient forest.

The darkness was thick and tangible. He slowed to a snail's pace, hands outstretched. He knew from conversations with Terl that the ground was treacherous in many outlying areas of the woodland where the forest gave way to peat bog. Moran had no desire to end his days entombed in peat.

He had just remembered the torch built into his mobile phone and was reaching into his jacket to retrieve it when he realised that, minute by minute, the quality of light was improving. He looked up through the lattice of leaves and branches and grinned with relief. He'd lost all track of time and couldn't for the life of him remember when he'd been so delighted to welcome the beginning of a new day.

Dawn was breaking over Cernham.

DC Bola Odunsi had had better mornings. He'd woken with a terrible sense of guilt at around five and no matter what he'd tried, sleep had slipped right out of reach. He kept telling himself that he'd done the right thing; what choice had he had?

Always keep the senior officer in the picture. Especially someone with Wilder's reputation. But the nagging doubt buzzing away in his brain would not be suppressed. What if Brit was right? What if Wilder *was* bent? But how? From what he'd heard she was on course for Superintendent short term, and maybe even ACC medium term. A high flyer. A model copper. Surely she was on the level?

Like Sheldrake? The buzzing voice tormented him. *Like sister, like brother…*

He'd got up at that point and made himself a lemon tea. Now it was quarter to seven and they were outside Tess' maisonette in Lower Earley. Nice area. He'd thought about buying here himself once. Why hadn't he? Bit too quiet, maybe. Too suburban. He wondered whether to voice his thoughts to Brit: what was all the fuss about? Why the panic? Everyone overslept now and again, even rank-climbers like Tess Martin. Everything was cool. False alarms all round.

Bola glanced at his partner. Brit was pale, tense-looking as he parked up and unclipped his seat belt.

He turned to Bola. "Well? Are you up for this?" Toby sounded like he looked. Bola shrugged it off.

"Sure. Stop stressing. You're freaking me out."

Toby approached the maisonette obliquely, keeping out of sight of the front window. Bola watched as his colleague edged closer, masked his eyes against the reflection, peered in and stepped back. He made an impatient motion with his hand, a *get your backside over here* gesture.

Bola obliged and stood behind Toby as he rang the bell.

Toby was examining the lock. It wasn't hard to see the deep scratches on and around the keyhole, the signs of attempted forced entry. Bola watched as his buddy went to the front window again and rapped on it.

"Tess?"

Across the road curtains twitched as the neighbours woke to the sound of Toby's voice echoing around the quiet close.

"Tess? Open up. Shout if you can hear me."

Bola felt sick in his stomach, regretting the egg on toast he'd made himself eat before shift.

Toby came back to the door, sized it up and looked at Bola. "OK. No choice."

"Seriously? She might be on her way to the station. You don't want to bust her lock. She'll kill you."

"Bola, she's not responding to calls, texts, emails, door knocking. What do you suggest we try next? Semaphore?"

Bola shrugged. "OK Brit. If you think—"

Toby's boot hit the flimsy woodwork just to the right of the lock and the door caved in.

Bola followed Toby into the maisonette, shaking his head and whistling softly under his breath. Brit was fired up all right, like big time.

The front room was in order. The kitchen the same. No sign of a struggle. They went into the bedroom, Toby first, then Bola.

Neither spoke.

The bedclothes were ruffled, as if somebody had been carelessly flung down. The pillow was in a normal position beneath the headboard, but it was the pillow both men were concentrating on; it was saturated in blood, some of which had stained the topmost part of the duvet and splashed onto the headboard. There was no sign of Tess.

"Oh God," Toby said quietly.

He turned around but Bola had gone. Toby found him

outside emptying his stomach into the flower bed.

"Where is George McConnell? Anyone?" Toby Glascock had reached screaming point. Everything was going to hell: Charlie banged up, Tess missing, George *awol*, the DCS unavailable, Moran still away – and the really weird thing was, no one else seemed to get it. The station was simply continuing as if it were a normal day, everyone going about their business as usual, sat at their usual desks, drinking their usual coffee, talking their usual bollocks.

He wanted to stand on his desk and shout at them. Yes, they were aware that Tess had, in all probability, been abducted by persons unknown. A break in. A kidnap. A robbery. God forbid, a rape. Every explanation or theory which could be bandied about *was* being bandied about. Except the one which mattered: the one which said Wilder was up to her neck in it. Maggs too, probably. But how could he say that? All Ts were being crossed, all Is dotted. And guess who was co-ordinating the search for Tess? Yep, in one: DCI Wilder, as senior officer on site, having dispatched Charlie into custody, was now free to take on the responsibility – or so the DCS had apparently told her in a brief moment of availability before he had been whisked into yet another press conference.

And to cap it all they were now surrounded by paparazzi as well as every prominent national correspondent Toby could think of, milling about with fluffy microphones at the ready, poised to pounce as unwary officers made their way in and out of the car park, slavering for any titbits of news or, better still, rumours and gossip.

It was a shambles. And who was going to fix it? Bottom

line: it was down to him.

"You OK, Brit?"

Toby looked up to see Bola's anxious face.

"No, frankly."

"What can we do, man? It's out of our hands."

"Is it?" Toby gave Bola a hard look. "Tess was going to check out Barry's Bikes this morning with George. I think we should go."

"I don't know. Wilder—"

"Screw Wilder."

"But—"

"Look, Bola," Toby said, "Wilder's up to speed with pretty much everything now. The helmet, the hair sample, the match with the lacquer above Banner's bed. Right?"

"Right," Bola said, studying his fingernails. "I guess she had to know all the details if she's invest—"

Toby waved Bola quiet. "Whatever. But I don't think she's exactly earmarked the bike shop as a priority."

"You what?"

"She won't follow it up. But we will."

"Fine by me."

As they walked to the lift Toby debated whether or not to share his more urgent thoughts with Bola – those thoughts which rested upon Charlie's divulgence of Brendan Moran's whereabouts to DCI Wilder. Wilder appeared to be very well informed about the team's recent covert investigations. Had she been briefed before Tess' disappearance? And if so, by whom? One thing was certain: if Wilder hadn't been busy this morning she'd have been all over them like a runaway express train. Sniffing around without her approval was, Toby reckoned, a bollocking offence at the very least. She knew everything, or that's the way it looked to Toby. He glanced at Bola as they waited for the creaking lift to arrive but the big man's face was giving nothing away.

Tread carefully, Toby. Very carefully.

Chapter Thirty-one

Now he could see where he was going Moran continued at a brisker pace. He was alert for the sound of the horn but since the maze it had been frustratingly – and ominously – silent. Neither had he much confidence that he was even headed in the right direction. He was sure of one thing, though: if he didn't find Rufus first, Rufus would certainly find him.

The newly-risen sun slanted through the treetops in a smoky kaleidoscope, highlighting a fallen trunk here, an exposure of rotting roots there. Moran picked his way through a constantly changing topography. In a small glade he caught a fleeting and heart-stopping glimpse of a nervous muntjac and followed it into a plantation of willow, which in turn gave way to denser clusters of oak and hornbeam. Nevertheless he felt exposed, the wooden club he still carried worryingly inadequate. As the wood deepened he found himself beneath the spreading umbrella of an ash, its trunk marked by a network of shallow ridges, almost like a map. Moran reached up and pulled at a loose branch. It came away easily and as he examined it he recalled from childhood days of forest lore that the ash was particularly suited for making arrows or spear shafts. He hefted the slim bough. It felt balanced and strong. Five minutes work with his penknife had sharpened the tip to a satisfactory point. He discarded the club and continued along the track, senses tingling for the slightest unexplained noise or movement.

The horn blast was so close that it stopped Moran in his tracks. As quickly as it had sounded the note fell away, leaving just the sound of the slow drip of moisture falling from leaf to leaf as a light drizzle began its pattering journey to the woodland floor.

"Rufus?" He cupped his hands over his mouth but his voice sounded puny as it was absorbed by the wood. "I want to talk. I mean you no harm. Is Celine with you?"

The response, a long throaty chuckle, told Moran two things: first, Rufus was very near, and second, a rational approach was unlikely to succeed. Somehow he had to get under Rufus' skin, work on the history, the reason this had all begun. The chuckle morphed into a low growling, like a restless tiger waiting for feeding time.

Best get emotional, Brendan, and be quick about it...

"Let's talk, Rufus. Speak to me. I want to hear about the girl. The first girl. What was her name? Rachel?" Moran remembered being struck by Lady Cernham and Richard de Courcy's inability to mention her by name. Always 'the girl', never 'Rachel'.

Ahead, from behind the wide trunk of an oak, a figure slid into view. Moran stood his ground as Rufus de Courcy, the embodiment of *Cernunnos*, Lord of the Hunt, approached. Moran planted his spear in the earth behind him and raised his empty hands. "I don't want anyone hurt, Rufus."

Rufus de Courcy was perhaps six and a half feet tall, powerfully built, black-cloaked, lithe and sure in his movements. Although his features were partially covered by a scarf, Moran could make out deep-socketed eyes below a misshapen and bulbous forehead from which rose two bony projections like the horns of a deer. The encounter with his brother's shotgun had clearly caused extensive cranial damage and disfigurement, and Moran guessed that his mother had played a central role in nursing him back to health – if *health* was an appropriate description of his present condition. However, in doing so she had denied her son the medical and psychiatric treatment he so desperately needed. A miracle, then, that Rufus had survived at all.

"Say her name again." Rufus had come to a halt a few paces away. "Say it and I'll kill you where you stand."

"No point in denying what happened, Rufus." Moran spread his hands. "You weren't to blame for her choices."

Rufus' eyes smouldered.

"Celine has no part in this."

"The sister." Rufus said. It was a statement.

"Yes. She wasn't here at the time. She was a child."

"She bleeds," Rufus said. "For her sister's sins. And for her own role as seductress."

"She didn't seduce anyone. She only spent time with your brother to find out what had happened."

"No." Rufus took a step towards him and Moran dropped his hand to the spear as Rufus pointed an accusing finger. "She is a seductress like her sister before her. And you too have welcomed her approaches."

"We talked. Had a drink together. That was it." And it

was, pretty much, Moran thought with a pang of regret.

"The act of seduction is not permitted."

"Where is she, Rufus? I–"

Rufus' cloak parted and in one quick movement Moran was looking at a drawn longbow with an arrow nocked and ready. It was an impressive display of expertise.

Rufus made a small movement with his head. "Run."

Moran held up both hands but dropped them as he realised what a pathetic defence they would be against a steel-tipped arrowhead. "Look, there's no need to–"

"Run, fornicator, *run*."

Moran briefly considered retrieving his spear but rejected the idea; any act of aggression on his part and Rufus would loose. He backed slowly; when death came winging towards him he at least wanted to be able to see it coming. A few metres further and he stumbled against a tree trunk. Cover. Moran put the tree between him and the longbow and ran for his life, dodging and weaving to spoil Rufus' aim. Something whacked his leg from under him and pitched him forward in a sprawling heap. He rolled and sat up, dazed. The arrow had buried itself in the hard rubber of his heel. No point wondering if it was a deliberate miss or a clever warning shot; Rufus' confident swagger as he closed the distance between them told him all he needed to know. Moran tugged at the shaft but it was stuck fast in his shoe; it would be impossible to run. He scrambled to his feet and faced his enemy.

Looks like time's up, Brendan…

He felt light-headed, almost relieved. No more decisions to make. No more fretting over law and justice. No more relationship problems. No more grief. No more dreams…

As Rufus raised the longbow Moran braced himself.

Chapter Thirty-two

Barry was a walking tattoo. At least, that's how he appeared to Toby at first glance. A thick, knotted beard obscured most of the lower part of the shop owner's face and those remaining parts of his body exposed to the air were a tracery of fantastical *Lord of the Rings*-style orcs and elves amalgamated skilfully with a generous smattering of metal and rock chick imagery. The letters of his Christian name were stencilled across the fingers of his left hand and Toby wondered why the right hand had escaped the tattooist's pen. Maybe he had plans for it.

"Help you?"

Given his alarming appearance, Barry's voice was surprisingly cultured.

Toby flashed his ID.

"Thought so." Barry grinned. "Just like the Mormons. Always travel in pairs."

"Do you sell this type of helmet?" Toby showed Barry an image from his iPhone.

"Special order. Had a few in but don't stock 'em anymore.

Low end lid, some cool high end features. People want 'em for the artwork, mainly."

"And when did you sell the last one?"

Barry scratched his beard. Toby wondered how many varieties of insect had made their home in its warm and comfortable micro-environment. "Now you're asking." The shop owner slid open a counter drawer and began to delve into the contents. "I keep a couple of month's worth of sales records in here. In case there's any comeback," he explained. "Let's have another butcher's."

Toby showed the image again.

"Oh… yeah, I think I remember this one. It was the last one of the first lot I bought in."

"You do? It was?" Toby felt his heart jump.

Barry was back ferreting in the drawer. Toby felt his hopes sink. With this standard of record-keeping the long shot was getting longer by the minute. Bola was wandering around the shop admiring the machines. The big DC stopped next to a massive Harley with gleaming metalwork and a dragon motif emblazoned on the tank and ran his finger lovingly over the paintwork.

"Nice, Brit, eh?"

"If you say so." Toby drummed his fingers on the worn counter.

"Got it," Barry said, flourishing a receipt in his oil-stained hand.

"You have?" Toby almost reached over and seized the crumpled piece of paper before he remembered himself and swapped his impatience for a question. "Name? Address?"

"Yep." Barry found and donned a pair of incongruously normal horn-rimmed glasses and peered at the invoice.

"Yeah, yeah. She was a hot one."

Toby's heartbeat had gone into overdrive. "She?"

"Yeah. Chinese chick. Had it all going on. Ten years younger and I'd have—"

"Name, Barry, please. Contact details."

"Sure." He held out the receipt. "It's all there. Serial number too – it's a certified helmet. Keep it."

"Thanks." Toby was at the door. "Bola?"

"With you, Brit."

On their way to the car Bola took out his mobile.

"Calling home?" Toby asked, blocking Bola's path to the passenger door.

"Texting the little woman. Why? Problem?"

"Save the social stuff for later, Bola."

"Man, what is it with you?"

"Put the phone away. Get in."

For a moment the two men faced each other in silence. Toby felt the atmosphere crackle between them, but he held his ground. After what seemed an age, Bola gave a short, humourless shake of his head and pocketed his iPhone. "Can I get in now?"

Toby nodded.

When they were moving Bola turned to him. "And may I ask where we're going?"

"Orts Road," Toby said. "I might have known."

It was an infamous name – the location of one of the biggest drug busts ever, an appropriate address for the calibre of villain Toby now believed they were dealing with: an expert motorcyclist in top physical condition who was also a highly trained assassin and kidnapper. Female, Chinese.

"Back up?" Bola asked.

Toby shook his head. "No time."

There never was.

The mid-terraced house was just like any other terrace in the road, or in Reading for that matter. Anonymous, nondescript. Perfect.

Toby's mobile buzzed. George.

"Are you sure you should take that?" Bola raised an eyebrow.

Toby answered it with a cold glance at his colleague. "Where the hell are you, George?"

George McConnell's voice sounded slurred, abnormal.

"Are you pissed, George?"

"No. Not right, though. Can't get Tess."

"Look, George, get into the station asap, would you? We're at this address – can you make a note?"

"Minute…"

George took an age to return.

"112 Orts Road. Got that?" Toby was half out of the car. "I'll update you later. If we're not back in an hour, send the troops in."

"OK."

The house was hot. Toby could feel it. Hand on baton, he rapped the rusted knocker. When there was no reply he motioned to Bola. "Your turn."

Bola's boot sprang the door in seconds. They were confronted by a narrow, uncarpeted hallway, front room to the right. It was empty, as was the dining room and kitchen. "I'll do the garden," Bola said.

Toby went upstairs. Bathroom empty. He heard Bola's call of "Clear!" from downstairs. First bedroom: empty. Main bedroom…

Tess was lying unconscious on a tatty double mattress, half-covered by a thin sheet. A congealed pool of vomit had congealed on the bare boards beside her. Toby yelled for Bola and went for Tess' pulse. It was faint, but there.

The ambulance took under five minutes; Toby muttered a silent prayer of thanks that they were only a stone's throw from the Royal Berkshire Hospital. He and Bola watched the paramedics attend to Tess. The head wound looked ghastly but Toby knew that a bleed from the head often looked much worse than it was. *Come on, Tess, come on…*

A minute or so later she responded to the paramedics' chatter. "All right, love, can you hear me? Do you remember what happened? No? Not to worry. Your mates are here. You're OK now. Just need to get you up the road so the A&E team can have a look at you. Easy, easy…"

They looked away as Tess was sick again.

"Still not sure whose side you're on?" Toby asked.

Bola avoided eye contact. "Point taken."

"Toby?"

Tess was sitting up, pale as the paramedics' white trainers.

Toby bent down. "Steady, boss. Don't push it. You'll be fine."

"Ha." Tess tried to laugh. "Oh God, bad idea." She fell back onto the mattress. Then "Ow," as a paramedic gave her a shot. Her expression changed as her memory began to kick back in and she tried to moisten her cracked lips. "There were two of them. Chinese girl –and a guy. Didn't see him, heard them in car. Talked about the 'last one'. It's the guv, Toby, they know where…"

As the medication began to take effect Tess was slipping

into a half-dozing, half awake state. "She's going to do it. He's going to leave with the woman. God, what's her name, I can't think. Can't think…"

The female paramedic quietened her and turned to Toby and Bola. "That'll have to be enough for now, I'm afraid."

"Will she be all right?" Bola's anxiety was all over his face.

Maybe, thought Toby to himself, maybe this is what the big guy needed, to clue him into what was going on.

"It's a nasty head wound," the paramedic was saying, "but it doesn't look life-threatening. Nevertheless—"

"Sure. She's all yours." Toby bent again. "We'll see you later, boss. Take it easy."

But Tess had slipped away, out for the count.

Back in the car Toby was onto the station. "Get me DC McConnell, please. No, wait, make that DCS Higginson. I don't care if he's busy. No, I don't care who he's with at the moment. No, I don't want DCI Wilder. We have a situation here. Are you listening?"

Bola was nodding with approval. "Stick it to 'em, Brit. Stick it to 'em."

Chapter Thirty-three

Moran's eyes were open. He still drew breath and nothing hurt or bled. He looked down. Rufus' second arrow had found the spot precisely between his feet. With a sick feeling he understood; Rufus wanted the end game to last as long as possible, to prolong the challenge. A wave of anger swept through him. As Rufus drew again Moran bent and snapped the shaft embedded in his shoe, turned and abruptly changed direction. He felt rather than heard the third arrow whistle past to his right.

There was cover – of a sort – ten metres or so straight ahead, a thick growth of tangled bush and briar. Moran pelted for it. As he dived, steeling himself for the tearing of thorns on his exposed skin, another arrow thudded into the ground to his right. A wild shot, or a further warning? No, he'd been warned already, and Rufus didn't do wild shots. Moran turned awkwardly, hindered by the tug of the briar's grip on his clothing, and saw that Rufus had company. The shot had been wild, but only because the hunter had been distracted. One word, a command, resonated flatly across the clearing.

"Enough."

Terl, red-faced, arm raised and forefinger pointing accusingly, was walking deliberately towards Rufus.

Moran ripped the brambles aside and lurched out of the bushes. Terl up held a warning hand.

"Leave this to me, Inspector Moran."

Rufus' cloak ruffled in the light breeze; Terl's unexpected arrival seemed not to have fazed him.

"It's got to end, Rufus. This all has to end. It should have ended years ago."

"Why?" Rufus' voice was quiet and measured. "We have a pact of blood. You and me. Together."

"No more, Rufus. I can't bear it, the guilt." Terl opened his big hands in supplication. "Enough blood. Enough killing."

When his words were met with silence, Terl turned his attention briefly to Moran. "Quarter of a mile that way," he pointed over Moran's head, "the bog begins. He'll have taken her there. That's where they all end."

Moran nodded. If they both rushed Rufus, maybe…

But Terl had other ideas. The publican's hand dipped to his belt and Moran saw the knife, a long, serrated hunting weapon, gripped firmly in the landlord's brawny fist.

"I've fought you before when we were kids, Rufus de Courcy, and God help me, I'll do it again if you don't give this up."

Rufus laughed. "And you'll kill me? With that?"

"If I have to."

"This is my land." Rufus' bow appeared like a conjuring trick and its nocked arrow pointed at Terl's heart. "I have the right to protect these woodlands from strangers and vagabonds."

Terl was shaking his head. "You're ill, Rufus. And I've been asleep all these years, bullied into silence by your family. But you made a mistake. You should have left Celine alone."

Helplessly, Moran watched the scene play out. He felt like a spectator in some Greek tragedy, impotent and sidelined.

"What is that harlot to you?" Rufus' voice was ice cold.

"She's a decent woman, Rufus. She only wants justice for her sister. Her murdered sister."

Moran could see that Terl was making surreptitious progress towards Rufus, slowly closing the distance between them. Moran understood. If Terl could get close enough the longbow would be difficult to deploy. But Rufus was no fool.

"Stop. Any closer and you die."

"You wouldn't kill me, Rufus." Terl's slow advance continued.

Moran heard the creak of the bowstring as it was drawn to full capacity. He had to intervene. Somehow. A stone, a rock, anything…

Terl hurled himself at Rufus.

It was over in an instant. Terl sank to the ground, clutching at the feathered shaft protruding from his ribcage. The knife fell to the ground.

Moran had only taken his eyes off Rufus briefly but the madman had melted into the undergrowth. He rushed to Terl's side. "Go the way I said. Towards the bog." Terl wheezed through gritted teeth. "You get to a fork in the path. Take the left."

Moran had torn the man's shirt open, ripped the cloth away from the wound. It wasn't good.

"Two trees … meet over the path. Between them the bog begins. Be … careful. There's a bog hole, solid for a few paces, then only … only the bog. He may not know…"

"Try not to talk." Moran examined the wound. The arrow had to stay where it was for now.

"He'll come for you. Drive you to the bog. That's his way. Use your brain." Terl grunted. "You're the policeman. Clever sod. You'll stop it, I know." Terl grimaced.

Moran picked up Terl's knife. "I'll send for help – that's a promise." He propped the landlord against a tree, straightened up, tucked the knife into his belt and, retrieving his spear en route, began to walk briskly in the direction of the bog.

Chapter Thirty-four

"Good to have you back, boss," Bola Odunsi grinned, showing the gap in his front teeth to good effect.

"Thanks, Bola." Charlie Pepper felt rough after another sleepless night in custody, but her elation at being released was carrying her through the fatigue very nicely so far. Her brief audience with DCS Higginson had also gone a long way towards making up for the treatment she had received at the hands of DCI Wilder and her snakelike number two, Maggs. Higginson had been straight and profusely apologetic that he had allowed himself to be distracted by what he referred to as 'politically sensitive' issues, and that his short-sightedness in failing to thoroughly vet the investigating DCI had led to her being held in custody on the strength of 'very questionable' circumstantial evidence. In the meantime he was spending 'some time' with DCI Wilder to 'establish the facts'.

"You've all done a fantastic job," Charlie told the team. She looked at each officer in turn. Toby was giving Bola the evil eye and DC McConnell looked like death warmed up.

Clearly, something was not as it should be, but for now she needed to get them focused on the task in hand, which was to nail this biker before she did any further mischief, and according to what Tess had been able to report, that mischief was likely to be directed at DCI Brendan Moran.

"So she has a head start, right? We have to assume she's heading west to – what was the name of the place where the guv's staying?"

"Cernham."

"Yes, Cernham. Thank you, Toby. So, we've contacted traffic, alerted Devon and Cornwall. Any joy?"

"No sign yet," George offered. "If she's using the motorway she's not riding. Maybe she's taken four wheels this time?"

Charlie pursed her lips. "Maybe. But this kid has style. I can't see her changing two wheels for four, somehow."

"B roads?" Bola suggested. "Scenic route?"

"Again, a possibility," Charlie agreed. "But whatever – they're going to be hard pushed to stop every bike heading for the West Country. Any success contacting the guv?"

A general shaking of heads.

"It's in the middle of nowhere, boss. No signal. Pub doesn't answer the phone. What can we do?" Bola shrugged.

"What we can do," Charlie said, "is get our arses down there."

She turned the key in the ignition and a face appeared at the car window. Denis Robinson, the Duty Sergeant.

"Sorry to bother you, ma'am."

"No probs, Denis. What's up?"

"Just had a misper reported." Robinson retrieved a

notebook and moistened his finger. Stressed and fired up as she was, Charlie nevertheless felt a smile creep across her face. Denis Robinson was a legend in the station. Old school through and through, he was an absolute stickler for order and detail.

"Go on."

"Thing is, it was the misper's previous address I thought you'd be interested in."

"OK. So let's have it."

Robinson read out the address and Charlie's smile faded. Banner's house. No, *her* house. In that moment Charlie realised that she was effectively homeless. No way was she going back there. Ever. "Who is it, Denis?"

Robinson squinted through his specs as he found the detail. "Now it's a foreign name. Can't say as I'll make a great job of the pronunciation."

Charlie knew what was coming. G.

"Ah, here we are. Miss Gosia Marenkovich."

"Right. Thanks, Denis. Is the reportee still here?"

"She is indeed," Robinson said. "I thought you might like a word. Polish. Name's … hang on… ah yes, Lydia Domasovec."

She turned to Bola in the passenger seat. "Hang on for me, guys. I need to follow this up."

Charlie followed Robinson to reception. A petite girl with a fragile, tear-stained face was sitting in Denis' side room nursing a cup of tea.

"Miss Domasovec, this is DI Charlie Pepper," Robinson told her. "She wants to have a little chat, all right?"

The girl looked up and gave Denis a wan smile. "Yes."

Charlie introduced herself and began with some simple

questions to establish her relationship with G. They were friends. Both had moved to the UK at the same time. After what had happened at Banner's house Lydia had invited G to stay as long as she wanted.

"So, what happened?" Charlie asked her gently. "She just didn't come back?"

Lydia shook her head. "A man came, a Polish man. He is very angry. He wants G to go with him. She must get her passport, pack her things. She would not do this. He says she must. G says no again. I close the door. The man goes away, but later I see him in the car in the street. He has taken G, I know it."

"Can you describe him?"

As Charlie listened suspicion became certainty. "Does he have a mole here?" Charlie indicated her right cheekbone. "He's very good-looking, yes?"

Lydia Domasovec nodded and began to cry.

Charlie felt her heart sink. Tess had told them that one of her abductors was a young male. She hadn't actually seen him, but had been adamant that the accent was European.

Polish, to be precise.

Lydia had just described Andreas.

"Come."

Charlie entered DCS Higginson's model office. Everything was the same: neat, ordered. The bone-handled letter-opener was in its place. All was right with the world. Except for the fact that DCI Wilder was sitting in the visitors' chair.

"Ah, DI Pepper. None the worse for your time in custody, I trust? DCI Wilder here was just explaining the background to her decision. So, you have an urgent message for me, I understand?"

"Sir." Charlie was seething, avoiding eye contact with Wilder. She had obviously succeeded in talking Higginson round, or at least was well on her way to it.

"Well?" Higginson made an open-handed gesture.

Charlie glanced at Wilder who was inspecting her fastidiously varnished nails. She seemed comfortable and at ease. Her hair was tied up in a school-matronly bun and her legs were neatly crossed at the ankles; altogether the epitome of calm, ladylike professionalism. Charlie wanted to hit her.

"It's all right, DI Pepper. DCI Wilder won't betray any confidences."

Oh, really?

"Very well, sir. If I may speak my mind?" Charlie had intended to save this for later but the circumstances seemed to demand she show her hand before Wilder could add any more spin to her story.

"Of course."

"If I may first of all point out some key deficiencies in DCI Wilder's investigative methodology?"

Higginson frowned. "Well, I—"

But Charlie had everything primed and ready; the words came like balls of steel fired from a spring-loaded catapult. "First, sir, I must point out that DCI Wilder failed to follow up a key witness statement that a motorbike was seen behaving in a suspicious manner within the calculated timeframe of the late DS Banner's murder. Furthermore, crime scene forensics has proved that a motorcycle helmet caused the abrasive marks on the wall immediately above DS Banner's bed. My team followed these leads and successfully identified the helmet owner, which in turn led to the discovery of the whereabouts of acting DI Tessa Martin. Thanks to their actions, acting DI Tess Martin is now in a stable condition in hospital. I find it incomprehensible, sir, that DCI Wilder and her colleague DS Maggs failed to follow this clear forensic evidence, instead choosing to hold me responsible for the murder on the grounds of purely circumstantial – and I believe planted – evidence."

"Planted? How exactly? Your prints were on the garrotte, DI Pepper. An incontrovertible fact that has yet to be explained." Wilder's tone was calm and controlled.

"Well, ma'am, I'll explain it for you," Charlie said. She could feel the heat on her face and her heart pumping. She retrieved a small bottle from her pocket. "This was found in the bedroom of the Orts Road house. It's Rohypnol."

Wilder was unfazed. "So?"

"The glass by my bed was noted as being empty by your sergeant, but I know that when I went to sleep it was full. Maggs poured it down the sink, didn't he?"

"I'm sorry?" Wilder was all 'what *is* this woman talking about?'

"But what Maggs didn't know," Charlie continued, "was that Dom Jensen arranged for the droplets of water on the bedside table to be analysed – the table was highly polished so the water droplets weren't absorbed by the wood. Dom's very thorough. And guess what? The water contained traces of Rohypnol – I can confirm this, sir."

DCS Higginson raised his eyebrows and glanced at Wilder.

"They also analysed the plastic wallet," Charlie continued. "My prints are there, but only four clear prints across one surface."

"I really don't see what you're getting at," Wilder said, attempting a complicit smile with Higginson.

"No thumb print," Charlie said. "You try picking up a plastic wallet without using your thumbs. You just wouldn't."

Higginson was leaning forward now. "So, let me get this right, DI Pepper. You're saying, and correct me if I'm wrong, that someone drugged you and took prints from you while you were in a narcotically-induced sleep?"

"That's right, sir. But the prints were too perfect. A neat row and no thumbs." Charlie shuddered as she thought of the assassin bending over her, taking her hand...

Higginson leaned back and folded his arms. "How extraordinary. Were you aware that DS Maggs had thrown the contents of the glass away, DCI Wilder?"

For the first time Wilder's composure wobbled. "I didn't appreciate that, I mean, I hadn't anticipated any need to–"

Trump card time, Charlie...

But still she hesitated. There was no going back once she'd made the accusation. That would be it. If she was wrong, it was a potentially career-ending move.

Sod it.

"And one other thing I feel I ought to mention, sir, is that DCI Wilder is closely related to ex-DCS Alan Sheldrake, your predecessor."

The implication was not lost on Higginson. His face darkened.

Charlie pressed on before Wilder could interrupt. She felt like a runaway train now; it was all or nothing. She prayed that the hunch she'd had while waiting for the lift was correct. "And I've just interviewed a young lady about a missing person, sir. One Gosia Marenkovich, a lodger in

Banner's house. The young lady is certain that Gosia has been abducted by a Polish man, the same man whose voice acting DS Tess Martin heard in the Orts Road house. Passports were mentioned, sir. I believe that Ms Marenkovich has been abducted by Andreas Pashkov and that they are attempting to leave the country. You see, sir, I believe that both Pashkov and DCI Wilder are involved in a conspiracy to murder DS Banner and frame me for the crime; Ms Marenkovich, as a potential witness, may be a threat to the security of their operation. I also believe that their motive is revenge for the conviction of DCI Wilder's brother, ex-DCS Alan Sheldrake, and that they are both closely associated with Huang Xian Kuai's drug operation. The Chinese girl is a trained assassin in Huang's team and her next target is DCI Brendan Moran. With me in prison DCI Moran's death would complete the act of revenge for our role in breaking the Huang-financed Ranandan drug operation last summer. Sir." Charlie finished, cleared her throat and waited for the explosion of denial.

But Wilder's reaction confounded Charlie's expectations. The DCI had sat as still as a petrified rock while Charlie had been speaking. Now her hands flew to her mouth and her normally measured voice cracked in a sob of despair. "No. You're lying! He wouldn't leave me, he wouldn't just abandon me!"

Charlie felt the tension drain from her body and for a split second she thought she might burst into tears. Higginson's attention, however, was all on DCI Wilder and his expression of horror and disbelief was one which Charlie would remember for the rest of her career.

Chapter Thirty-five

The strident, quavering chirp of a redpoll startled Moran as he headed for the divided path Terl had described. The little bird was perched on a branch fifteen feet or so above him. An alarm call – but was he the cause of the redpoll's agitation, or had the bird seen something else? Moran stood still and listened. There was another sound, lower, repetitive.

The sound of someone moaning in pain.

Celine...

He hurried on, abandoning the path but keeping it in sight until a wooded archway, a meeting of two bowed birches, came into view. As Terl had told him, it framed a choice: left was the bog, right was – unknown. But the noise, he was sure, came unmistakeably from the left.

Moran's instincts urged him to rush to Celine's aid, but two words prevented him from doing so: *decoy* and *trap*. Rufus wouldn't be far away and it looked as if Terl had been wrong about Rufus' ignorance of the mire. Moran wasn't surprised. He remembered Rufus' words:

This is my land...

Moran went right, skirting the fork in a wide circular approach which he hoped would take him between and behind the point at which the paths split and where he might get a better view. He made himself slow down, all too aware that he was competing with a lifetime's expertise, and he could only pray that Rufus hadn't had time to pinpoint his position. If he had the game was already over.

Presently he noticed that the ground was beginning to soften and he had to tread with care. The wood was thinning, giving rise to lower, marshy areas which sucked at his feet and reminded him again of Terl's warning. It was time to turn inside the base of his imaginary inverted triangle and backtrack towards the fork from this new direction. But the landscape had changed subtly, the gnarled and stunted trees providing scant cover but hindering the speed of his progress. His ears picked up the sound of a woman's sob. He froze. Had he imagined it? No, there it was again: a soft, despairing sigh. He'd reached the bait.

Steady, Brendan… Don't lose it now…

He caught a slight movement ahead and to the left. A trick of the light? He fixed his eyes on the spot. No, there it was again…

Moran's heart thumped hard in his chest.

Got you…

Rufus was standing between two alders from where Moran guessed he had a clear view of the path and, most probably, Celine. The location was well chosen and it was only the merest luck that Moran had spotted him

He took a deep breath. One chance, no more. He couldn't close with Rufus – the man was too quick. If he exposed his position Rufus would track him and make good use of the longbow. Moran lifted his spear and hefted it. Although his athletic youth was a distant memory the javelin had been his forte. Could he trust his aim thirty-five years on? He stole another glance. Rufus was a shadow in the stillness. Moran focused in on the shape of his antagonist's body. The cloak fell to Rufus' knees but the stance the hunter had adopted meant that his left thigh was exposed. Moran knew he had to land a crippling blow. Nothing less would do.

But there was another problem. This would be a throw from a standstill, not at a run as he had been used to. The distance itself wasn't a problem. Moran estimated he was around twenty-five metres from his target, a comfortable range.

Yes, for a seventeen year old, maybe…

The other question was: would the spear fly accurately? It had the weight, but would it fly true? There was no way to be sure, no official rating – it was just a cut of wood. It looked to be straight enough, but Moran knew that three attributes made a successful throw: balance, weight *and* skill. Plus there was always the possibility that Rufus would move. Moran felt the sweat cold on his forehead as he steadied his aim, felt the solidity of the wood, drew back his arm. At that moment Rufus turned and looked straight at him. The eyes blazed. Moran released the spear with a cry, putting all his effort and half-remembered expertise into the throw.

Time stood still. If Rufus had seen it coming he was either rooted to the spot in surprise or confident of a miss. Still the spear flew, spinning as it drew closer to its target. Moran's heart lurched as it dipped and, as if flicked by an imaginary hand, drifted to the right to find ground in the damp earth by Rufus' feet.

That's it. You lost.

Moran found himself walking towards the motionless Rufus. The sensible thing to do would be to turn and flee – even though he knew Rufus would catch him in minutes, if not seconds.

So when did you ever do the sensible thing, Brendan?

There was still the fragile hope of negotiation, or at least the chance to buy a little time…

"Fornicator." Rufus towered over him. Before Moran could get a word out gloved hands encircled his throat and he felt himself lifted off the ground. Stars danced a spangled polka and his vision blurred. He felt his legs kicking in a helpless vacuum. A long way off, someone screamed.

And screamed again.

In a way he couldn't articulate, this second scream seemed different. Moran felt the grip on his throat loosen and he hit the ground like a sack of sand, writhing and fighting for air. When he was able to draw breath his vision slowly cleared and he understood why he was still alive; Celine was on her haunches beside him, wild-eyed, panting, both hands wrapped firmly around the javelin's shaft, the business end of which was buried in Rufus' thigh. Celine yelled another sob of scarcely-believed triumph and threw her weight behind the ash pole. Rufus' agonized shriek shocked Moran into action and he scrambled to his feet retching and gasping as Rufus made a scrabble for the longbow which had fallen from the folds of his cloak. Moran kicked it away and Rufus fell back, hands clawing at his wounded leg.

"Leave it. Pull it out and you'll bleed to death." Moran inspected Celine's handiwork from a safe distance. The spear had penetrated deep into the muscle. Rufus bared his teeth and half-sat up. The scarf had fallen from his face so that Moran could see the full extent of his facial injuries. An image of a church gargoyle came to Moran's mind. The shattered, twisted jawline, the protruding forehead…

"Brendan." Celine had released the spear and was leaning on a tree trunk for support. Her shoulder was bloody and torn, her face the colour of goats' milk. She collapsed to her knees and slid to the ground with a gasp of pain. There was a lot of blood. Moran was at her side, gently probing the wound. "Let me see."

"Be careful. The ground – it's not safe…"

"I know. Don't talk. I need to get you back to the cottage, have a proper look at that shoulder–"

She was drifting in and out of consciousness. He felt her pulse. Not good. The wound looked superficial but he was no medical expert. Celine's eyes flickered, widened…

"Watch him – he's–"

Moran spun around to see that Rufus had dragged himself to the low dip in the path, leaving a red trail from his injured leg behind him. He let him go. "I'm going to lift you. It might hurt. I'll be as gentle as I can."

"Rufus–"

"We'll pick him up later. He won't get far – if he gets anywhere at all."

Moran felt a momentary sensation of nausea as he swung Celine up into the classic fireman's lift. Hardly surprising – the combined effects of the de Courcys' narcotic, lack of sleep, food and water were all beginning to take their toll.

As he stumbled away from the bog he looked over his shoulder. Rufus had managed to crawl out of sight, leaving just a solitary blood-flecked gauntlet on the crust of moss as a sign of his passing.

By the time Moran reached the road he was close to exhaustion. He briefly considered knocking on doors until he found a house with a landline so that he could make the necessary calls for assistance – until he remembered where he was; it was quite likely that any unvetted resident would shop him to the manor.

Nothing about this place would surprise me any more...

At last the village centre came into view. No one rushed to his assistance. The pub was locked and the lights were off. The Post Office as he passed it was the same. His car was still parked outside the cottage and he wondered if he would be able to get it started or if de Courcy had crippled the machine for good.

One thing at a time, Brendan...

His knees were threatening to give way as he reached the front door and turned his key in the lock.

The door swung open and he found himself looking into the twin barrels of Richard de Courcy's shotgun.

"Took your time in the end," de Courcy said in a conversational tone. "But I *am* impressed that you're still alive. Lie her down on the sofa, would you?"

Too tired to object, Moran complied. "She needs help."

"Oh yes. Always has done," de Courcy said wistfully. "And she'll get plenty, believe you me."

"This is finished," Moran said wearily. "It's over, de Courcy."

"Says who?" de Courcy was examining the wound on Celine's neck, with interest rather than out of any concern he might have had for her wellbeing.

Moran sat in the armchair. "I've sent a message to my team in Berkshire. They'll be in touch with Exeter by now." Moran consulted his watch. "I reckon you've got until lunchtime."

De Courcy laughed. "You're bluffing. What did you do? Send a homing pigeon?"

Moran shook his head. "No. I sent a letter. I told them that if they hadn't heard from me by Friday morning they were to send in the marines."

And why the hell didn't you think of that before, Brendan?

"You wrote a letter? What a resourceful chap you are." De Courcy grinned and Moran saw the madness in his eyes. "I'd better push on, then. Thanks for looking after her." He nodded to where Celine was groaning softly as she regained consciousness. "What happened, by the way? How did you get the better of Rufus? You're the first, you know."

Moran's pulse quickened as he realised that de Courcy intended to take Celine with him. "You're not going anywhere."

"No? But I have the gun." De Courcy jabbed the shotgun into Moran's chest then stepped back out of range of Moran's legs.

"You're leaving your mother to face the music?" Moran said. "Hardly honourable behaviour."

"Honourable?" The shotgun was back, this time pointing between Moran's eyes. "I've honoured this estate all my life, looked after things. My brother, my mother. The bastard, Harrison."

"Your half-brother, you mean. He's still a de Courcy, whatever name he chose to adopt."

"He is *nothing*. And he'll *never* be a de Courcy..."

Moran watched de Courcy carefully. The man's face was reddening, forefinger tapping on the trigger guard. Behind him Celine was stirring again, but this time her eyes were open and he could see that she was casting about for something to use as a weapon while de Courcy's back was towards her.

"Blood is blood." Moran shrugged. "And you're leaving him as well? And Rufus?"

"Rufus is *alive*?" De Courcy blanched. "You didn't *kill* him?"

"I don't make a habit of killing people," Moran said, keeping his tone even and reasonable. "Unlike your family." Moran let de Courcy wrestle with what was left of his conscience and took the opportunity to signal a negative to Celine. She relaxed but her eyes were wary.

"The killing. It was not my doing." De Courcy had lowered the shotgun, was speaking now almost to himself. "All started with that girl, that summer…"

"Give me the gun, Richard." Moran held out his hand. "This must stop now."

"No, no." The wild look was back in his eyes. "I always have a plan, you see. Always."

Before Moran could think of a counter argument de Courcy had seized Celine's arm and dragged her to her feet. "We're going. Get in the car."

Celine stumbled and almost fell. Moran leaned forward but de Courcy warned him off with the gun. "Stay where you are."

De Courcy ushered Celine out of the cottage. Moran heard his car door open and close, the bonnet likewise and a moment or two later the engine sprang into life.

He went to the window. *Now what, Brendan?*

De Courcy drove hard and fast. The car hurtled along the narrow lane like a bullet. He glanced at the fuel gauge and cursed. Have to stop at the garage. No problem. Take two minutes, that's all.

He pulled into the tiny forecourt. As usual, no other cars were about. The woman was semi-conscious. He could risk filling up without dragging her into the shop with him. Just to be safe he took the cartridges out of the shotgun and put them in his pocket.

As the petrol sloshed into the tank de Courcy felt a surge of elation. *I'm leaving at last. Finally … to hell with the money. To hell with all of them…*

He walked quickly to the shop and reached into his jacket for his wallet. The forecourt assistant smiled as he approached. Someone new. A girl. De Courcy wondered what had happened to Manjit. Always here, in all weathers, all times of the day. No matter what…

"Hello," the girl said. She was quite pretty, Chinese by the look of her. Not many Asians in these parts, apart from Manjit.

"I've been waiting for you," the girl said. She reached under the counter and de Courcy found himself looking at a squat, unwavering hand gun. He frowned. "I don't under–"

"You don't have to, Mr Moran," the girl said, and blew de Courcy's brains all over the shop floor.

Celine heard the shot and ducked down as a girl emerged from the shop and walked quickly past the rusting water and tyre pressure gauges to the rear of the building. Celine poked her head up again and heard the motorbike before she saw it swing around the corner and exit the forecourt in a cloud of exhaust.

What the heck?

Her neck throbbed as she got out of the car and for a moment she thought she might faint, but a quick bend to the knees cleared her head. When she straightened up another car was turning into the forecourt. The driver got out, a big black fellow, and wandered over to her.

"You OK there, miss?"

"I'm not sure, to be honest," Celine said truthfully. Her head was throbbing again with dull, drum-like beats.

"Woah. What've you done to your neck? Hey! All right, lean on me, that's the way." He caught her as she swayed and fell into his arms. Just before she lost consciousness she heard the big guy call out to his fellow passengers. "Toby?! Boss! Over here, quick!"

Chapter Thirty-six

"Want to take your own car, guv?" Charlie raised her eyebrows, knowing what the answer was likely to be.

Moran scowled. "Funnily enough I've kind of gone off driving for the time being. Once our buddies from Exeter turn up I may be in the market for a lift – if it's not too much trouble?"

Charlie grinned. "No probs."

They were sipping tea in Moran's cottage. De Courcy's body had been taken away half an hour previously, Celine had been rushed to hospital, and a forensics team were apparently on their way from Exeter, along with a five-man team led by one DS Wilmot.

Charlie had sent Bola Odunsi and Brit to keep an eye on Lady Cernham pending the arrival of Wilmot's team. As for the rest of it, she had trouble even beginning to get to grips with the events of Moran's last few days in Cernham.

"This Rufus." She finished her tea and rinsed the mug in the sink. "You don't think he'll be any trouble?"

"He'll have gone to ground. He's badly hurt. Trust me – I

saw the damage."

"And how many bodies do you reckon we're dealing with?"

Moran sighed. "Two in the maze. At least four in the bog. Somewhere. Terl got off lightly – couple of centimetres to the left, the medics reckon, and he'd have been a goner. But Lady Cernham will have to confirm the exact tally."

"God, I can't believe it." Charlie shook her head. "Here in picture-postcard land?"

"I know. *Straw Dogs* revisited, to be sure." Moran went to the sink and ran himself another glass of water. Now that he was half-way to rehydration his headache was slowly receding.

"Straw what?"

Moran laughed. "Nothing. An old film, before your time." He drained his glass, trying not to make his concern at Charlie's appearance too obvious. She looked terrible – pale-faced, with dark smudges beneath her eyes and a harsh, jerky timbre to her voice. And no wonder. It said something for her resilience and determination that she was here at all and not resting up, as the police quack had no doubt recommended. He was irrationally angry with himself. What a time to take leave! But how could anyone have predicted what had happened in his absence? *Stupid question, Brendan.*

Anyway, it wasn't over yet, not by a long chalk. He squirted a jet of washing-up liquid into the glass and ran the hot water tap. "Anything from traffic?"

"Nope, not yet. Whoever she is, she's damn good."

"We'll find her. And this other guy – what was his name?"

"Andreas."

"Andreas." Moran put his rinsed glass onto the draining

board. As if in response the door knocker sounded and Moran grunted as he saw who it was through the window.

"Ah, DS Wilmot. Come in." Moran gestured graciously.

"Thank you, sir. I understand there's been an incident."

"There has indeed, DS Wilmot. And this time I can show you a body or two. I haven't been able to arrange them all neatly for you, but I can point you in the right direction if you'd find that helpful?"

"I would, sir," Wilmot said, avoiding eye contact. "If you wouldn't mind."

Moran patted the young officer lightly on the back. "No trouble. Have you ever visited Hampton Court, Sergeant?"

"Left," Moran directed.

Charlie glanced at him, brow furrowing. "Wrong way, guv. Civilisation's over there." She jerked her head to the right.

"Maybe, but I have a feeling."

They waited, engine purring, at the T junction. The small garage was alive with police officers and forensic teams.

"No CCTV, I suppose." Charlie watched the activity which had transformed the sleepy forecourt into a major crime scene investigation.

Moran grunted a laugh. "You're kidding. They're lucky to have electricity, let alone something as sophisticated as cameras."

Charlie shivered. "It could have been you, guv. So easily."

Moran acknowledged Charlie's concern with a grim smile. "Just a bit of luck, Charlie, that's all. Now then, left it is."

"Where are we going?"

"To the seaside." Moran settled back and closed his eyes.

*

The shrill beep of Charlie's mobile woke him. For a second he was completely disoriented until he felt Charlie's hand lightly touch his shoulder. He sat up bolt upright.

"It's OK," she whispered, before returning to her call.

"DI Pepper."

Moran stretched and blinked as the sun slanted into the car's interior. It was warm. A seagull cruised gently past the windscreen, intent on some titbit dropped from a passing sightseer's sandwich.

The seaside. A hunch.

Charlie was talking, issuing instructions.

"Have you got that, George? OK. Get to it. Toby and Bola will be with you in a couple of hours. Keep me posted."

She clunked the phone down in the plastic pocket by the gearbox.

"News?" Moran's voice sounded thick to him, the occluded tones banging darkly in the centre of his skull. The headache was back and his mouth was dry and metallic.

"George. He's following up the Domasovec info. Higginson's roped him in to interview Wilder."

"Has he, by God?" Moran fumbled for the window button. "That'll teach him to go out on the tiles during the working week."

"I think he was set up, guv. That creep, Maggs, duped him into some sleazy drinking club session."

"No excuses. George should know better." Moran felt himself coming round as the sea breeze wafted into the car. "I'll have a wee word when we get back."

Charlie checked herself in the mirror and grimaced. "Death warmed up and left to cool off."

"You look a hell of a lot better than I feel," Moran lied.

"Come on. Let's have a wander."

As they walked the short distance from the car park to the tiny lane Moran remembered from his visit with Celine, Charlie slowed her pace and hung back.

He turned. "What's up?"

"You think she's here." Charlie's face had lost the little colour it had had. "Don't you?"

"Where would *you* go? All major routes will be on the lookout for her. She knows that. If I were her I'd stay local for a while until things have cooled off a bit. Wouldn't you?"

"Yes. I suppose."

Charlie looked as though she might be about to faint and Moran saw the fear in her eyes. "Are you OK?"

"I just keep seeing Banner's room. Imagining her touching me, taking my prints. She could have killed me in my bed, like Banner, like–"

Moran put his arm around her shoulder and she turned into him, buried her head in his chest and let the sobs come. "It's all right. You're all right, Charlie." He heard himself muttering reassurances. The close physical contact reminded him of his need for emotional caution. He felt attracted to her in her vulnerability, more so than he would have expected. Maybe it was a reaction to the past twenty-four hours? Or maybe…

Maybe you're just an old fella with an eye for the ladies, Brendan…

He pulled away with an effort. "Come on. Let's get ourselves a coffee."

Charlie sniffed, wiped her eyes and nodded. "Sorry, guv. Very unprofessional."

"Don't be daft. You've had a hell of a time of it."

They came out of the alley into the lane, which was lined

with souvenir, bric-à-brac and coffee shops. It was busy, but not overly so. Moran wondered how much money they made over a typical season. Enough to eke out some kind of existence, he supposed. Could he see himself in a place like this? A shopkeeper? B and B owner? Maybe. One day…

"Guv. There." Charlie pointed.

He snapped back to the present. A motorcycle was parked against the wall on the opposite side of the lane, blocking the narrow pavement. Tourists tutted and shook their heads as they negotiated the obstruction. Moran assessed the machine. It was just a bike. Could be anyone's. But his senses were tingling nevertheless. It was a racy kind of bike – not that he knew much about biking, but it looked like the sort of machine a young person might use to get around in style and with a fair bit of speed.

He assessed the layout of the lane. Behind them it sloped gently down to the sea front. At the last shop the lane widened. A car could block the lane at that end if necessary. Up ahead, past the bike, the lane narrowed. They would need something else to prevent a bike getting through. Unless he took measures to make sure it didn't get started at all…

The other issue, of course, was the question of safety. The girl was armed and neither he nor Charlie had anything more dangerous than a folded newspaper to use in self-defence. What they did have ,though, was the policeman's old friend – the element of surprise.

First things first, Brendan – establish identity.

Charlie's hand was on his arm. "If it's her, she knows what you look like."

"Does she? Maybe she needs to visit Specsavers, then. If

Richard de Courcy was in a position to agree with me I'm sure he would. She only had my car registration and, I'd guess, the description of a middle-aged man, medium build with greying temples. Anyway," Moran adopted what he hoped was a confident and optimistic expression, "she killed me earlier on, so she won't be looking for me here, will she?"

"This isn't one to tackle on our own, guv."

"Listen, you go back to the car, drive it to the end of the lane and get ready to park across it on my signal. And keep your head down."

"What are you going to do?"

"Take a wee look, that's all. It's probably a false alarm anyway. Go on, off you go."

Looking a shade doubtful Charlie walked away towards the connecting alley between the lane and the car park.

The shop window was full of surfing equipment and beachwear proclaiming the benefits of the surf bum lifestyle – or so it appeared to Moran. It wasn't his kind of shop and the wall of music which assaulted his ears as he entered did little to change his mind. There were perhaps a half dozen visitors browsing and chatting, mostly youngsters, but one or two older couples wandered in bemused fashion between the various displays, chuckling in low voices at some of the odder items of youthwear while at the same time giving Moran the distinct impression that they felt rather daring at having entered the premises at all.

And then he saw her.

In black leather. Trying on a pair of sunglasses, the reflector type favoured by US cops. Her hair was shoulder length, glossy and raven-black, and her physique, although diminutive, had quite obviously been honed to hard muscle in the gym.

Moran ghosted past her, but not before he had caught a glimpse of her eyes in the small, square sunglasses mirror. Dark, emotionless eyes. The eyes of a killer.

He moved on to the counter. On the wall to the rear above the shop assistant's head were mounted a triad of spear guns and a selection of wicked looking diving knives. Moran offered a prayer to the woodland god who had saved him earlier and felt for his wallet. It was still in his jacket, and so was his credit card. Forty-eight pounds seemed a lot to pay for a knife, but then again he was working under special circumstances and he needed something quick and effective.

He chose quickly. Titanium was strong and the point looked deadly. For a brief, surreal moment Moran caught a vision of Higginson's expression as the DCS glanced through next month's expenses sheets. Moran made sure the girl was still focused on her sunglasses before making a quick purchase and an even quicker exit.

Moran waited until he was sure that no passers-by were looking his way before he buried the knife in the rear tyre. The air rushed out with a *whap* that turned a few heads, but by then Moran was strolling up the lane doing his best to imitate a tourist. He reached the turning point at the top of the lane and about faced in time to see Charlie idle the car into position at the far end.

One minute. Two minutes. His throat was so dry that he was tempted to nip into the newsagents for a mineral water but he couldn't risk taking his eyes off the shop door. Any time now. *Come on…*

She bounced out of the shop and clocked the damage immediately. Her head went this way and that, looked down the lane towards Charlie and then turned back towards him so that it seemed to Moran that their eyes locked for a second or two.

She knows.

He wouldn't have predicted what happened next. The girl mounted the bike, fired the engine, swung it around and opened the throttle full tilt towards Charlie's end of the lane.

Damn…

He signalled but Charlie had already begun to accelerate towards the weaving motorcycle. Although destabilised by the lack of tyre pressure the assassin still somehow managed to exercise enough control over the machine to steer it. *So much for your bike knowledge, Brendan…*

He started to run. Charlie was coming up the lane and there wasn't a great deal of room on either side for the bike to pass. The Chinese girl would still go for it, though. But which way? The gap on the left looked slightly wider to Moran and the rider evidently thought so too. Moran stopped, breathless, clutching his sides. He wasn't going to get there in time to make a difference. He could only watch.

She's going to get away…

Sparks flew as the bike made contact with a section of shop frontage. She was directly opposite Charlie's car window…

Charlie swung the wheel and the car caught the bike just behind the saddle. The bike tilted sideways and fell into the shop alcove in a shower of glass and noise.

Good girl, Charlie…

The car had passed the alcove and Moran prayed that Charlie wouldn't be tempted to get out. It seemed not; the engine revved and the car lurched backwards into the alcove.

He heard it make contact with a rending scream of metal on brick.

OK, good move…

He was nearly there. The car jerked forward into the lane, but with a teeth-clenching grinding of gears Charlie reversed again; a further explosion of masonry dust and splintered wood greeted Moran as he finally reached the car.

By now a shocked semicircle of tourists had gathered to watch events unfold. The car rolled forward yet again. Moran caught sight of Charlie's wide-eyed, tear-streaked face through the shattered windscreen, her mouth set in grim determination. Moran held up his hand but she wasn't looking. The gears ground into first.

As the car moved he got a good view into the alcove. The girl had been crushed into the shattered plate glass window and left half-sitting, half-lying in and out of the shop, legs dangling. The bike itself was a twisted pile of metal.

Moran grimaced as the car smashed into the alcove a third time. He ran forward and wrenched the passenger door open.

"Charlie, enough!"

The Chinese girl was slumped over the bonnet, trapped between the car and the shop front. She wouldn't be walking for a long time, let alone riding a bike. Moran reached over and gently removed the keys from the ignition. Charlie had let go of the steering wheel. Her body was shaking from head to foot like a woman in the grip of some terrible fever.

He placed his hand gently on her shoulder. "All right, Charlie. That's enough. It's over now. It's over."

Chapter Thirty-seven

"So you've made your peace with the Devonshire constabulary, Brendan?"

Moran reflected on this suggestion for a few moments. "I think they are satisfied that I acted in their interests, sir, if that's what you mean."

DCS Higginson glowered. "You know what I mean, Brendan."

"If it's not impertinent to suggest as much, sir, I'd say that they have every reason to thank us several times over." Moran ticked off the reasons using his fingers for emphasis. "Namely, assisting in the arrest of Matthew de Courcy and his mother, apprehending a murder suspect, disabling a self-confessed murderer, liberating a village from what amounts to a reign of terror…"

"All right, all right. You know what I'm getting at. It's a damned mess, the whole thing. And a political nightmare." Higginson fiddled with his letter opener. "These cross-constabulary incidents are a never-ending tangle of red tape. And you seem to specialise in the bloody things."

Moran inclined his head in acknowledgement. Better stop there. He'd made his point.

"Anyway." Higginson tapped the letter opener like a drumstick. "How's DI Pepper? Timely arrival of hers, I understand?"

"She'll mend. A few weeks off. Somewhere to live."

"Quite, quite. The thing is, Brendan, I've received a complaint."

"Oh?"

"Via Devonshire. It seems that a member of the public who witnessed the arrest of your Chinese girl claims that excessive force was used by an arresting officer."

Moran noted the 'your' in reference to the assassin. So, she was *his* assassin now, not Higginson's. "My officer acted in the best interests of public safety, sir. The assassin was armed – I can prove that. And dangerous. I don't think I need to prove that."

"Nevertheless, Brendan, there will probably be an enquiry. I'm just letting you know."

"If I may, sir, DI Pepper has been through a lot in the last few months. I would strongly advise back-pedalling the complaint under the circumstances. She's a good officer with huge potential. Something like this might send her–"

"I can't do that, Brendan. You know the form. It's like a parking ticket. Once written…" Higginson opened his palms in an 'out of my hands' gesture.

Moran bit his tongue. It was madness, but no point trying to fight it now. He did his best to hide his anger and changed tack.

"And DCI Wilder, sir," Moran sat forward. "Have you formally charged her?"

"I'd like to do more than charge her." Higginson shook his head ruefully. "But Internal have been in touch. They'll be taking her on."

"I see."

Higginson noted Moran's expression. "Problem?"

"It's just that we have a loose end, sir. I was hoping—"

"Ah, this other chap from the house. Andreas."

"Yes."

"Miles away by now, I'd have thought." Higginson held the letter opener between two forefingers, moving it from left to right in an unconscious gesture of impatience. He clearly wanted to be onto his next task.

Moran soldiered on. He needed Higginson's buy-in for this – better not highlight the potential for yet another cross-constabulary outing, though...

"But if I can track him down, sir, it might put the seal on any further activity from the Huang network. At least in our neck of the woods. And I just feel that, for Stephen Banner's sake, for all of our sakes—"

"Quite, quite so. DS Banner's funeral's next Thursday, by the way. Bloody Home Secretary's attending, so it'll be all protocol and form. But look, can't we get anything out of your Chinese girl?"

"Still unconscious, I'm afraid. And I rather think that the two gentlemen I met in the hospital corridor will have considerable more clout than you or I – with respect, sir – when she does eventually come round."

"MI5. Surprise surprise."

Moran nodded. "So, is DCI Wilder still in our hands, so to speak?"

"She's being collected tomorrow morning," Higginson

267

said, poker-faced. "I may not notice if you want to pop in to wish her well. Or whatever."

"Thank you, sir."

"I don't believe we've met?" Moran tested his weight on the flimsy wooden chair, rested his elbows on the bare table and indicated the chair's opposite number. "Please."

DCI Suzanne Wilder's reputation was known to Moran and the unmistakeable vestiges of authority were still evident in the way she held herself and by the manner in which she scrutinised him as she accepted his invitation to sit down.

"You'll be Moran."

"That's correct."

"What do you want?"

"I don't like loose ends. I wondered if you could help me out."

"Why should I?"

Moran poured himself a glass of water, took a sip and sat back in the chair with his arms resting on his stomach, fingers interlocked, thumbs tapping. "Because I want to talk about Andreas."

Wilder looked as though he had slapped her. Her expression darkened.

"Easy one to start us off, eh? How did you meet?"

"He was one of my brother's contacts."

"I see. And you were introduced so that you could plan my sergeant's murder and the discrediting of my DI? Did Sheldrake tell you where to find him, or did he find you?"

"Does it matter?"

"It might. And a helpful attitude, as you know, may go a little way towards the reduction of any sentence you're given."

Wilder looked around the small room, as if to finally satisfy herself that she had reached the point of no return. "Don't be ridiculous. A couple of months off a life sentence isn't much good to me."

"You haven't really got much to lose, have you?" Moran offered quietly.

Wilder sighed. For a moment her poise seemed to fail her. Then the stony expression returned. "All right, I'll tell you. But not because I'm kindly disposed towards you, or that I believe it will make any difference to what happens to me."

Moran knew the reason. It was always the same when half a partnership was in custody and the other running free, especially if the one in custody had been stitched up and left to fend for herself. Wilder wanted revenge. And if you added an emotional context – as there clearly was here – then heavy persuasive techniques were seldom necessary. Just the right degree of prompting. Having said that, Moran still knew he had to draw on every last ounce of professionalism during the interview – not because he was fearful of failing to extract the information he needed, but rather to keep his anger in check so that he wouldn't succumb to the temptation to lean over the desk and strangle Wilder where she sat.

"Fine. In your own time."

"Andreas was brought in to clean up the mess after the Ranandan brothers were killed. My brother recommended I get in touch with him. I found out where he was living – easy enough if you know who to ask – and together we planned the operation."

Operation. The premeditated murder of a police officer.

Moran swallowed his outrage, held his peace and waited for Wilder to continue.

"We spent a lot of time together. He was lonely, I suppose. The natural thing happened. And then a few weeks ago that Polish slut moved in and screwed everything up."

"Everything?"

"Almost everything. Andreas became distracted. He was good at his work, but she had done something to his head. His attention to detail was compromised."

"Well, you still managed to kill my sergeant and frame my senior officer."

"Yes, but the details weren't rigorously checked. DI Pepper's arrival at the house was *not* anticipated – we had someone else lined up for the room, but suddenly we had to move quickly, improvise a little. That damned glass of water. Andreas would have made sure of all that if he'd been thinking straight."

"You're saying that this Gosia girl seduced him? Stole him from you?"

"He denied it, of course. Men do, don't they?" Wilder's eyes were black and bitter. "But he promised that when we were finished we would go back to Poland together. There was plenty of work for us there."

"Via Huang, no doubt."

Wilder looked at him steadily. "I'm not saying anything about him. Not now. Not ever."

Moran shrugged. "As you please. Go on."

"What else can I say?" She shrugged. "May I have a cigarette?"

"Not yet. Where would Andreas be heading? How would he leave the country?"

"One of two ways. Either by private plane, or maybe Eurostar. That's a favourite. He likes his comfort."

"I see. Any guesses for his present circumstances?"

Wilder rubbed at a stain on the table top. She looked up and for a moment Moran could see the pale reflection of a once handsome woman. Not beautiful, but handsome; there was a difference. When she spoke her voice was flat and emotionless. "If she's with him he won't use the plane. Eurostar would be my guess. Maybe even the ferry. But he's probably gone already. He's good at what he does, when he's on the case. You'll not find him easily."

"Thank you. I don't expect we'll meet again."

"No."

Moran got up and left. He went straight out to the car park, found a trio of external plastic rubbish bins and kicked hell out of them until his feet protested and he had to find a seat on the concrete lip of a nearby parking bay to get his breath back.

It seemed a long time since Moran had held court from his customary spot in the incident room – just to the left of the whiteboard by the glass windows which separated his private office from the rest of the team. It seemed a long time, but in fact it was only eight days.

George McConnell, Bola Odunsi and Brit were seated in an attentive semicircle. Moran wished that Charlie was well enough to be involved, but he had sent her on compulsory sick leave to stay with her parents in Coventry. He hadn't mentioned Higginson's complaint; Charlie didn't need that right now. He was still two officers down; Tess Martin was doing fine but out of commission for the foreseeable future.

Moran regarded his depleted team. George was looking apprehensive. He knew that Moran wouldn't let his mid-week all-nighter go by without comment. However, Moran had decided to let the Scot stew for a while; it would make him keener to please.

"Lend me your ears, good people," Moran began. "We have a fugitive and a possible abductee to track down."

"Friends, Romans or countrymen?" Brit asked innocently.

Moran frowned, feigning bafflement.

"Shakespeare, guv. Julius Caesar."

"Ah. I thought it was Dumas."

Now it was Brit's turn to look perplexed.

"Alexander Dumas," Moran smiled. "The three musketeers. That's what you three look like from where I'm standing. Anyway, let's get on. I've had a wee chat with Wilder."

The three exchanged glances. Bola Odunsi screwed one hand into a fist and punched it into his open palm.

Moran continued. "Wilder informs me that we should be looking to the Channel Tunnel. Or, less likely, a private plane."

"Want me to check the smaller airfields, guv? He could be off anytime," McConnell offered.

"I don't think so. I think that Andreas will take his time leaving the country."

"What makes you think that, guv?" Brit asked.

"Because Wilder would have me believe that he's already left. She can't quite bring herself to shop him completely."

Understanding dawned on the trio's faces.

"So." Moran found a chair and sat down. He felt drained of energy and his headache was never far away, lurking in the background like some unwanted party malingerer. "We think about other ways. My chart-topper is the ferry."

"Portsmouth, Plymouth, Poole, Dover…" Bola began.

Moran raised his hand. "I know. A lot of ground to cover. And out of our jurisdiction."

"Back to the Orts Road house, guv?" McConnell suggested. "We need a starter for ten."

"Nope. No need."

All three frowned.

Moran paused, enjoying their confusion. A moment later he relented and produced a folded slip of paper from his pocket. "Booking form. Brittany Ferries, Poole, Tuesday morning, seven thirty. Three tickets."

"Where'd you get that, guv?" McConnell's face was a picture of bewilderment.

"Inside a motorcycle pannier I happened to come across at the seaside." Moran put the form carefully back in his trouser pocket. "Lucky I checked, eh? Oh, and another thing." He produced a mobile phone, wrapped in a clear plastic bag, from the same pocket. "You any good with these, Bola? Someone told me you were a bit of a dabbler."

"Sure." Bola frowned. "What's the problem with it?"

"No problem, it's just that there don't appear to be any viewable text messages. Unusual − but then again, we're dealing with unusual folk here, are we not?"

George whistled. "The chink's iPhone? The entire spook community will be looking for that, guv."

Moran held up his hand. "Please, George. No disparaging racial slang."

McConnell mumbled an apology but couldn't resist a further objection. "There'll be an enquiry into this, guv.

They'll throw the book at you."

"Only if they know we have it, George." Moran smiled. It felt odd to do so, as if he were trying to remember some long-lost form of expression. "And I'm betting it won't take DC Odunsi here very long to find anything worth finding."

"I'm on it, guv." Bola grinned, the grin of a man who knew which side he was on.

Chapter Thirty-eight

"Bit nondescript, isn't it?"

Moran had to agree. Poole wasn't really his cup of tea – or maybe it was just that he'd had enough of the seaside for the time being. "I think it's more picturesque by the harbour. But not a bad place to hide, Toby, wouldn't you say?"

"Yep. There must be hundreds of B and Bs in the area."

Moran shuffled the pages of McConnell's report and grudgingly conceded that the little Scot had gone some way to making up for his lock-in misdemeanour. He'd asked George to do a little digging into Gosia Marenkovich's background, and what had come out was most revealing. He was also pretty *au fait* by now with Andreas Pashkov's field of expertise, which ranged from specialist communications systems to the supervision of industrialised torture and murder. Pashkov probably wasn't his real name, though, any more than Gosia Marenkovich was the real name of Charlie's other erstwhile flatmate. As Toby followed signs to the ferry Moran found himself wondering if Andreas was as diligent an ID checker as he was a killer. For his sake, Moran hoped so, but then Moran wasn't going to lose any sleep over it.

And talking of sleep, Moran felt a lot better in himself. He'd managed two nights of five hours apiece and had been able to put the previous week's events into some kind of manageable perspective. However, he knew from past experience that certain scenes from his time in Cernham would not be shaken off easily, especially during the wee small hours. But that was for later. Today was all about closure, if not of the entire Huang Xian Kuai operation, then at least of Thames Valley Constabulary's sideshow role, which had been heralded the previous summer by the sudden disappearance of an undercover policewoman.

And which, I hope, will end here…

"Second largest after Sydney." Toby interrupted his thoughts.

"Pardon me?"

"Poole is a natural harbour, guv. Only bigger one is Sydney."

"Well, I'll be blowed."

"Lovely beaches, too. The St Tropez of the south coast. That's what they call it."

"Whoever 'they' are."

Toby grinned. "Yeah. Ah – there it is. The Thistle Hotel, right?"

"That's what Bola came up with."

"Once a geek…"

Moran guffawed. "The thing about technology is you can never be sure that 'deleted' really means 'deleted'. Fortunately for us."

Toby backed the car into a tight parking space with the

ease of long experience. As he killed the engine he paused, a slight trace of concern passing across his face. "You're not expecting this to be a heavy scene, are you, guv?"

Perhaps Toby was thinking of Tess Martin, recovering in hospital – or Charlie, traumatised and resting up in Coventry with an as yet unknown disciplinary hanging over her. Or maybe Banner, whose funeral they would all attend the following day. Perhaps he just needed reassurance that they weren't about to become another statistic in Huang's international game of brutality.

Moran studied his shoes for a moment, wanting to compose a helpful reply but caught nevertheless in a moment of self doubt. What if he was wrong? What if he'd misread the information, failed to take some critical but unknown factor into account?

At last he turned to Toby, who, in that moment of vulnerability, looked younger than his twenty-five years.

"No, Toby. No, I'm not."

Toby's eyes brightened. "That's good enough for me, guv. Let's do it."

"Well, they did ask not to be disturbed." The receptionist looked visibly taken aback as Moran produced his ID.

"They, or her?"

Out of the corner of his eye, Moran saw Toby cock his head at the question. As did the receptionist.

"I'm sorry?" she said.

"Did they both ask? Together, I mean. Or did the girl come down later by herself?"

"I don't know. I'll have to check."

She bustled into the back office, clearly put out by the

stupidity and pointlessness of the question.

As they waited for the receptionist to return, Moran's mobile buzzed.

"Moran."

"Guv?"

Bola. "Go ahead, Bola. What's up?"

"Had a call from Devon – a DS Wilmot? Wants you to call him urgently."

"Did he say what it was about?"

Moran caught the momentary hesitation at the other end. "They have an issue. About the guy you wounded."

"Oh? What, exactly?"

"They can't trace him. And the weird thing is, Lady Cernham and her son – er, stepson…"

"Matt 'Harrison'?"

"Right. The thing is, guv, they both deny that this guy exists."

"They *what*?"

Bola's voice grew more animated. "I don't mean, like, they say he *never* existed, guv. Just that he's been, well–"

"Come on. Out with it."

"That he's been dead for nearly eighteen years."

Moran shook his head in bemusement. Toby was reading the snack bar menu and examining local taxi cards on the reception desk. "Tell Wilmot I'll get back to him as soon as I can."

"OK, guv. But he's got *his* guv'nor breathing down his neck, you know. They'll want a proper statement."

"*Another* statement? I've given them Chapter and verse already."

"Sure. Sorry, guv. Don't shoot the messenger, you know?

How's it going, anyway?"

"I'll tell you when we have something, Bola. Don't worry."

Moran signed off and a moment later the receptionist returned. "Just the girl, as you said," she reported peevishly. "Although I don't see—"

"Thanks," Moran said. He consulted his watch. "Nearly ferry time." He returned his attention to the receptionist. "Anyone booked a taxi to the ferry this morning?"

"Of course. It's a ten-minute run to the ferry port. Lots of people book a taxi for this time of day. They're starting to arrive now, if you look outside. But Mr and Mrs Wachowski aren't due to check out today, so I don't see why they would want a taxi to the ferry."

Moran waited for her to suffix her statement with 'stupid', but she allowed her body language to do the talking.

"Good. Well, we'll take a seat, shall we, Detective Constable?"

The receptionist looked puzzled. "You don't want the room number?"

"No thanks. Sorry to be a nuisance."

Moran wasn't expecting a 'not at all', and he wasn't disappointed. They took a seat in the foyer and Toby picked up a copy of the Times. It was getting busy and soon a check-out queue began to form, the nearby lift door opening and closing and disgorging anxious, watch-checking parents with carefree toddlers and older siblings in tow, be-suited businessmen, and a fair smattering of elderly, white-haired couples moving at a frustratingly slower pace and no doubt increasing the stress levels of those keener to press on with the next leg of their journey.

Not long now, Brendan…

It was ten minutes in the end, just as Moran was toying with the idea of a second encounter with the receptionist. She came not from the lift but down the stairs, casually dressed in T-shirt and jeans, clutching a worn travel bag and wearing a neutral expression. She looked just like any ordinary young woman – attractive, but not memorably so. The hair was a touch shorter, but the face was the same as the photo Charlie had showed him. Gosia Marenkovich joined the queue and withdrew a purse from the side-zipped compartment of her bag. He nudged Toby who was deep in some sporting article and they went across the lobby together.

"Good morning, Ms Marenkovich. My name is Detective Chief Inspector Brendan Moran and this is Detective Sergeant Toby Glascock. May we have a quick word?"

To her credit, Gosia Marenkovich's reaction was as calm as the English Channel, clearly visible through the hotel foyer's plate glass window, appeared to be.

"Of course," she replied. "It is about the house again? I am going on the ferry this morning, to France, you see. But if you are quick it is fine."

"We'll do our best." Moran smiled. "Are you travelling alone? You see, we were told that you were – how can I put it? – a little reluctant to leave your friend's house?"

"My friend? Ah, yes. Lydia."

"That's the lady."

"She worries so much. She's a good friend."

"You were with a man, Ms Marenkovich. We had reason to believe he intended to harm you." Toby's voice was kindly but firm.

"A man? Oh, yes. Andreas. It was all fine. We fixed

everything. A misunderstanding."

"Ah. I see." Moran said. "And where might we find Andreas?"

She shrugged. "I don't know. He is doing his own thing now. I couldn't say where he is."

"You were lovers?" Toby asked.

If she was shocked at the directness of the question she didn't let on. "In a way, I suppose. But it was difficult. We don't agree about many things."

"Which room were you staying in?" Moran said. "Mind if we have a look?"

Gosia's composure faltered. "My room? Why? It is finished here. All finished. There's nothing to see. I don't understand."

"If you wouldn't mind." Moran indicated the lift.

Gosia moistened her lips. "OK. Sure."

Moran allowed Gosia to lead and they followed her to the lift. He felt a rising tension. He could still be wrong.

First floor.

Second floor.

Gosia seemed to flinch as the lift pinged for the third floor.

"After you," Moran eased her an encouraging smile.

They passed two straggling families attempting to bundle the kids down to checkout. A mother raised her eyes to heaven as she zoomed past to intercept a stray toddler's bolt for freedom. A wave of giggling floated back from the direction of the stairwell, followed by the sound of a palm on flesh. The giggling stopped abruptly.

"Thought that was illegal," Toby observed drily.

"Wait till you have kids," Moran advised. "You'll soon change your tune."

An ear-splitting yell of protest announced the returning mother, her toddler's escape attempt successfully thwarted.

Gosia had stopped outside one of the bedrooms. She glanced to the end of the corridor where the fire escape doors framed a bright rectangle of seaside light. *Three floors up? Not a good idea.*

Gosia was rooting in her handbag, making pretence of having mislaid the key. Her last line of defence. She looked up and recognised Moran's expression for what it was. *Yes. I know.*

Her face seemed to collapse. Her arms dropped to her sides as Moran held out his hand. "The key, please, Ms Marenkovich."

"Shall I, guv?" Toby's shoulder was at the door.

"It's all right. Here. Take it." Gosia placed the key in Moran's open palm. "He deserved it. The bastard. I hope he rots in hell."

Moran opened the door and Toby went in. Moran encouraged Gosia with a gentle nudge to the shoulder.

She had made no attempt to hide the body. Andreas Pashkov lay naked on the bed, looking to all intents and purposes as if he were merely taking a nap.

"Ah," Toby said.

"Take a seat, Ms Marenkovich." Moran was checking Pashkov's wrist for a pulse. To his surprise he found one; it was erratic and faint, but discernable. He nodded to Toby. "Still with us. Just."

"You know, don't you?" Gosia sat on the only available chair and demurely clasped her hands, resting them on her lap.

"About your father? About what Huang did to him, and

many others? Yes."

"I don't care now what will happen to me."

Toby was on the landline to the emergency services. Moran sat on the edge of the bed, facing her. "For what it's worth, I understand your motive. What I find rather chilling is the premeditated way in which you planned your revenge – but I must congratulate you on your detective work. It can't have been easy to locate Pashkov's next assignment and arrange a house share so that you were in a position to seduce him."

She shrugged. "Not so hard. A man is easy to deceive."

Moran donned a pair of rubber gloves and examined the half-empty glass on the bedside table nearest to Pashkov's body. He sniffed the contents and raised an eyebrow. "If I didn't know better I'd say this was the same potion Pashkov used in DI Pepper's drinking water. Am I right?"

She nodded.

"From Pashkov's own medicine chest?"

Another nod.

"Well, if that's not irony I don't know what is. You—"

Gosia launched herself at Pashkov's unconscious body and flung herself full-length onto the bed, straddling him. Before Moran could react her hands had found Pashkov's neck. Moran got hold of her shoulders while Toby, in less gentlemanly fashion, grabbed a handful of hair. She was strong and determined, but between them they managed to drag her off the bed and onto her feet. Her eyes spat hatred.

"He will die. Even if he lives I will find him and kill him."

Toby held her firmly in an arm lock, breathing hard. "Not where you're headed you won't. Shall I escort Ms Marenkovich to the car?"

The wail of an ambulance siren drifted up from the car park. "Do that, DS Glascock. I'll see if I can smooth the cross-constabulary politics a little for the Chief."

"Good luck with that one, guv."

Toby took her arm and Gosia Marenkovich allowed herself to be led from the room without a backward glance.

Chapter Thirty-nine

"Ah." DCS Higginson looked up as Moran knocked and entered. "The culprit returns. What in the name of all the saints have you been up to, Moran? I've had chief constables from two constabularies bending my ear today. Perhaps you'd be good enough to brief me?"

Moran sat down without invitation. He was past caring about niceties, rank and protocol. "We have Gosia Marenkovich in custody, the last link in the chain of events which started with DS Banner's murder. I think we can say that, for the time being, the aftermath of last summer is over."

"But this Huang character is still at large, isn't he? Dorset is flapping like a runaway kite. They don't like the idea of international drug operators coming and going freely among their tourists and elderly residents."

"Sir, Huang is an invisible man. I don't personally believe that he is an immediate concern for either constabulary. Better to leave him to the likes of the two Ronnies at the hospital."

"You're saying that he's untouchable?"

Moran sighed. "By ourselves, yes. He's sitting pretty at the top of his food chain, and the only fish we get to see are the minnows and sprats."

"Like Pashkov."

"A large sprat, but yes, like him."

Higginson was shaking his head. "And that girl, Marenkovich. Ordinary, you say? Normal background?"

"Yes, sir. Her father got involved with Huang when he ran into financial trouble. He was approached because of his useful professional contacts." Moran shrugged. "I don't know all the details – I don't need to – but something went awry. A whistleblower tipped Huang off that money was being skimmed, whether by Marenkovich's father or another of the gang we'll probably never know. Anyway, the result was a bloodbath. It was all over the Polish nationals. Gosia Marenkovich was sixteen and she'd already started a career as a model. The press made a big splash of it: 'Beauty queen's dad in warehouse drug cull', that sort of thing."

"One thing puzzles me." Higginson's brow creased thoughtfully. "You say that Marenkovich's friend reported her as an abductee, yet that clearly wasn't the case."

"She's a clever girl," Moran said. "Contingency. If things got messy she had a witness to say she was taken forcibly. Then she could plead self defence, emerge with her clothes in disarray after she'd killed Pashkov."

"But she didn't take that option. Strange."

Moran made a *comme ci, comme ça* gesture. "Sure, but it would have been a lot of hassle to carry it off: court case, more publicity. And, of course, the risk that her identity would be discovered. Prosecution then have their motive, and she goes down for life. In the end she just decided to disappear. But we turned up, and by then it was too late to play that particular card."

"Indeed. Dorset is far from happy though. Their CC feels we could have avoided any unpleasantness by informing them earlier. And he told me so in words of one syllable, Brendan."

"I appreciate that it's a little delicate, sir," Moran replied, mildly encouraged by the 'Brendan'. "But there was always the risk that we would put them both to flight by acting hastily. And Pashkov may live, in which case we're only talking assault with intent."

Higginson gave him a knowing look. "Far be it from me to accuse you of hastiness, Brendan."

"On the other hand, if Pashkov dies, then whichever way you look at it it's a kind of justice," Moran said, running a hand wearily through his hair. "Maybe not the one we've signed up to, but a kind of justice, nevertheless."

"I wouldn't want to think that it meets with your approval, Brendan," Higginson said pointedly. "Nor that any delay on your part could be construed as an encouragement to allow the kind of justice you refer to to prevail."

"Of course not, sir."

"Good. Now, Devon, if you please."

Moran scratched his cheek. The stubble rasped under his nail. "I've provided a comprehensive statement. I've also undertaken to assist the Devon constabulary in whatever manner they see fit concerning recent events in Cernham. In doing so I'm sure that the mystery will be solved and the matter brought to a speedy conclusion."

"OK, that's fine for the record. Now tell me what you

really think."

Moran allowed himself a half-smile. Higginson might turn out to be a half-decent appointment after all. "I think Devon have a very resourceful and troubled fugitive on their hands."

"You don't buy this denial stuff from the family?"

"No, I don't. I saw Rufus de Courcy in the flesh. I know what I saw."

"I'm sure," Higginson nodded, sounding anything but. "Anyway, I'm happy to release you for a couple of days to keep them sweet."

"I appreciate that, sir."

"Good. That'll be all."

Moran wearily got to his feet.

"And Brendan?"

"Sir?"

"Take a few days off afterwards, would you? Somewhere sensible, where nothing happens. Get my drift?"

Moran wordlessly closed the door behind him.

Chapter Forty

As Moran passed the cottage he felt an unexpected chill run down his spine. The feeling of helplessness he had experienced as de Courcy bundled Celine into his car, shotgun cradled under his arm, came back to him like a stinging rebuke. But de Courcy's actions had saved Moran's life, only to cost him his own.

Justice. Of a kind...

Moreover, Celine was all right. Shaken, naturally, but well enough to have been discharged after twenty-four hours under obs.

The pub was still closed. Would Terl return? Would anyone still want to drink there? But that wasn't Moran's problem.. It was up to the residents of Cernham how they wanted to move forward after recent events. A stark choice, Moran thought as he walked briskly past the churchyard: move on, or move out.

It was late morning and Moran found that the simmering anticipation he had felt as his journey drew to a close had not diminished with his arrival. If anything it was stronger.

Perhaps it was more than anticipation. Perhaps it was nervous excitement? He allowed himself a rueful grin. Well, why shouldn't he feel a little excited? Maybe this was the beginning of something he had given up hope of ever experiencing again – and maybe, just maybe, it was also the end of the long, anguished, empty years since Janice's murder at the hands of the IRA. With a small shock he realised that his eyes were dry following the articulation of her name. He couldn't recall a time when that had ever been the case.

Healing. After all these years, healing…

His thoughts were curtailed by the sight of DS Wilmot approaching from the direction of the Manor, several uniformed policemen in tow. The sergeant waved a half-hearted gesture of greeting and Moran could tell even at a distance of fifteen metres that Wilmot was intensely preoccupied.

"DCI Moran. You're here. Good."

No small talk, then, which suited Moran well enough. "So, what's the latest?" he enquired. "Have you found him?" Pointless question. The answer was written all over the sergeant's face.

"Have I hell," Wilmot said miserably. "We've combed the bloody woods for miles and there's not a sign. We found your American, though. All six pieces of her."

Moran's stomach yawed. "Where?"

"Harrison's garden. Under the woodpile."

"I see."

"I'm sorry I didn't take your report more seriously," Wilmot said, avoiding eye contact.

"It's done now," Moran said tersely. "Hopefully a lesson

learned. But your immediate concern should be Rufus de Courcy's whereabouts. What about the Manor itself?"

Wilmot shook his head and the two accompanying uniforms adopted appropriately regretful expressions. "No. Nothing."

"There could be hidden rooms, perhaps even secret passages connecting the Manor to its outbuildings and gardens. It's old. Some parts date back to the eleventh century," Moran said. "Have you pumped Lady Cernham for information?"

Wilmot made a gesture of exasperation. "Her? We've not got anything useful from her, nor Harrison. She's lost it completely, and he's suicidal. Can't leave him alone."

"I'm not surprised," Moran said. And he wasn't. Harrison had been in a no-win situation since birth. Neither was his quality of life likely to improve in the near future. Maybe prison would serve as some kind of release for him – it was hard to predict. "Well," he continued, trying to sound optimistic, "I'm sure you've worked out a way of moving things on even without their co-operation."

Wilmot rubbed his temple. "You're the key right now. We'll go over the whole thing again until it makes sense. You might remember something new, something that seemed irrelevant before. I don't know." Wilmot shrugged.

He looked very young in his misery and Moran imagined the weight bearing down on his shoulders from his seniors. The DCI was still off sick, apparently, and Wilmot was senior most suitable. It wasn't so much a short straw as a stick of dynamite. The press were literally camped around the village's perimeter like modern-day Greenham Common protesters. Milling film crews, gabbling reporters and pushy newspaper hacks desperate for the first shot at a headline had homed in from all points of the compass like migrating geese. It had taken Moran fifteen minutes to negotiate the media circus, and he had only managed to break through without being mobbed because of the timely intervention of a squad car.

He nodded sympathetically. "I'll do my best, but I'm not at all sure there's much I can add. There's Celine as well. Ms… Mrs…" Moran realised that he had no idea what Celine's surname was.

"Mrs Keene, sir," one of the uniforms said, trying to be helpful. "Keene by name only though," he added.

Wilmot gave him a withering look before turning his attention back to Moran. "Mrs Keene is up at the Manor. In fact, one of my officers is talking to her right now, but she doesn't remember much about what happened except that you carried her back to the village. Everything else is a 'blur'." Wilmot did the standard 'rabbit ears' impression to indicate apostrophisation, which Moran invariably found irritating.

"It's a bit of a blur to me as well." Moran gave a short humourless laugh; his nightmare incarceration in the ice house was still a hazy but strangely vivid memory. Something else was bothering him, though: the name, Keene. That rang a bell. Moran frowned. She'd never told him her surname, so why did it sound so familiar?

"Listen," Wilmot said. "I have to make a report. I'll meet you at the Manor in half an hour." He looked at his watch. "No, make that an hour. There's tea and coffee, some bits to eat. Make yourself at home."

"Fine," Moran replied. "I'll see you there." He was in no

hurry, and although the prospect of returning to the site of his recent trials was less than enticing, the knowledge that he was soon to be reunited with Celine was compensation enough to bring a smile to his lips. He began to walk towards the de Courcys' ancestral home, marvelling at how, over so many years, the family had been able to exercise such murderous control over the village and its environs.

It was a beautiful spring day and the only sound to break the silence as Moran made his way along the lane was a final barked instruction from Wilmot to his constables as the sergeant prepared to file an empty return to his superiors.

As Moran made his way up the drive he noticed two uniformed officers guarding the entrance to the ice house. How many unwary souls had shared his experience of imprisonment? More than a handful, he speculated. Perhaps they'd never know the full tally unless the bog could be completely drained, and he had no idea if such a mammoth task could ever be accomplished. It seemed unlikely. Moran's feet crunched on gravel as he made his way towards the front entrance, his approach monitored indifferently by yet another uniformed policeman standing in the time-honoured attitude adopted by all police officers called to perform the solitary and dull duty of guardsman. Moran introduced himself and the constable stepped to one side and ushered him in.

"Quite a place, sir. Never seen anything like it."

"I know," Moran said. "I've been here before."

His footsteps echoed in the hall's empty expanse. He half-expected to hear Rufus' muffled threats and shouts booming once again from the long room, but the only sound as he pushed open the salon door was the tinkle of china upon china as Celine reacquainted her cup with its delicate saucer and rose to greet him.

"Brendan. It's good to see you."

She looked stunning, dressed simply in a Laura Ashley style cotton skirt and top, her hair loose upon her shoulders and her mouth smiling a greeting which promised warmth, companionship, and maybe something else too. Her eyes sparkled with delight.

"Good to see you, too." They embraced briefly. "How's the neck?"

"On the mend." She shrugged. "I'll heal just fine, so the medics tell me. Come and sit down. They've just brought tea."

Before he could ask who 'they' were, Celine explained. "A few ladies from the village are helping out. The police are using this as a base. Of course, we've had forensic teams in and out like a TV crime drama. It's all happening here."

"And they still haven't found him."

"No. They haven't." Celine reached for the teapot and Moran took a seat on the sofa beside her – the same sofa Lady Cernham had occupied as she had unburdened herself of her chequered family history. That night seemed a long time ago, but, Moran reflected, it could never be far enough away for comfort.

"I hope they're not giving you a hard time," he said, accepting a cup and saucer of such intricate delicacy he was almost afraid to touch it. "Thanks."

"Pleasure." She smiled again and Moran's world lit up. "No, just the usual questions, you know."

"Oh yes, I know," he nodded, then looked up, surprised.

"What?"

Celine was laughing. "Nothing. Just the way you said it. You sounded like a jaded old detective who's seen it all."

"That's a pretty accurate description."

They both laughed.

"Tell me," Moran said, "Mrs Keene. How do I know your name when you've never disclosed your surname to me?"

"Probably because you rented my cottage last week."

The penny dropped. "Really? Why didn't you say? You never mentioned you were the owner."

"You never asked."

Now or never, Moran. He had to know. "And the Mrs?"

"An anachronism. He died years ago."

"I'm sorry."

"Don't be. I was young, so was he. We probably wouldn't have stayed together anyway. He got sick. Cancer."

Moran nodded sombrely, but inside the elation was building.

"Shall we take a walk while you're waiting for our friend, Wilmot?" she suggested.

"Why not?" He finished his tea and they went out into the mid-afternoon sunshine. The lawn rippled in the light breeze, but it was a breeze carrying with it a breath of summer. Celine linked her arm in his and they went down the steps, following the line of the balustrade towards the maze.

"Not the maze, I think," Moran said. In any case the entrance was barred by chequered police tape.

"No. What an experience." Celine shivered. "That old couple. Horrifying."

"They were archaeologists, apparently," Moran said.

"Wilmot's theory is that they found a body rather more contemporary than they were expecting to find."

"Oh God," she said in a low voice. "Another of *his–*"

Moran nodded. "And their remains show injuries commensurate with serious trauma. A car accident is the favourite."

"But not an accident." Celine's mouth twisted in distaste.

"I don't know that they'll ever prove anything, but for my money I'd guess they were run off the road by a Land Rover or similar, belonging in all probability to Richard de Courcy."

Celine shook her head slowly. Moran was enjoying the way the sun danced in her hair as she moved. "It's horrible, isn't it?" she said. "How they got away with it for so long."

"And how do you feel now that it's nearly over?" Moran asked gently. "Your sister can rest in peace. You must tell me about her – if you can bear to?" he added quickly.

"Of course. I'd like to."

"You must have suffered, suspecting – knowing – the truth, and being with de Courcy must have–"

"I can't speak of him," Celine interrupted. "An evil man, that's all. An evil man who got his just desserts."

"Of course. In your own time, perhaps. We can take things at your own pace. That's fine."

"Is it?" She stopped and turned to face him. "Is it fine, Brendan?"

Moran heard a scrunch of tyres on the drive. More forensic activity, no doubt. Or maybe Wilmot had finally tired of tramping up and down from the village to the Manor.

"What do you mean?" Moran felt the first flutter of

anxiety. He had been too heavy-handed. *Idiot.*

"Can you live with the truth, Brendan?"

"I'd prefer to live with the truth than with a lie," Moran replied, frowning. What was she getting at? "What do you mean?"

"They'll not find him, Brendan."

Her voice carried such certainty and conviction that Moran felt as though he had been forcibly struck. He took a step back, shaking his head.

"Oh no. Tell me you didn't–"

"Do you think that I've lived the last fifteen years of my life for nothing, Brendan? That I've made the sacrifices I've made just to let it all go, as if it didn't matter what the de Courcys have done? As if my big sister hadn't been *murdered?*"

Moran stood a small distance away, hands by his sides, almost speechless. Eventually he managed one word. "How?"

"You told me yourself I was a resourceful woman, Brendan. And I told you when I came to you in the ice house that it was going to end. That I was going to put a stop to it once and for all. I wasn't spinning you a yarn. I wasn't makin' it up."

The Irish lilt grew more pronounced as she went on. Moran could only listen, aghast.

"I used a tracker. It's small. You can get them online these days. I fixed it on his clothes when he cut me. After we crippled the bastard I went after him. He'll not be troublin' anyone again."

"Where's the body? I have to tell them, Celine." Moran's day had turned to night. There was a hard lump in his throat and he had difficulty speaking normally. "You know I have to."

"Do you? Do you, Brendan?"

Now he could see the moistness in her eyes. She blinked a tear away angrily, folded her arms. "I could be happy with a man like you, Brendan. And you with me. I know it. I can *feel* it."

"Yes," Moran said simply. "Yes, I know."

"I saved your *life*."

"Yes. Yes, you did."

"Your choice. Do your duty if you have to. Throw it all away, why don't you?"

She turned then and walked away, arms still folded, retracing their steps, leaving Moran alone by the gently fluttering police tape.

"So." Wilmot's weariness was barely camouflaged now. His eyes were red-rimmed, and a dark line of fatigue beneath each told the story of the pressure he was under. "So, you want to revise your statement."

They were sitting in Wilmot's car, an old Rover 75 which smelt of oil, paper and sweat. The sergeant's mobile office. Moran sat next to him in the passenger seat watching a robin flit from one branch to another in the apple tree which leaned into the lane from above the adjoining hedgerow. He cleared his throat before replying, not trusting his voice.

"Yes. That's correct."

"Let's have it, then."

Moran heard himself speaking but it was as though he were listening to some detached third-party recording. Wilmot prompted and sought clarification where necessary, allowed Moran to collect his thoughts without interrupting, and gave him his head when the words came quickly and without hesitation. When he had finished Wilmot clicked off the recorder and exhaled deeply.

"They gave you quite a dose, apparently, so I'm not particularly surprised."

"No," Moran agreed.

"As you say, it was probably a combination of the drug, the setting and your understandable anxiety concerning Mrs Keene's safety which prevented you from recognising Richard de Courcy as the primary antagonist."

"Yes."

"Mrs Keene has also confirmed that to be the case. Funny the way the mind can play tricks, especially under duress." Wilmot turned to gauge Moran's response.

"Yes, I'd have to agree."

"Oh well," Wilmot said, trying not to let the relief spill into his tone too much, "at least we can stop chasing ghosts, eh?"

"Quite." Moran tried to raise the corners of his mouth and failed. "Although I doubt very much whether Lady Cernham will ever divulge what happened to her youngest son's body after he died."

"You never know," Wilmot said. "My guess is that they buried him in the grounds somewhere nearby. Anyway, we can search at our leisure now. It's all history."

"Indeed."

"Bloody aristocracy, eh? All that money and what happens? They make a complete balls-up of their lives."

"Succinctly put," Moran said.

"Well, thanks again, DCI Moran. Safe journey."

"Thanks."

Moran got out of the car and walked slowly past the pub to his own borrowed pool vehicle. The sun was low in the sky and a full moon had already risen above the horizon. A fresher breeze stirred the trees overshadowing the graveyard and Moran turned up his collar. He sat in the car for a long time before he felt able to start the engine and begin the long journey home. The question he had asked himself at the start of his holiday now returned to mock him:

To continue or not?

But the question had gained an addendum, an accusation:

…but you can't now, can you? Not after what you've just done…

Epilogue

Seven months later

Celine settled down at the bureau to examine the documents she had received from the solicitor. It was all exactly as she had intended. As the only surviving – and legally free – relative of the de Courcy family, the outcome had never really been in doubt. In fact, all things considered, the necessary legal loopholes had been negotiated more smoothly than she had dared hope. Tenuous though her claim might have been, it had nevertheless proved undeniably demonstrable: a simple DNA test had shown beyond doubt that Matthew de Courcy and she were from the same gene pool, the biological wheels having been set in motion by darling Rachel's dalliance with the late Lord of the Manor.

And here she was, the new Lady of the Manor. She wondered what Rachel's *amour* would have had to say about that, were he still alive. But that mattered not a whit, as her mother used to say. Celine removed her half-moon spectacles and chewed an armature thoughtfully. She'd have to make changes, for sure, but all in due course. Best let the dust settle for the time being, allow the village to get used to a new regime.

The clock on the desk told her it was approaching four. The time sure was flying by. So much to do, so much to think about. But it was time for the afternoon visit. She took a set of keys from the desk drawer and made her way to the hall.

Her footsteps echoed brightly in the empty space. Solitude wasn't a problem; she'd had plenty of practice over the years, after all. It would have been something if Brendan had stayed. Really something. But then, had he done so, her options would have been limited, so perhaps everything had worked out for the best after all.

She unlocked a door and descended into the bowels of the old house. Once there would have been servants' quarters here, perhaps a hot and frantic kitchen with cooks and maids running to and fro. Not anymore. These half-forgotten rooms and basements hadn't seen much of interest for decades. Until now, that is.

As Celine turned the key and entered the chamber she felt rather than heard the rustle of fearful anticipation. This was the part she enjoyed the most – not the physical part, although that was satisfying enough in itself, but rather the mental anguish that the simple fact of her presence was able to induce.

Rufus de Courcy was chained to the wall in a standing

position, hands manacled above his head. As she approached he cowered, tried to turn himself away from his tormentor. Celine watched his efforts impassively. She selected a nine-strand whip from a small arsenal of equipment she had procured. As she flexed her arm and made a few practice strokes, Rufus broke the silence with a series of animal-like bleats. He pulled and tugged at the chains but they were firmly embedded; she'd made sure of that. Taking care to stay out of reach, Celine went to work. It was tiring, exhausting even, but whenever she felt herself weaken all she had to do was remember Rachel's beautiful, smiling face. Her big sister, whom she had worshipped...

She was careful not to inflict too much damage – that would defeat the object – and she was confident that her medical expertise would suffice if there was any immediate danger to life. For example, the leg had been an unpleasant wound, but antibiotics, regular cleaning and daily dressings had soon cleared that up. With any luck he might last six months or more, provided, of course, she wasn't too heavy-handed. But would six months be enough? That was a tricky one. Six months for her sister's life? It didn't seem much.

"You should count yourself lucky," she told Rufus, "that I'm only a frail woman."

Celine took another breath and bent to her task.

Moran watched from a distance as DS Wilmot's team made a cautious approach. He didn't anticipate trouble, but he hoped Wilmot's attitude would be at least sympathetic if his worst fears were, in fact, realised. There was still the possibility that he was wrong, of course; there was *always* that possibility... Wilmot had needed a lot of persuading to follow up what amounted to a hunch – and a tenuous one at that.

They were at the main entrance. He remembered the last time he had stood where the policemen were now standing – en route to the gardens, arm in arm with Celine, hoping against hope that it would somehow work out. How had he *known*? He'd quizzed himself many times, rejecting the idea as absurd, unlikely, ridiculous. But the conviction wouldn't go away. Just one simple fact kept it alive: that she hadn't answered his question.

Where's the body?

Moran shivered. Three weeks till Christmas and the skies promised early snow. He watched from the gate, unable to make contact with the gravel drive, something holding him back…

The great door swung open and Celine's familiar figure filled the space. She folded her arms as the police sergeant explained the purpose of their visit.

Search warrant, reason to believe…

Her body language told him all he needed to know. He saw her head turn a fraction as her eyes strained to identify the solitary figure hovering at the edge of the estate. For a brief instant their eyes met and then he was walking away, his breath forming smoky clouds of condensation in the grey gloaming.

The DCI Brendan Moran Crime Series

Black December

Creatures of Dust

Death Walks Behind You

The Irish Detective (Omnibus)

A Crime for all Seasons (Short Stories)

Silent as the Dead

Gone Too Soon

Standalone novels

The Trespass

The Serpent & the Slave

The Ley Lines of Lushbury

Sign up to Scott Hunter's newsletter to be notified of special discounts, offers and news, and to receive a FREE eBook

www.scott-hunter.net